MIDIAN

Red Sea

(GULF OF AKABA)

Ezion Geber

MT SINAI
(HOREB)

WILDERNESS OF PARAN

WILDERNESS

OF SIN

Rephidim
OASIS

Marah Oasis

Elim Oasis

(GULF OF SUEZ)

REEDS

Miles

palacios

100

Memphis

On

E

RIVER NILE

0

ALONE ATOP THE MOUNTAIN

By the Same Author

THE GENIUS OF PAUL
THE HEBREW SCRIPTURES
WE JEWS AND JESUS
HEROD: PROFILE OF A TYRANT
OLD TESTAMENT ISSUES
THE ENJOYMENT OF SCRIPTURE

ALONE ATOP THE MOUNTAIN

SAMUEL SANDMEL

Doubleday & Company, Inc.
Garden City, New York, 1973

ISBN: 0-385-03877-1
Library of Congress Catalog Card Number 72–93399
Copyright © 1973 by Samuel Sandmel
Printed in the United States of America
First Edition

For Charles Sandmel
Ben Sandmel
David Sandmel

✳ A WORD TO THE READER

The source materials drawn on are not only statements in the Pentateuch, but also clues derived from the text, and the legacy of scriptural interpretation as found in the ancient rabbis and Philo of Alexandria some two thousand years ago.

The rabbis and Philo fashioned out of Scripture an embroidered portrait of Moses consistent with their own age. Like them, I have used Scripture but also have gone beyond it, to fashion a portrait of Moses hopefully consistent with our age.

ALONE ATOP THE MOUNTAIN

✳ CHAPTER I

My good friend Caleb assures me repeatedly that I have become a legend. I am old enough now for that. He tells me, too, that our people say that I have not lost my virility. Perhaps they mean this in a general way. Caleb nudges me, as if to ask if it is specifically true, and I pretend not to understand, and then we both laugh, as good friends will.

Surely our people must mean my mind. They could not mean my body. I am a tired man, ready for rest.

Not that I have turned over the reins. Not yet. Not even to Joshua.

According to Caleb, our people have begun to link my name with Abraham, Isaac, and Jacob. I am, of course, flattered at this, but wonder if they mean to compliment me, or to bury me. In bygone years they were scarcely so complimentary; it was more usual for them to speak of Moses the tyrant, or else of Moses the bungler. If I have now entered into the high company of our patriarchs, our people may consider me, too, part of our bygone past.

Do I seem ungracious? Perhaps. Yet I have never been able to deceive myself and I still cannot do so. I have been cursed with too good, too accurate a memory. There are things which our people would probably prefer me to forget; more to the point, there are things which I myself would rather forget.

The set of legends about me have grown to the point that apparently my minor frailties are forgotten. I am now no less than a superman. This is a unique achievement on the part of a bungler, and of a man who to some was even worse than that. Yet I am simultaneously, according to the legends, the most humble of men. I enjoy this ascription of humility.

But I am not humble, nor have I ever been. Perhaps I have

been arrogant, but I hope not too much so. I hope I have been fair and straightforward. No completely humble man could ever have done what I have, or have gone through what I have. The legends have transformed me even more than so many of the events did.

How I enjoy these legends! There is, though, an omission in them, about which I have a number of times questioned Caleb. None of the legends seem ever to speak of me as laughing. Therefore, since I am the austere old man, austere I have always been, and humorless, and sure of myself, and infallible—at least that is what I hear about me from Caleb. Perhaps the people have to think that about me. But Caleb knows, and has always known, that I have often laughed, though, of course, there were times when I could and times when I could not. When we recollect together the events as they really took place, and then compare them with the version or versions that have cropped up among our people, we can still both laugh, and that is fortunate.

In the case of Caleb, this is as gratifying to me as it is surprising. He seems completely without bitterness. There was that event which I had expected would make him bitter, and with good reason; I had expected that he would not be able to hide any bitterness he might have felt. I sometimes wonder if it was the shattering turn of events to me which dissolved his own shattering disappointment. I am tolerably sure that he has no rancor in him, and, if this is so, it is the product of that great heart of his. He is, and always was, my closest friend. It was I, not someone else, who caused him his searing distress. I had to do it.

We sit and talk, as old and trusted friends do. We talk almost every afternoon and early evening. We would talk in the mornings, too, but that is the best time for Joshua bin Nun and me to confer, as more and more I turn things over to him. In the morning the people are busy, cleaning up the debris from the night before. The young men have their daily drill, precisely as I mandated them to, for they shall face some horrible battles when they cross the Jordan into Canaan. The mothers are kept busy planning for the little tots to romp in the valleys, or to climb part way up Mount Nebo; I have forbidden them as yet to ascend all the way to the top, for I myself must be the first person to reach Pisgah, the peak, for I am so humble that I reserve for myself the privilege of being the first to look westward onto the Promised Land.

Today Caleb regaled me with still another story about my infancy, about my remarkable precociousness. My foster mother, the princess of Egypt (so runs this new story), took me to visit her august father, the Pharaoh. The monarch dandled me on his knee, he admired my beauty, he patted my head, and he remained happily ignorant that I was one of the hated Hebrews. The princess told him for the twentieth time how bright I was, and he determined to put me to the test. He sent for the slaves to bring in a brazier of hot coals. These he had set before me, near my left hand; he took his jeweled crown from his head and set it near my right hand. Which would I choose? Would I be stupid enough to offend his majestic self-esteem by putting his crown on my tiny head? The story seems to break into two versions. In the one, I put out my baby hand and I lifted the heavy crown toward my head, but when I saw the open displeasure in his face, I slowly set it down on the table and I picked a hot coal instead, and put it to my mouth. The other version tells simply that I glanced at both the crown and the coals, and looked up at the Pharaoh and saw the expression on his face and, without picking up the crown, unhesitatingly picked up a hot coal. In both of these versions, it was the hot coal in my mouth that made me heavy of tongue so that I was to need, in my maturity, the fluency of my older brother, Aaron, who was to be my spokesman in the great enterprise.

The story is out of the whole cloth. But if someone were to say so, thus Caleb informs me, he would hear the reply (as he says he has heard it) that a babe simply does not and cannot remember such things; and therefore Moses' not remembering the incident in no way makes the story untrue. This is, of course, sound reasoning. Yet I must say clearly that the story of the crown is fiction. Caleb has often told me the basic tale as they now tell it: the wicked Pharaoh had decreed that all Hebrew male children should be thrown into the Nile—his wise men had told him that he would lose his crown to a Hebrew child. (Wicked kings are always destined to lose crowns to innocent babes.) To try to save me, my mother, Jochebed, had disdained the help of available midwives, who were obligated to report all Hebrew births to the palace. My sister, Miriam, helped her out in my birth. A watertight basket was secretly prepared for me, and I was put into it, and the basket put in the River Nile. When the princess, the daughter of Pharaoh, came to the Nile to bathe, she heard the sound of a baby crying, and she knew it was a Hebrew child—was it because of the tear in the voice that she knew it was a Hebrew? The princess took me from the Nile, adopted me as her own, and, to make it a very, very good story, she hired my own mother at a most generous salary to nurse me and tend to me. My sister, Miriam, so the story went, solicitously watched from a hiding place to see what would happen to me when the basket I was in was put in the Nile. This story is partly true and partly false. I could enjoy it, were it not for the part that Miriam is supposed to have played. To be candid, to attribute to my sister, Miriam, some virtue such as solicitude is to distort her character; she was a selfish, mean, and grasping woman. I know that our people adulate her. Fine. Perhaps as a girl she was different, but I have no recollection of anything kindly that she ever did. Indeed, all my recollections of her go in the opposite direction.

Whether it was the princess, or one of her maids who found me, I do not know. I was found; that is true. That she adopted me is not true; that she was my patron and generous and solicitous is true. I was not raised within the imperial palace, but in one of the quarters of the ladies of the lower nobility, along with some orphans and bastards. My mother was never actually my foster mother, though that does make a good story. There was a regular arrangement, however, for the princess' own lady-in-waiting to take me secretly to my mother, and for me to stay there for long intervals of time. This began when I was a little boy, and that is why I was always able to speak the Hebrew language as well as Egyptian. Until my father died, my mother lived with him within the slave camp; when the camps became overcrowded, she was moved into a hut just outside the camp, while Aaron and Miriam remained inside. Our people never seem to get it completely straight that we became so numerous we spilled over from the camps, to the hovels just outside them; sometimes our people talk as if there were camps and nothing but camps, and sometimes as if there were no camps at all. If you ask how that could have been, the answer is that our people were so completely cowed that the camps, and their fences, were not really needed to imprison us. So, I spent a good bit of time with my mother, and it was she who would point out to me where Aaron and Miriam were in the camp. I scarcely remember my father; I remember my mother very well. I remember too that at times both my mother and the lady-in-waiting used the same words in cautioning me that my secret must never be found out.

As a boy and as a young man, the princess used to send for me from time to time. Because she was a princess, I almost never looked directly at her; therefore I have no clear recollection of her. I have asked myself innumerable times why she had continued to show her concern for me. The explanation may be that, having had me saved from the Nile and from her father, she felt an obligation to me. I remember gifts which she gave me, especially of Egyptian clothing. She it was who paid for the tutors whom I had. I have an impression that her kindness to me was her way of defying her father; one of my tutors used to ask me, in between lessons, whether or not it was true that she hated her father. If I had known, I would not have answered him. The tutor knew only that she was my patron; he did not know I was a Hebrew. I remember only two conversations with the princess. I had long forgotten the first one, and it came back to me only very, very much later. She had said to me, "I enjoy having my slaves, but there should be no slaves. People should be free. Even a princess should be free." Perhaps I was then fourteen or fifteen; I do not remember. She was most generous and kind to me, yet

I cannot say that I really knew her. When, years later, I returned to Egypt after having fled, the princess was already dead. The second conversation which I remember I will tell about later.

That I am a Levite means that I come from the most peculiar of our tribes. Among us the arts of reading and writing have flourished. From among us teachers were drawn to serve all tribes. My mother, Jochebed, taught me to read and write our language, telling me that my father, Amram, had been one of the last of the public scribes who before the enslavement patiently wrote documents such as wills and contracts; he possessed an unusually beautiful handwriting. He could draw, but seldom did so, except in making fun of the Egyptian ways of drawing—they knew only profiles, never a full face. My mother told me that our forebear Abraham had come to feel and to teach that it was a short, and blasphemous, step from drawing a picture to worshiping it, and that he who worshiped his own creation could scarcely be worshiping his creator. So my father, Amram, did no drawing and no painting. Among us Levites there were no artisans, no architects, no builders. We were the spiritual tribe, the thinkers, the scholars. My mother wanted me to be a learned man, even in Egyptian lore. It is strange that I, the man of action, the man of practical affairs, should have come from the tribe of impractical people. Not strange that my brother, Aaron, came from it, for apart from his very personal qualities—about which I intend to be candid—he was in so many ways the epitome of our Levite disposition.

The calamity of enslavement, you must understand, was as bitter as it was incomprehensible. The excuse was that the Pharaoh was persuaded that we were an alien community, and that, were Egypt to be involved in a war, we would have to be reckoned among Egypt's foes. This is, of course, preposterous, for our Egyptian loyalty was beyond any question. Moreover, we had come into Egypt on invitation, in the gratitude of an earlier Pharaoh to our Joseph whose brilliance had preserved the country and his throne. We had not been those migrants who settle in the debris of the cities and whose habitat is the slums; no, we were joyfully given permission to settle in luxurious Goshen. We prospered, and in turn we brought prosperity to Egypt. Egypt was our home, our fatherland.

Then what was the reason? I have pondered it, but I do not know. I have sometimes thought that it was not anything that we had done, not some malfeasance that, understandably, some individuals among us had been guilty of. It was, instead, what and who we were. Or rather, it was what we were not. We were not huntsmen, or philanderers, or traffickers in slavery. Our vice was that we shunned the Egyptian vices.

Do not retort that I have an overexalted opinion of our people. Not I! Not I, Moses! Not I, after the passing of almost four decades in the Wilderness. Not after my personal tribulations. I have been the leader of humans, and therefore I have known, even from my people, agonies the like of which the Egyptians could scarcely ever have experienced. In a word, the Egyptians, even when capable of kindness, have been cruel people, but we Hebrews, even when capable of cruelty, are a compassionate people. That was our trespass.

There was no escape for us. I do not mean the efficiency with which the enslavement was introduced and maintained. I do not mean the way in which the borders were sealed, our mobility within the country terminated, our shops confiscated, and our artisans barred from the guilds; this was all done with that quiet efficiency which characterized the Egyptians. But when I speak of no escape, I mean that our people were transformed into slaves with no destiny before us but to remain slaves. Had any of us hoped to become genuinely part of the Egyptian community, even if he was as Egyptian as the most suave among our Ephraimites, there was no prospect or possibility for him, for the terms of the enslavement declared that because we were Hebrews, we could never share in the life of free Egyptians. Personal qualifications meant nothing; personal disposition meant nothing, and those of our Ephraimites and Manassites who tried to pass themselves off as Egyptians discovered that the Egyptian police were efficient and ruthless and without compassion.

Whether anyone besides me among the Hebrews was able to avoid the enslavement and the bitter toil—our task was to build unnecessary cities—I cannot say. Perhaps judicious bribes here and there gained a few individuals some respite. I am persuaded that there was little of this. Indeed, I think I can safely say that all of us Hebrews were enslaved, all of us but me. Perhaps my being the only free Hebrew was what put on me the burden which I assumed.

If the question arises, how did I manage to see my sister and brother from time to time, risking to enter where they were prisoners, and fearfully to make my exit, then the answer is that my Egyptian was totally free of accent, my cloak was Egyptian, my trousers were Egyptian, and I walked about as if I were some royalty, however minor. I suppose that my bearing, and my imitation of the arrogant gait of high-placed Egyptians, accomplished the matter.

An unpleasant truth is that I was more revolted at the treatment of the Hebrews than aware of a sense of my identification with them. The palace and the quarters where I lived were filled with slaves, whom I could order about and, if I felt so inclined, could chastise, though I never did. I felt no kinship with the palace slaves, but I began to question why some men were free and others slaves. I was too pleased that I was free to be concerned deeply that my people were not, and I recall no strong feeling that these were my people. It was slavery itself, not the enslavement of the Hebrews, that seemed to me inconsistent with the great culture of the Egyptians. If I was passingly troubled for the Hebrews themselves, I was by no means in anguish for them. But I had no thought at all of their liberation, not only because I did not care deeply enough, since I myself was free, but also because I saw no ready way of ending the slavery. Not unless the Pharaoh might pass away, and the prince—I knew him slightly—would be prevailed upon to change the abominable policy.

Yet I must have cared, for I once tried a gambit. I asked for an audience with the princess; this was the second conversation. I haltingly, and naïvely, suggested to her that, since she had spoken against slavery, she approach her brother simply (so I said) to ascertain his attitude. She laughed; it was unnecessary, for she knew it. He was worse than her father. Moreover, slave labor was a boon to royalty, especially to kings who built needless cities and palaces and temples.

So, there were slaves all about and my people were slaves, but I was free, and it was easier to glory in my own freedom than to engage in futile concern about the slaves who did not seem to be my people.

I have heard from Caleb the Hebrew tale of our midwives who courageously saved the male babies; I have heard the gloating accounts of how the Hebrews managed to multiply, despite the Egyptians. Strange that the reality should have taken this curious turn. The fact is that only a small number of babes was sporadically slaughtered, and these only to intimidate our people. The Egyptians had no wish at all to limit our numbers; to suppose that they would want to kill off potential progenitors is silly, for what they wanted was increase, the more slaves the better. The exploits of the two midwives, Shifra and Puah, in concealing Hebrew male babies, may have some truth in it, since there were some scattered infanticides which took place. But can one suppose that only these two midwives could have attended all the thousands of women in our twelve tribes? Our people constantly convert history into pleasant and puzzling legend! No, the Egyptians' plan was to keep us alive and to encourage our natural increase, for we were good workers, especially under Egyptian compulsion.

Perhaps if there had seemed to me some tiny hope for our cowed and dispirited people, I might have found within me some stray thought that contemplated the word freedom. Perhaps from the word freedom, however quietly I might have whispered it to myself, I might have found in myself some sense of relationship with my people. I confess that it probably seemed to me, to the extent that I thought about it at all, that such a bond could have meant only my despair, and I was reluctant to join my people in their hopelessness. I felt completely apart from them, and I never gave even a moment's thought to the supposition that their travail was mine.

What occupied my mind was my studies. I learned mathematics and astronomy, and I was flattered that my tutors praised me and amused that one of them declared that my aptitude for mathematics was typically Egyptian. I was nearly twenty and I suppose that I was no less attractive than the usual young man. One tutor —an old lecher—kept asking me about girls and women. I am afraid I let on to him that I was a rake; of course I was not. No; I was a Levite, a student, a quiet, retiring young man whose enjoyment was in cultivating his mind. It was proposed to me to study law, but I was not interested. I was told that I should turn to architecture; I was not interested. Nothing that was practical beckoned to me; I gave no thought to my future. I kept myself busy drinking up knowledge, learning and learning and learning, but without any idea of why, except that I enjoyed learning, anything and everything. Immersed in my schooling, I cultivated my various studies and thought little of my people, except on the rare occasions when surreptitiously I went to visit Miriam and Aaron. To visit Miriam was something of an ordeal, for piteous as was the lot of all the Hebrew women, she was persuaded that her lot was by far the worst of all. It was not; it was only bad. The gifts of goodies I secretly handed to her, she received without a word of thanks. I was torn between pity for her and annoyance at her self-pity. Perhaps I was unjust; perhaps, in view of what happened later, I can never be just to her.

But Aaron was a different matter. Aaron's hands were as inept as his tongue was agile. Few things are as easy to make as clay bricks, but Aaron managed to fail. The bricks should have been oblong; his were round. He was assigned by an exasperated guard to the lowest of the chores, that of piling up the bricks. Normally, ten men would be required to push over a stack of bricks; Aaron's stacks fell over of themselves. For this he was cuffed and beaten, and he was often in pain, but his chief response was his bewilderment that his stacks fell over so consistently. I said, "You do not concentrate on what you are doing." He smiled through his pain: "When I am piling up bricks, I am thinking about animals. Why is a camel a camel, and a horse a horse? And could one mate a camel with a horse? And why do crocodiles lay eggs, but hyenas copulate?" Twice he told me that he would have made a splendid doctor, and I knew it was true, and I wept inside me for him at the same time that I marveled at the agility of his tongue. Words came from his mouth as breath from most men's nostrils! I talked to one of the guards, suggesting that he make Aaron a teller, a tabulator of the increasing store of bricks. The guard shook his head. "That slave can add a column of figures, but he never writes down the right figures to add." Aaron, I told myself, needs to be free. But there lay ahead a greater likelihood that I would become a slave than that he would ever know freedom. My bond with Aaron was that of family, that he was my older brother, not that he was a fellow-Hebrew.

The beginning of my identification with my people came, so I recall, from a pair of incidents. One day, on my way to Aaron's camp, I passed a large patrol of Egyptian soldiers, gathered around a fire where a cook was finishing the preparation of the lunch. He called out that all was ready, and the soldiers rushed to the food. One of them, large and strong, stationed himself before the food. With one hand he helped himself, with the other he pushed the soldiers away. I stopped to watch. There was no sharing here; each fought to get food for himself, and a small, thin soldier, weeping that he was hungry, got nothing but jeers from the others. When I came into the camp where Aaron and Miriam were, a guard was carrying a small tray of fruit. He set it down carelessly, made a gesture toward a group of Hebrew slaves, and he sauntered off. The Hebrews ran to the tray. A big man among them pushed his way to the tray. "We divide!" he proclaimed. The slaves pulled back, and the big man lifted up the tray and carried it from man to man. All received the same petty amount, even a small man who was too weary to stand and who lay on the ground at the side. The big man carried the tray to him and the small man helped himself to his portion.

I witnessed this sharing. I saw it for the compassion that it was. These were my people, abused, beaten, broken in body, yet they were sharing with each other. The passing thought came to me: Must I not find some way to express my compassion? Must I not share my freedom with them?

I recall the passing impulse to cry out, "I am a Hebrew. Enslave me! Let me share my brothers' misery!" But I said to myself that I must remain free. And then I told myself that one free man might be the means of bringing freedom to all of them. If I were not free, they could never be free. At first I was not aware of what I was thinking. But after I walked out of the camp, words rang within me: "They must be free. They are my people, they must be free, and I must be the one to free them."

That is how it began, from a furtive thought, a momentary resolve. Yet the fact was that I knew neither what to do, nor how to do it. I only knew that, for the first time, I sensed that I could be at one with my people.

I expected this all to pass away. Yet, most strangely, when I went to bed, my mind was filled, not with the usual mathematics, but with marvelous plans. Plans for sneaking weapons into the camp. Into all the camps. Plans for how a network of men would be created who would prepare themselves for some future uprising, when they would, at a prearranged signal, fall on their captors and free themselves. They would become a veritable army, big enough and strong enough to challenge even Pharaoh's soldiers. I conceived no single plan that night; instead, I conceived a hundred, not one of which would ever have worked.

It was the next afternoon that the second incident took place. A Hebrew slave was digging in the sand, slowly and wearily, and near him there was a guard, condescendingly watching him, and scornfully berating him, with the vilest of language. The Hebrew slumped to the ground. The Egyptian guard came to him, shouting insults and prodding him with his toe and then kicking him. When he lifted his shovel to hit him, I could stand it no longer.

I was never a man of powerful physique, and surely the Egyptian would have had no difficulty in making me a ready target for his blows. Nevertheless, I jumped on the Egyptian, and, taking him by surprise, I threw him to the ground. Somehow he fell upon his own shovel, and somehow the vein in his neck became severed, and he began to bleed. He tried to get up, but he collapsed back to the ground. To a mixture of my horror and my satisfaction, he quickly expired.

The Hebrew slave crept away, in relief and in silence—by silence I mean that he did not bother to thank me, though at that moment I was not aware that he had not. It was more urgent to do something with the Egyptian's body, so that a good interval would elapse before his superiors would discover him missing and institute a search and an investigation. I buried the body in the sand, and, looking about to make sure I had not been seen, I walked away, slowly at first, but when I had left the scene, I walked briskly to my quarters at the palace.

That I killed the Egyptian is true. That I killed him deliberately, as the story about me goes, is not true. I had no intention of killing him; indeed I jumped at him without thinking. I spent a sleepless night, torn by the abiding satisfaction that I had killed and the fear that in some way the slaying would be traced to me. I was harassed by the awful horror that I had killed a man. Curiously, it was the latter which, most of all, made my night sleepless; the previous night, when I had dreamed of sneaking weapons into the camps for a mass uprising, the implication of the weapons—that they would be used for killing—failed completely to occur to me. The killings which would ensue on a mass uprising had not seemed real; the reality of my killing the Egyptian weighed on me. I tried to tell myself that it was only an accident; I went on to tell myself that surely freedom would never come to the Hebrews without some killing. But I could not deny to myself that I, Moses, a Hebrew and a Levite, had killed a man. I had killed, though my mother had told me that Hebrews must not kill. Our father Jacob, when his sons Simeon and Levi had slain the Shechemites in their vengeance for the rape of their sister, Dinah, had not praised them; indeed, he had not hesitated to say "Cursed is their anger, for it is unrestrained." And Levi, the ancestor of our tribe, had felt Jacob's severe rebuke so keenly that we Levites had it fully ingrained in us that no trespass was as heinous as killing. Hence, it was no consolation that it was a hated Egyptian I had slain. Toward dawn, I was able to console myself in that I had rescued a Hebrew. I did not then know that I had taken my first step in an intention, in an as yet unformed plan, to free the Hebrews.

In the daylight, my chief concern was whether or not the Egyptian's body had as yet been found. I had to find out, so I put on a different set of clothes to change my appearance a bit. I made my way back to the place where I had buried him. Afraid to linger, afraid to look too closely, I satisfied myself with the vague reassurance from a hasty glance that the body was still where I had left it.

I walked away, relieved. As I proceeded, I saw an Egyptian guard lazily sitting on the ground, while across a field two Hebrews were digging in the clay. When I passed near them, I heard them quarreling. Suddenly they took to fighting, and I ran to the unconcerned guard and said, "Those two slaves are fighting." The Egyptian spat on the ground. "Let them kill each other." I went back to the men who were fighting. They lay on the ground, one pummeling the other. I pulled the man on top off of the other. "How can you beat your brother?" I asked. The Hebrew slave, squirming in my grasp, cursed at me. "Who made you a prince and judge over me? Are you trying to kill me the way you killed that Egyptian?" He said to the man whom he had been beating, "This is the one, the one I told you about."

I turned loose of him and quickly walked away. The Hebrew slave had already told others about the incident of the day before! Without doubt, the news about it had spread in his camp, perhaps even in other camps. And the man had recognized me. It would not be long, it could not be long until the Egyptians too would hear and, having heard, would find me. Find me, and exact a disproportionate price from my body. It was then I remembered that the Hebrew had not thanked me.

I returned to my quarters. I tied a few of my possessions in a blanket. I no longer had any thought in my mind that the Hebrews must be freed; my only concern was to save myself. I had to leave Egypt, run away from the Hebrew slave who had not thanked me.

After dark, I crept out of the city, and walked eastward until dawn. When it was daylight, I found a half-burned house where I stretched out my blanket and tried to sleep until the safety of night would return.

Then, with acute bitterness, I remembered again how the one Hebrew had beaten the other and his sneer as he mentioned my killing the Egyptian. I hated him, Hebrew that he was. For such a person, freedom was too precious a gift; let this man stew in his slavery. I, Moses, I would be free. Free of Egypt. Free of such Hebrews as that slave.

I had identified myself with my people only long enough for it to end in chagrin and flight.

A few nights later, I came to the border and slipped across it. Now I could travel in the daytime. Egypt was behind me, the plight of the Hebrews was behind me. I was free, free of ever being a slave, free of any concern for the slaves, free of any concern for my people.

That is how it was.

Perhaps that is how it had to be. Perhaps it had to be a half-outsider, a repulsed half-insider, who was to bring our people freedom. Perhaps my being a half-outsider was a boon, for I was always to need both a sense of identification with my people and, for their sake, some sense of distance from them. A sense of distance which could bring a clarity to one's mind and, with it, an unmistakable sense of purpose.

✳ CHAPTER II

Our people tell little about my years away from Egypt. Perhaps it is enough for them that I went away and came back. Or, since I was as yet not their leader, they may have had small interest in me then.

They seem to know only three things, according to Caleb. One is that when I arrived in Midian, I helped the seven daughters of the priest Jethro at a well. We Hebrews have no end of stories that take place at wells. When our father Abraham sent his servant Eliezer eastward for a bride for Isaac, Eliezer met Rebekkah at a well. Our father Jacob, too, had an incident at a well. Alone, he rolled away the enormous covering-stone which usually required a host of shepherds, this for our mother Rachel. My own achievement, according to the legend, is that I drove away some male shepherds who were keeping Jethro's daughters from the well. One notices that when the stories are about men dealing with men, they take place in the wide squares, at the gates of the city where the courts hold their sessions, but when the stories are about men dealing with women, they take place at a well.

That I, Moses, enabled the seven daughters of Jethro to draw water is something that I do not remember ever happening. I have heard this story, of course, from Caleb. "I am led to understand," he said with a smile, "that you arrived in Midian, a penniless refugee, and you helped the seven daughters of the priest of Midian, a man of wealth and high position, draw their water, and very promptly you married one of them. Noble people, the Midianites! They take in a refugee and immediately marry off a daughter to him!"

I too smiled. "It is a good story, Caleb."

He snorted. "Yes. But was that the way it was?" Before I could answer, he burst into a laughter that mystified me. "Your father-in-law," he went on, "appears in our stories with at least four names: Jethro, Jether, Hobab, and Reuel. If our people cannot get his name straight, how can they expect to get the incident at the well straight?"

As I have told Caleb, there was indeed an incident at the well, but a minor one, a different one. I arrived there on foot, my sandals all but worn out, my clothes torn and ragged, my money gone. For two days I had not eaten, and, hungry as I was, my thirst was even greater, for Midian is an arid pasture land, and I had run out of water through not finding a spring or a well to refill my goatskin. It was to slake my own thirst, not to save the girls, that I came to the well. As to my saving the girls, how could I, weakened as I was, challenge a number of shepherds? I remember helping the girls water the sheep, but only that and no more. When the girls thanked me, I understood their words, for their language is in many ways like our own. Their pronunciation is strange, and I was to discover that they had turns of phrases and uses of grammar—or should I say abuses?—which are different from ours. When I replied in our own language, they seemed to have some difficulty in understanding. I then replied to them in Egyptian, but they clearly did not understand it at all. I reverted then to Hebrew and spoke slowly and possibly louder than I needed to, and this time they did understand.

I did not count the girls; perhaps at the well they numbered seven, or perhaps they did not. (Caleb assures me that they could not have numbered seven there, for that would have been too great a coincidence in that the number seven is by far our favorite number. My Egyptian tutors had instructed me about numbers. Divisible numbers, except twelve, are profane, but prime numbers, except five, are mysterious and sacred. One, two, three, seven, eleven, and thirteen are full of omen, but five is not, since it is so common, because of fingers and toes. Four, six, eight, nine, and ten are without omen, since twice two equals four, twice three six, twice four eight, and thrice three nine. But twelve is a wondrous number, divisible by three and by four and even by six. Our father Jacob had twelve sons, and our tribes therefore number twelve. The Egyptians, when they say that numbers are sacred and mysterious, really mean that they are magical. I asked once about the number ten, and it stuck in my memory that my tutor had scorned it as the most profane of numbers, merely equaling the total of fingers and of toes.)

So, Caleb suggests, the girls there may have numbered four, or six, or eight, but seven is surely what they did not number. I do not recall how many daughters Jethro had, but certainly at least seven.

When I asked for food and for lodging for the night, saying that I had come from Egypt, one of the girls pointed to a barren hill and said something to me about a tent just beyond it. The tent was occupied by a very old couple, the man nearly deaf, and the woman infirm. I made my request for food, but he did not seem to hear, and she not to understand. I pointed my finger to my mouth. She addressed to me a single questioning word in her dialect: Food? I spoke the similar word in my Hebrew. She motioned me to a rug, and I gladly sat down, and she set to work to feed me: flat bread and beans and roast lamb. It had been that way for me throughout my flight. Wherever I went, I was treated well, with good hospitality.

Why had I chosen to flee eastward? The south, to Ethiopia, was ruled out simply because the extent of Egypt, north to south, was so great that it would have taken weeks, possibly months, to traverse it. The choice therefore was between west and east. Our father Jacob had come from the east, from Canaan, and for that reason I went eastward.

But Canaan was not my goal, for no other reason than I had no goal. I was fleeing from, I was not fleeing to. Canaan did not occur to me at all. I had a very dim recollection that it was said among us that He had promised Canaan to Abraham and his descendants. But Jacob and all his household had left Canaan to go to Egypt, and I suppose that if I thought at all, I assumed that the promise of the land of Canaan was intended for some distant age, not for mine. Besides, He had spoken to none of us since His words to Jacob; He had not talked even to Joseph.

My coming to Midian, then, was mostly accidental. To the extent that it was not accidental, was the fact that I went from place to place only after being sure there were no Egyptians about. Therefore I entered the desert, looking for tiny villages of people whose languages were reputed to be near enough to Hebrew so that they might understand my speech. Throughout my journey, there was never a nomad's camp which denied me water or food or lodging. To a person fleeing, a person whose people were enslaved in Egypt, this hospitality was almost overwhelming, not so much in any excess of generosity. Indeed, some who shared with me did so out of their meager possessions. Rather, the hospitality was overwhelming in that it existed everywhere that I touched. I did not know then that the welcome I encountered was for the solitary passer-by.

When I arrived in Midian, I had no intention of staying, but simply assumed that, after a day or so, I would push on somewhere else, though whither, I neither knew nor thought about.

I had stayed the night near the tent of the old couple. I wanted to press on, but when they invited me to stay, I saw an opportunity to rest from my weariness. Perhaps—I am not certain—I wanted some time to pause and to think through where I ought to go. I scarcely moved the next day; I am certain that I did no thinking beyond being grateful that the Egyptians were now so far behind me I needed fear them no more. The next day the old woman handed me a blanket and told me to wear it while she washed and mended my clothes. On the following day, wearing my clean but patched clothes, I followed a young boy, who had come for me, to Jethro's house. I waited while, in front of the house, a circle of men sat around Jethro. I could tell that he was the man about whom they were gathered, but I could not yet see him. He was apparently receiving reports about the sheep and giving assignments to the men gathered before him. All was orderly; later on I was to learn that all had been equally systematic.

The men dispersed, and after a little wait, the boy brought me into Jethro's house. It was richly furnished with colorful rugs and drapes. Jethro was a small man, with a long black beard; his eyes were black and they seemed bright and clear; his voice was soft and low.

"You are an Egyptian?" he said to me.

"I come from Egypt. I am a Hebrew."

"A Hebrew? Then we are kinsmen, for our forebear Midian was a son of the great Abraham. Did you know that? No? But, welcome. What is your name?"

"Moses."

"Moses? Is it an Egyptian name?"

"Perhaps. It was not I who chose it."

"And what brings you here?"

"I am simply traveling."

"To where?"

"I have no destination."

"What were you doing in Egypt?"

"That is where we Hebrews are now."

"Not in Canaan?"

"Not since the time of Abraham's grandson Jacob."

I told him briefly about Joseph in Egypt and the removal there of Jacob and Joseph's brothers. I told him, too, of the enslavement, as briefly as I could.

"And the Hebrews are enslaved there? And you left?"

"I did not leave. I fled." I told him about my peculiar background, about the Egyptian I had slain, of my need to flee.

To my amazement, he made almost no comment. Instead, he said, "Raised as you were, did you receive any Egyptian education?" I told him about my studies, my concentration on mathematics and astronomy. To my surprise, he arose and said, "Come with me." We went out of his tent. He pointed to a sycamore tree. "Can you measure how high that tree is without climbing it?" I said, "There is a way. First measure a distance from the tree to wherever you may stand. Then measure the angle from that place to the top of the tree." I used the Egyptian word for angle, and he did not understand. I tried to think of the Hebrew word for angle; I could not. Indeed, I am not sure, even now, that there is one. I said, "I can show you if you give me something to write on."

"You can read and write?"

"Yes."

He called to a boy who presently brought a large piece of a broken pitcher and a quill and some ink. I asked him where I was to write, for hitherto my experience was limited to writing on papyrus. "We write on sherds, broken pieces of pottery." Then he added, "I can read. I can write a little bit."

I sat down on the ground. I drew a sketch of a wall and showed him the angle formed by the wall and the flat ground, repeating the Egyptian word angle. He repeated it after me. I drew another sketch of a wall on a hill, with the ground falling away, and I said, "Big angle." He nodded, as if he understood. Then I drew obtuse angles and acute angles and right angles, and he continued to nod. I drew a tree, then, and flat ground at right angles to it, and I asked him if he understood, and again he nodded. Then I drew a right angle, with its base equal to the flat ground in the previous drawing, and a vertical line in place of the tree. He nodded. I completed the triangle and said, "Now we can solve the problem," and proceeded to do so. He called the boy. "Bring more sherds." He said to me, "Do it again." I did it all again.

He said, "I know now how to do it. I do not mean that I am sure I could do it myself, but now I know how. I was sure there must be a way." His eyes glistened; he smacked his lips. "This is wonderful! This is wonderful!"

He importuned me to do the whole thing still another time, and I did. Then he pointed to a smaller tree, and he said, "That tree is a smaller one and we stand farther away. Can it still be done?" I said, "If we have a known base line and two known touching angles, we can do it, and in the same way."

We did more examples, and he showed no sign of weariness. At last, though, the lesson was over. He clapped his hands in joy. "I have enjoyed this! How I have enjoyed this! We must do more, much more!" We went back into the tent, and we had some fruit and a hot drink. After a while he said, "Sometimes, at evening, we count off two weeks after full moon, and then expect the new moon. Sometimes it comes, sometimes it waits for the next day. Do you know why?" I explained to him the moon's revolution around the earth and about the dark of the moon. He only shook his head. "You understand it, and you explain it well, but I do not grasp it." Then he smiled a quiet and shy smile. "I do not grasp it —yet. But if you were to explain it again tomorrow, and again the day after tomorrow, maybe then I would grasp it. Must you travel on, or can you stay?"

I said, "I can stay."

"Good! Then you will stay on with us, and we will talk about these things." He took another piece of fruit and began to eat it. "You will learn that among my people I am reputed to be wise. Oh, I am old enough not to be ignorant of the ways of men. But there is so much that I thirst to know, not about men, but about the stars and about trees and animals and creeping things. Travelers pass by with tales of the East and the learning that is there, and tales of the West and the knowledge that is there. Some day, I tell myself, I will go either east or west, and I will learn their language and even how to write it, amd master their knowledge. Now, in you, the West has come to me, and through Abraham our father we are kinsmen."

So I stayed on, the guest of this remarkable man. He was their leader. He was even their ruler. A ruler, but not like Pharaoh. I became his teacher; how much more he taught me! Often I sat in the circle of his shepherds and listened as he heard their reports and assigned them their duties. I marveled at the clarity and order of his mind. I learned, too, that he was their judge, and I attended while litigants contested before him. I noticed, when he acted as judge, that he customarily kept his eyes closed. When we had come to know each other better, I asked him why. He said, "I close my eyes so as not to see the litigants. What must occupy my attention is not the people before me, but the justice which I must try to discover. It is hard, Moses, very hard. It is even harder to recall from one case the justice which must carry over to other cases. And so few cases are identical."

"Have you no books of law?"

"Have you not yet learned how rare among us has been writing and reading? No, we have no written books. We rely on memory, and our memory is no less than wondrous. Indeed, we boast that our memory is exact and that we transmit our past without deviation. Yet when litigants are before me, I see how unclearly they remember what happened even two days ago, and then I become suspicious of the reliability of our corporate memory. No, we have no law-books, but only a tradition. A tradition which we sometimes think we inherited from Abraham. Have you traditions from him?"

"Yes, many traditions. How he left his native Ur in despair of the folly there. We hear of him that in Ur the people made idols and then foolishly proclaimed that the idols had made them. That he settled for a time in Haran, but there too he found a folly, for the people worshiped the moon, believing that the moon was the creator, but Abraham knew that the moon was a creation. Yet he would have stayed in Haran had not He instructed him to leave."

"He? Who is He?"

"He? He it is who made the sun and the moon and the earth—indeed He made everything."

"What is His name?"

"His name?"

"Yes, what is His name?"

"I have never heard that He has a name."

"He must have one."

"I have never heard it. Or heard that He has one."

"Our god has a name, Shaddai, the powerful one."

"Ours has none. Or, if He has one, I have never heard it."

Jethro seemed troubled. Then he smiled. "Never mind. We Midianites do not think too often about Shaddai. It frightens us to think about him. Also we have our idols, and when our holy season comes, we worship them. And we worship the sun too. Mostly, though, we worship Shaddai who makes our flocks increase in the spring. I have been only passingly curious about our worship, Moses. I am a devout man; therefore I resolutely push away from me the passing thought that our idols, since they are lifeless, cannot bestow life. I worry that the sun allows itself to be covered by clouds. Yet when these doubts assail me—no, they do not assail me, they only come into my mind as unnoticeably as a servant entering my tent. But I tell myself, when the doubts appear, that beyond the idols and the sun, I know nothing, absolutely nothing, except that we speak of a power called Shaddai. The few occasions when I have tried to think about Shaddai, I have become so frightened that I have pushed the thoughts away."

I said, "Among us Hebrews it is known that our God spoke to Abraham, to Isaac, and to Jacob."

Jethro said, "We know nothing of Isaac and Jacob; they are your ancestors, not ours. We trace our heritage of law to Abraham. Do you not?"

I tried to remember what I heard from my mother. "I do not recall any such tradition."

"Have you no books of laws?"

"I know of none. If perhaps we had them, they disappeared in the time of Joseph and his brothers when we lived under Egyptian law, as now my people live under Egyptian lawlessness." The last words I spoke with some bitterness, and this surprised me, since for the most part, I had begun to forget Egypt.

He said to me, "When spring comes and the new lambs are born, we are thankful, and we are also frightened. We are thankful for the increase, but we are frightened, too, that so many lambs die. We fear that the destroyer who kills the lambs may kill us too. We gather at our altars, and give back some lambs to Shaddai—whoever he is—who gave them to us. Some of the blood we gather, and we smear it on the doorposts of our houses or at the portals of our tents, to keep the destroyer away. You will witness this in the spring." He shook his head. "I am more at ease as a judge than I am as a priest. A judge knows with what he deals; a priest does not know, he only believes." He looked at me. "Do you know your God or do you only believe about Him?"

I shrugged my shoulders. "He has not spoken since He spoke to Isaac's son, our father Jacob."

"But do you not think about Him?"

I said, "I have had no reason to do so. Even when I was concerned with the enslavement of our people, I did not think about Him. If I had thought about it, I would have wondered why He allowed it and still allows it. No; I have not thought about Him."

"What could you tell me about Him?"

I laughed. "I can tell you nothing, because I know nothing."

"But surely you must know something."

"Only that He spoke to Abraham, Isaac, and Jacob and that He created the world and He rules it."

"How do you worship Him?"

"I am not sure. Except that He commanded circumcision upon us."

"But what are your holy days?"

"We have none."

"No laws? And no holy days?"

"I know of none."

"We circumcise too. But we have no tradition that our Shaddai commanded it."

"I remember hearing that it was our God who so commanded us."

Jethro fell silent for a moment. Then he spoke: "I shall tell you something, Moses." He pursed his lips, and he rocked back and forth. "Nothing in the world is more important than understanding. Than for a person to know who he is and where he came from and where he is going. Some or all of these questions I find I cannot answer at all, and I do not even dare to think about them. But they are more important even than angles and the height of trees, and how chickens lay eggs, and how hawks are able to fly. I have a thirst for knowledge, Moses. But I have no thirst to know about my God; only a passing curiosity. I am afraid to have the thirst. I am afraid of my God."

That is the way we often talked, moving from one subject to another, always very quickly, never really finishing one thing before we began another.

When each spring came, I would take part in the ceremony of the lambs, in the sacrifice of the few so that the many would live. I even went around with Jethro as he smeared blood on the doorposts of the houses. I saw how serious he was, and I tried to match his earnestness, but I could scarcely believe that a smear of blood would keep the Detroyer away. Besides, when I tried to find out who and what this Destroyer was, Jethro either could not or would not answer me. It puzzled me that in some ways his curiosity was boundless, but about the Destroyer and about his *Shaddai*, he forcibly restrained his curiosity.

In due time he spoke to me of his daughter Zipporah. "She is shy, but she is intelligent. She is loyal, loyal beyond my other daughters. A selfless girl. For a man other than you, she might be too quiet, too silent. The usual man could never learn her qualities. She would make you a good wife, Moses."

I said, "Is she willing?"

"I have asked her. Yes, she is willing. Not eager. But she will marry you."

"May I see her?"

He called to his servant to summon Zipporah. I thought I would see a woman; instead I saw a girl. Her complexion was very dark and her hair coal black, and her eyes were brown. She seemed tiny, not in height, but only because she seemed slender, and I wondered if her body was as yet fully developed. Yet as I looked at her I became aware of a desire for her. When he said to her, "Moses asks if you are willing to marry him," and she answered, "I would be honored," her voice was clear as a flute, and as musical. I wanted her to stay so I could talk with her. But she gracefully withdrew. I said to Jethro, "She is lovely. When can I see her again?"

"At your marriage. I must talk with her and let her tell us when."

A week later Jethro took me to a little house he was giving me. Three days later we were married, to the music of harps and pipes, and then we were escorted to our house and allowed to enter into its privacy.

Perhaps, if it is of any interest or concern, I should say that we both came to the marriage bed in full purity. That this was so for me may surprise you, for my position at the court brought me more than one opportunity and more than one forward Egyptian girl. What it was that deterred me from those opportunities, I cannot say. Perhaps it is that I am a Hebrew, and the open lust of the Egyptians, and their relentless satisfaction of it, repelled me.

I was soon to discover the brightness of her mind, the tinkle of her laughter, her endless search for ways to serve me and to please me. When I said to her, "You are my wife, not my slave," she only smiled. I came to be completely in love with her.

Especially when she told me we were to have a child. How that thrilled me! How that pleased Jethro! He already had grandchildren; I fancied that somehow my child would become his favorite. I felt myself now to have become a genuine Midianite. I had never really been an Egyptian; the Hebrew part of my life was well behind me. No, I was a Midianite.

Then a month before the baby was due, Zipporah startled me. "If it is a boy, will you yourself circumcise him?"

"I have not thought about it."

"I have spoken to father. Among us Midianites, it does not need to be the father who does the circumcising. But he thinks that among you Hebrews, it must be the father, because your God so commanded Abraham."

I went to Jethro and spoke to him. He said, "Did you not say that your God commanded Abraham to circumcise himself and his children?"

"I will do as you Midianites do."

"Zipporah wishes you to do as the Hebrews do."

"But why?"

"Because she has bound her life to yours."

"But am I not virtually a Midianite?"

"In all things but one, Moses."

"What is that?"

He looked directly at me. "Whenever we talk, and we mention Egypt, there is a difference in our voices, a difference in the tones in which we speak. To me, the Egyptians are the wicked people who have enslaved those Hebrews. To you, the pain of that enslavement is constant."

I shook my head. "I never think about it any more."

He nodded. "I suppose you do not. But when we mention Egypt, I hear your voice and I see your face. Deep inside you, the Hebrews are still your people, and you still suffer their agony."

"I do not think I do," I said.

"And Zipporah suffers it too."

I said, "I have forgotten Egypt and my people. I have even forgotten the Hebrew man whom I helped and who scorned me."

"You say you have forgotten, exactly in the same moment in which you remember. But it is Zipporah, not I, who has asked about the circumcision."

Back at my home, I spoke to her. She said, "Of course we must do it in the Hebrew way."

"But you are the mother, and a Midianite—"

"I am what my husband is. If you are a Hebrew, I too am a Hebrew."

Somehow, estranged from the Hebrews as I felt myself to be, her words warmed me. I said so, and I caressed her. Then she said, "At night you are sometimes very restless. I whisper to you, 'What is the matter, Moses?' You do not answer. I have held a lamp to your face and seen it to be a face wracked in pain."

I said, "Sometimes I think that I dream about Egypt, and the cruelty, and the beatings, and the way our people are slaves. But in the morning, I never remember the dream."

"It is in your heart, not in your mind, Moses."

"Perhaps." Then I said, "If it is a boy, and you wish me to perform the circumcision, I will do so."

"I wish it."

But when the boy was born—we named him Gershom—he seemed sickly, and even after the sixth day he seemed to continue to lose weight. I spoke to Jethro. "It is my opinion," he said, "that one should not circumcise such a sick baby."

So, after all, we did not hold the circumcision. I confess that it did not greatly disturb me, for I did not think something of that kind could be very important. Zipporah, however, was disturbed, and only the concern for our sickly child kept her somewhat calmed. Then the baby began to get well, and she asked me a few times if I thought he was now healthy enough, and each time she asked, I answered, "Not yet." So she was troubled.

With Jethro there was almost daily a session in which he would ask me about some phase of Egyptian lore, and promptly we would become diverted into an animated discussion of customs, or laws, or religion, or science. Indeed, had it not been for these stimulating discussions, which constantly disclosed to me the orderliness of his mind and his acute ability to make the separations and distinctions which are necessary for accurate understanding, he might have exhausted my knowledge! I never found him tiring. In mathematics, especially when we discussed abstract principles, he often insisted that he did not fully understand; even at those times when he was able to repeat without error complex things which I had told him, he would say that it was only the words he was repeating, not the idea, and that he was too old to be beginning to learn. But if he was a beginner as a student, in human wisdom he was not only sagacious, but almost a poet in his ability to sum up his observations in short, rhythmic sentences. Ancient proverbs lay at the tip of his tongue, much as spices do at the hand of a merchant. Often, though, when he cited a proverb, he would first extol it as an epitome of wisdom, and then, with a twinkle in his eye, assure me that the proverb lacked only one quality, truth. "Proverbs and the wisdom of the folk are for prudent people, not for the venturous. They are for men who wish to live without risk, not for the man with daring."

"And what kind of man are you?" I asked, laughing.

"I am the man who as a boy presumed to dream of going to Chaldea or Egypt, but never dared to. These days, I dream that I have been there, knowing all the time that I have not. It was not that I was cowardly, Moses, at least not in the usual sense. I am the man in whom common sense prevailed, and such men distinguish themselves in their lack of accomplishment."

I said, "What kind of man am I?"

"I do not know. Not yet. I think you are a man of unusually high intelligence. I think you believe you are a placid man. You are not; you are a man of the heart, a sensitive man. I think you have learned to restrain anger, and you have needed to restrain it because it is so powerful in you."

I said, "I know of my anger. I killed an Egyptian."

"Yes. But you are not a killer, Moses."

"I do not think I am. But I think I am placid, Jethro."

"You could be a venturous man. Once you were."

"When?"

"When you slew the Egyptian. When you had the thought that you must release the Hebrews."

"The killing was only an impulse. The release of the Hebrews —that was only the shadow of a thought, and never a real intention."

Then Jethro seemed to hesitate. "You are a sensitive man, Moses, and I wonder if you will understand what I am about to say." He paused. "We meet every day. Your brothers-in-law shepherd the sheep; you sit and discuss eternal truths with me. I have arranged it so." He looked straight at me. "It is not a good arrangement, Moses."

I felt my face begin to flush. "Have people said to you that I do not do my share of the work?"

"They would not dare speak to me. Their wives speak to Zipporah."

I said, without hesitation, "She has said nothing to me."

"To them she has said enough."

After a moment I said, "I shall do my share of the shepherding."

He nodded. "We shall still find time to talk, Moses. In the evenings."

I said, slowly, "If I were a Midianite, rather than a Hebrew, the wives would have never spoken to Zipporah."

"You are wrong. They would have spoken. With even more boldness."

I said, with some warmth, "Until this moment I have felt myself to be fully a Midianite."

"Neither you nor I can stop idle and jealous tongues from wagging."

I got up, and left him, and went to Zipporah. "Why did you speak to your father, not to me, about your sisters and their words about my not doing my share?"

"Father should not have told you."

"But why?"

"It would have made you angry. The way you are angry now. And angry even at me."

I looked at her. Her beautiful face was distorted into the face of an unhappy baby, and her eyes were filled with tears. "I am not angry," I said to her. Yet I was angry, very angry. I kissed her; I dried her tears.

I went out to walk in the hills. Was all this because Jethro had favored me? Or was it, rather, because I was an outsider? And was I not simply an outsider, and a Hebrew at that? My mind told me that it had nothing to do with my being a Hebrew, but it had to keep telling me that, for the notion persisted in recurring to me.

If I say so myself—to quote a proverb I had heard from Jethro, "Let a stranger praise you, and not your own lips"—I became the best of all the shepherds. It was I who was up first in the morning and who came back last in the afternoon. I said to Zipporah, "Have your sisters ceased to complain about me?"

She laughed. "They complain that you work so hard that their husbands must now work harder."

I still met with Jethro, but not as often as before. And at times, when we met after the evening meal, I was tired and he was fresh, and I think that these were times when I nodded and even dozed during our talks.

It happened one morning that a tiny lamb jumped onto a large rock, a rock that had just fallen from the top of the mountain. As the lamb jumped on it, the rock suddenly rolled, and the gentle lamb became frightened and jumped again, and now another large rock rolled and smote the lamb. It lay bleating, a prisoner of this second rock. I walked to it and with difficulty moved the rock away. The lamb lay still. I lifted it to its feet, but it fell over and bleated in pain, and I knew that one or more of its delicate legs was broken. I picked it up and carried it to the fold. I tied some smoothed twigs to the tiny legs. I walked away and the lamb followed me. The next day, Zipporah, to whom I had said nothing, mentioned this lamb to me. "And what is it that your sisters now say?" I demanded.

"Their husbands do not admire you," she said, "but I do. They would have killed the lamb; you rescued it."

It was a trivial incident. I wondered if I had made myself ridiculous in carrying the lamb back to the fold. But I told myself that what I had done was proper. Was I not the shepherd?

Yet I grew more and more weary with the chores and especially with the daily habit of rising so early and returning late. But one day the thought occurred to me that I had responded instinctively to a stricken lamb, but I had managed to stifle the concern which I should have felt for my stricken fellow Hebrews. I reasoned to myself that the lamb and the Hebrews had nothing to do with each other. Yet as often as I told myself that the connection I was seeing was simply not there, exactly that often did that connection seem to assert itself. And as I continued to tell myself that this connection did not exist, I began to admit to myself that there had persisted in me a deep and abiding concern for my people, a concern I thought had disappeared. I began to have moments in which I chided myself for seeming to have developed an unconcern, and then counterbalancing moments in which I justified the unconcern, either by telling myself that I was simply tired of my chores, which made demands on my body but not my mind, or by asking myself the comforting question, what could I do?

To that question, I could give the comforting answer in the single word, nothing. Except that one day I asked myself if it was true that I could do nothing. Then in place of asking what I would do, I began to ask myself questions about myself.

Was I an adventurous person? Or was I one who prudently ran no risks? And what was my life to be? That of an able shepherd, passing seasons and years and decades in being a shepherd? Or was there something that I could possibly do about my fellow Hebrews? Could I—I, Moses—who had fled and become merely a shepherd, return to Egypt for the great task of releasing my people from slavery? How would I do it? I did not know.

To none of such questions did I give myself sensible answers, or answers which were clear enough for the issue to arise whether the answers were sensible or not. Then, for some unexplained reason, I again remembered the bleating of the injured lamb, and it echoed in my ears as if it were the cries of pain of my people.

One night, Zipporah shook me and awakened me out of a deep sleep. "Moses, Moses! What is wrong?"

I said, half-awake, "What is the matter?"

"You have been calling in your sleep, saying 'Do not despair, do not despair. My people will be free!' "

I said, "I was dreaming. I do not remember the dream."

"You dreamed of the Hebrew people. Of your people." Then she said, in the same breath, "Of my people." She sat on the bed. "You must set them free, Moses."

I took her hand in mine. With my other hand I caressed her cheek. "It is not possible, Zipporah."

"It must be possible, Moses."

I shook my head. "It is not possible. I know Egypt. It is not possible."

"Will not the Hebrew God help you, Moses?"

I said, "He has not spoken since the days of Jacob."

I lay back in my bed. Sleep would not come to me. I was forlorn, discouraged. Zipporah was still sitting on the bed. I felt her caress my hair; I heard her say, "Moses! It is too soon to be completely sure. But I think—I think—that we will finally have another child." Her words broke the despair and brought me rejoicing. Yet the next night, when I returned from Jethro's house in the village, I could see that something was amiss with Zipporah. At first she would not speak. Then at last she said, tearfully, "I should not have spoken last night. We are not going to have another child. Not now. Not ever!"

In the next days, she conferred with midwives, and she tried their countless remedies, but all in vain. Gershom was the pleasantest of little boys, but I wanted more children. Strange, I thought, that here in the freedom of Midian, more children were denied us, while in Egypt, Hebrew children in abundance were being born to live the life of slavery. How good it was that Gershom was here, not there! But what of the countless Hebrew children there?

One day a traveler came by, an Ishmaelite, who had been in Egypt. "What is with the Hebrews?" I asked.

"They are slaves. Miserable slaves."

"And the Pharaoh?"

"The old Pharaoh is dead."

"And the new Pharaoh?"

The Ishmaelite smiled a knowing smile. "People now long for his wicked father."

All the next days those words kept running through my mind. "People now long for his wicked father." My poor people! I pushed my way southward with my sheep, and in the distance I saw the outline of the mountain Horeb; the afternoon sun was shining on its west side. Then I saw a marvelous thing, a bush on fire. Bright as was the sunlight, I could nevertheless see that the bush was on fire. I looked at it, wondering how it could be burning and how it could be seen so clearly. I waited to see the flames die down and disappear. I waited a long time; the flames did not die down, not even a little. I began to walk to the bush.

Then He spoke to me. Not, at Caleb tells me, people say an angel spoke, but He Himself spoke. "Do not come near. Put off your shoes, for you are standing on holy ground." Then He said, "I am the God of your fathers, the God of Abraham, the God of Isaac, and the God of Jacob."

I should not have been frightened, but I was. Frightened as are those who, having heard of this, insist that it was an angel who spoke to me, for they are fearful of even saying that it was He Himself. I hid my eyes, afraid to look at the bush any longer.

The chief recollection which I have today is surely that I was overpowered by fear, a fear beyond any possible measuring, a fear beyond my ability to describe its intensity. That our people sometimes speak of an angel's speaking to me, and go on to recount an orderly conversation between Him and me, is perhaps easy to explain, in the tendency of people to simplify things and to put a barrier between them and what is holy. On those occasions when I have tried to give myself a simple and calm account of what took place, I have been unable to. When I repeat some of the words which were spoken, I am not certain that these were the exact words. The truth is that my tongue became frozen, or else it uttered a babble of syllables, and I am reasonably sure that at one point He replied to my intention rather than to my sentences. It was not by any means an orderly conversation, not on my part. While it was happening, I knew myself to be bewildered, and little as was the control which I had over my tongue, even less was the control over my ears. They heard and yet did not hear, and they seemed to gather in sound and at the same time to impede my comprehending His words. Moreover, I must confess that that awesome moment now flows together with the questions which later Jethro threw at me relentlessly, or the reassurances which Zipporah gave me, so that I cannot any more easily separate what went on between Him and me, and between them and me. I must nevertheless try to keep these matters somewhat apart.

Neither my fear nor bewilderment was ever jostled aside by that stronger force, incredulity. At no time did I fail to believe my beleaguered ears. You may therefore trust the truth of what I tell, even if I cannot vouch for the accuracy of the words.

He said to me, "I am the God of your fathers, Abraham, Isaac, and Jacob. I have seen the affliction of My people in Egypt. I have heard the groans which the oppressors force from their mouths. I have determined that My people shall be free. You shall go to Pharaoh, and free My people. You shall bring them here to this mount, to worship Me. Then you will lead them into a land of milk and honey." I felt within me an instantaneous exultation. He spoke further, "It is you whom I will send to Pharaoh."

I remember clearly what my answer was, for my exultation momentarily ceased, and anxiety abruptly took its place. I said,

"Who am I that I should go to Pharaoh, to bring the Hebrews out of their slavery in Egypt?"

He wasted no words in saying who I was. Rather, He said, in the simplest of ways, "I will be with you."

It was not an answer, yet it was a full answer. I, no matter who I was, was to go, and He would be with me.

How this story has grown since then! There is a matter pertaining to my rod, a rod which supposedly turned into a snake and then back into the rod, a symbol of His miraculous power. That is a harmless legend.

I was, as you will understand, perplexed. For me to have devised some mission of my own was quite different from His sudden speaking to me after so long a silence, and from His sending me. Who would believe that He had spoken to me? Would the Hebrews believe it? I stammered some words to Him. I said, "If I come to the people of Israel and say to them, 'The God of your fathers has sent me to you,' and they ask me, 'What is His name?', what shall I say?"

He said, "You ask My name?"

I said, "Yes."

What he then said is strange, and even today it is still partially mystifying to me. It seemed then, and seems now, devoid of logic, or, at least, of human logic. He gave this reply: "Tell them that I am Who I am, that I am He Who exists." But He went on: "Tell them that *I am* sent you."

In my confusion and the absence of comprehension, I repeated His words: " '*I am* sent me!' " I could scarcely credit my ears. I would have grasped it if He had said, "Tell them that *I* sent you." But that *I am* sent me—I said no more than to repeat His words; I think I babbled for a moment.

He said, "I am Yahve. That is My name. Yahve, He Who is, He Who causes things to be. I cause existence; I am He Who is."

I said, "But Your words: Say that *I am* sent you—"

"A little joke, Moses."

I babbled on, greatly astonished.

He said, "O Moses! Are you to be like other people and deny

me a humorous word? Am I available only to the long-faced, the gloomy, the dispirited?"

Then I said, "I do not understand. In such a serious moment You make a play on words—"

He said, "You must beware of men who cannot smile. I send you to lead My people. I send you to travail, not to joy. The joy you must carry along with you. Beware, Moses, of men who cannot smile. And My people must learn that unless they can laugh, even in times of distress, they can lose themselves."

That I can repeat what He said shows that I heard Him. Can you readily believe how baffled I was?

He went on: "I am Yahve. I appeared to your fathers, Abraham, Isaac, and Jacob, as the God Shaddai; I was never known to them by My name, Yahve. To you, first of all men, I have revealed My name, for upon you I put a charge greater than has ever been put on any man."

"But surely other slave peoples have been freed—"

"I put on you a greater charge than freedom. You cannot yet understand; in time you will."

How right that was! How terribly, agonizingly right!

Yet my mind had not moved forward; it was still back in His words to me that I was to go to Pharaoh. I managed to say, "There is a question which I must ask, but I am fearful of speaking."

"Speak without fear."

"You tell me to go to Pharaoh. Why is it I whom You send? Can You not free Your people without me?" Having spoken, I found myself in acute terror, and I said, "Forgive me."

"I forgive you." I record here not so much His words as my poor remembrance of them. "I created men, not gods. There is no God besides Me. I have set a limit both on man and on Myself. I do not debase man by doing his work for him." There was a silence, and then He went on, "If this is not yet clear to you, with your own intelligence in time you will understand."

As I now ponder it, this last matter was scarcely cogent or related; it is the kind of thing that Jethro enjoyed discussing. How it chanced to come into the conversation, I am only now beginning to grasp. I think that random thoughts which I had never put into words before then now coursed through my mind in somewhat vague form. Or perhaps they were not even vague thoughts, but only some hints of one's unshaped thoughts. Or, better still, His words were answers in advance to questions which in time I would need to ask, if not of Him, at least of myself.

I said to Him one more thing, but let me defer it for just a bit. Let me instead recall that I cannot at all remember how the awesome encounter ended, nor can I recall how long it lasted. I seem to recall that it ended as abruptly as it began.

As I moved away from the mountain—whether walking, or crawling, or running, I do not remember, just as I do not recall putting on my shoes, though I did—I did not think clearly or consecutively. My thoughts ran more side to side than ahead. What I could not think through to a decision then, I cannot think through to a decision even now. Perhaps I can explain this matter which was, and is, beyond all deciding, and then I can go back to the point at which decision was possible. To proceed: On the one hand (so I believe I argued with myself), He was sending me. He, God, was sending me; me, Moses, a man. The mandate to go was from Him: yet the task was something which I, at least in part, was to accomplish. The divine and the human, then, were to be intertwined. How was I to understand, both then and also later, which part was in His hands, and which was in mine? I have spoken of the rod which turned into a snake as a legend; our people speak of it as one of the signs by which I could glimpse His power. Yet even while I dismiss this as a legend, there is the other matter our people tell about, of my hand which in a trice became leprous and in a trice was cured. This, you must know, is not a legend; I attest that it happened. I saw my hand become infected; then I saw it cleansed of infection. I saw this with my own eyes. If you say that my eyes deceived me, bear in mind that I who affirm the leprosy of my hand do not hesitate to smile at the legend of the rod. You must not charge me with lying, but at most with being mistaken. I know that I was not mistaken.

If, then, He was sending me, perhaps some of His power was going with me. But since I was not He, then some of what I must do, perhaps even much of it, I must do as a man does things. Where was the boundary to be? And where—and when—would He intervene in those things beyond me? To be bereft of knowing where and when He would do so, made me feel my own great burden.

Perhaps it was this sense of burden which prompted me, as He was speaking to me, to say something more to Him. What I said was, "Send whom You will, but not me!" Perhaps it was this same sense of burden that made me go on to describe myself to Him as heavy of tongue. I should not have said that. In answer, He replied that He would designate Aaron as my spokesman. Let me not blaspheme; He surely meant Aaron to be a help to me. Could He have failed to know Aaron as I was to come to know him?

But had I really wanted Him to send someone else? I think not. I think that I was only expressing my fears and uncertainties. I am sure that I did not want someone else to go; it was my privilege, my opportunity. I wanted to go!

As I keep saying, I do not know whether these thoughts came to some clarity in my mind then, or if these were only at that time impressions which fleeted through my mind without coming to rest there.

I was going to lead them from Egypt, lead them across stretches of land and over narrow or broad channels of water, and I was going to bring them into some land where they would settle in freedom and live in freedom, and live in peace and prosperity. To free them in Egypt was to be only the beginning; the end would come only when I, Moses, would have proudly led them somewhere. I, Moses, was to be their leader, from the beginning until the end, their leader until the time of the full accomplishment. Do you notice that my thoughts were of what I, Moses, would do?

That I would lead out people into some land did not mean that

I knew where I would take them. Canaan was completely unknown to me and I felt no special connection with it.

I like to think now that when I made my way to Zipporah, my fears quickly gave way to joyous expectation, but it was not that way. No, I felt some exaltation, but I felt absolutely no joy, not even as the conviction was forming in me that I, Moses, would set our people free. No; already then I thought vaguely of impediments and obstacles and problems. I was a man of hopes, but also a man of fears.

I made my way to Zipporah, unaware that I was moving. I told her of the burning bush as if it was still close by. She responded as if she had been daily expecting me to exerience it, and then to come home and to tell her of it. She said, quietly, "He is sending you. We must go."

"We? No, you cannot come with me."

"But I can. And I will."

"It can be dangerous, Zipporah. I cannot expose you—"

"If He is sending us, He will watch over me."

I shook my head. "No, beloved. You may not."

Her eyes filled with tears. "You cannot leave me behind. He is your God, He is mine. Your people will be mine. And I must go to Egypt to taste their enslavement so that I am truly part of them." She took hold of my hand. "Our Gershom is no longer a baby, and he will come too. And he has no brothers or sisters who need my care—" Her voice trembled, for she had desperately wanted a second child.

I said, "We shall see. But I must immediately speak with your father."

Indeed, I wanted to go to Jethro that very moment, but she had prepared my meal for me, so I lingered to eat it. Usually we talked as we ate; that evening we ate in silence. I could not speak, simply because too many thoughts and anxieties and plans kept coursing through me. Only when I was about to leave, and she asked if she should go to Jethro with me—before I could answer, she herself said No—did she disclose why she had been silent. She said, as I stood at the portal, "Moses! Our Gershom is not yet circumcised!" Fear and plaintiveness echoed in her sweet voice. She added, "It must be done. You must do it." I gave her no answer but a kiss, and I left.

Jethro heard me out, at full length, without any interruption. He said, then, "You must go, Moses."

My heart warmed to his approving words. I said, "I knew you would say that."

He said, "It has been in your mind, as I have known even better than I think you have."

I said, "I was fearful that you would discourage me. Or, as the father of your daughter, and, as priest and chieftain, you might try to forbid me."

He shook his head. "I would not presume to forbid you. Shall I forbid a man from going to free his enslaved people? Not I." Then he said, "So He spoke to you?"

"Yes," I said. "And His name is Yahve."

"Indeed?" He smiled. "I have observed that people are able to believe what they want to believe."

I said, "I assure you that He spoke to me."

He looked at me, and with a nod of his head, said softly, "You have told me that He has not spoken since the days of your forebear Jacob. Now, most opportunely, He has spoken to you. And told you His name!" A smile flitted over his lips. "Remarkable!"

I said, "Do you not believe me?"

He paused. He spoke sharply. "Moses, do you believe yourself?"

I rose up. "I am not lying."

"Sit down, Moses. I have not said you were lying. I do not think you were, or are. Or, if you are, it is to yourself you are lying, not to me."

I said with some anger, "Why do you say this to me?"

He said, "Did you see Him?"

"No. Only the bush."

"Then you did not see Him?"

"He is invisible."

"How convenient! Invisible! Is He audible?"

"I heard Him."

"Is His voice tenor, baritone, or bass? Or does He have a eunuch's soprano?"

"It was a voice unlike a human voice."

"Was it your ears that heard? If I had been in the vicinity, would I too have heard? Or did you hear, not with your ears, but inside you?"

I said, "I do not know. I only tell you that He spoke to me."

He seemed to be pondering my words. Then he scowled. "You led your sheep to a mountain, the mountain we call sacred. The mountain on whose top we see the lightning play and from whose summit we often hear the acute crash of thunder. The mountain near whose peak is the cave, the cave which our people never enter, for it is a dangerous cave. There, so we have heard, a man can sometimes see the god. Were you at the cave? And in it?"

"Not at it. And of course not in it."

"You were only on the side of the mountain?"

"Yes. On the west side."

He thought for a moment. Then he smiled. I said, "Why do you smile?"

He did not answer for a moment. "What is He to do, and what are you to do?"

"About what?"

He said, emphatically, "About each detail. About every detail."

(Was this not what I had myself wondered about, as when I had asked Him, "Why must you send me? Cannot You release Your people without me?" But, had I really asked Him that? Or do I now transform the question which Jethro was asking me into a question which I had in actuality not asked Him? I no longer know.) But Jethro went on. "Will you yourself break all the sets of chains, or will He? Will you yourself organize an uprising of your people, or will He?"

"I do not know. I have not yet thought about it."

He called to a servant to bring in some fruit. "He is sending you. He is not going instead of you."

"But I am sure He is going with me."

"Will someone speak to the Pharaoh? If so, will it be He, or will it be you?"

I said, "Jethro, I have not thought these things through. Your questions are all the same, for you keep asking what He is to do and what I am to do. I too—"

"Yes, that is what I ask. Not for me to know, but for you to know." The fruit was brought in, and he had the servant pass the bowl to me first, but I did not want any. Leisurely he inspected the bowl and then made his selection. "I should not imagine that it would be difficult for Him to see the Pharaoh, since He is God. I should suppose, though, that since you are only a man, you may discover some obstacles. There are officials; there are ranks and levels of the nobility; there are armed guards."

"I have not thought about it."

"No. It is too soon. You are still too much filled with the day's experience." He leaned back, and he closed his eyes. "It is a great enterprise, Moses. A very great enterprise. I hope you will succeed."

"But of course I will. He is sending me, and He will help me."

"My questions—the ones I have now already begun to ask myself—are not about Him, but about you. What you are to do, and how you are to do it. I could easily tell myself that were you to attempt this unaided, to attempt it entirely on your own, it would be impossible. You must not underestimate the difficulties."

"I shall know how to deal with the Egyptians. I assure you that I know them, and I know Egypt."

He shrugged his shoulders. "Perhaps you know them. Do you know your Hebrews?"

"My Hebrews? I do not understand your question."

"They are slaves. Their bodies have been damaged. And they cannot help but have the minds of slaves. I think that I have known enough slaves to know a slave's mind. I no longer have slaves; once I had them. I freed my slaves, not because I am a kindly man, but because I lived in fear of them. One slave whom I freed I remember. He was first my father's slave; I inherited him, and I promptly freed him. First he was grateful. Then I learned that, free, he hated me who had freed him more than he hated my father, who had berated him and lashed him." He took another piece of fruit. "Perhaps as you begin to form your plans, you may want to discuss them with me. I can promise you a willing ear."

"Zipporah wants to come with me to Egypt."

"Naturally."

"I cannot take her."

"She would be an encumbrance?"

"It is not that so much as the danger. I could not be sure of her safety."

"Say nothing to her about her safety. That will only increase her insistence on going. Tell her, lovingly, that you must go alone."

"And may I leave her, and Gershom, in your care?"

"Yes."

I thought that he wanted to talk some more. I did not want to, for I had suddenly become unbearably weary. For some elusive reason I felt my sense of elation disappear, and I wanted desperately to go to my home, to lie on my bed and to fall quickly asleep. I rose, anxious that he might detain me. He did not. He rose, too, and he walked with me to the door.

"Had you said, Moses, that you had been to the cave and in it, I would have said you deceive yourself. The bush that burned—it has inclined me to believe you." As I stepped into the dark he said, "May He who spoke to you bless you, Moses."

These heartening words of his restored to me some of the elation I had lost. Indeed, I had begun to wonder what I would do if he, whose opinion I valued and whose esteem I cherished, and whose approval I needed, had either gullibly accepted my story, as if I had gone through some everyday occurrence, or else had charged me with delusion and self-deceit. I tried to tell myself that the truth of that afternoon was entirely independent of both overhasty belief and of cynical disbelief. Yet I knew that I wanted to be believed, and that I had wanted Jethro to believe me. Zipporah, I knew, would believe me, even if I told her lies. I wanted Jethro to believe me, not alone because it was true, but because very passionately I wanted him to believe me.

If Jethro had doubts, which I think I allayed, Zipporah had none at all. When I returned to her, I quickly gained the impression that her anxiety about Gershom's circumcision no longer was in the forefront of her preoccupation. Indeed, what soon became clear and unmistakable was her joy, not that He had finally spoken, but that it was I whom He had spoken to. To her this seemed just as it should be; it seemed to her that there was nothing to be surprised at that I, who had fled from Egypt and had had the conviction that, at least consciously, I had forgotten my people, should have been the one to whom He spoke. She exulted in the privilege that had come to me; she assured me that I had received an honor that was due to me; and she wondered if she was worthy of being the wife of the one to whom He had spoken. I told her that she must not abase herself. She answered that it was not abasement of herself, but only the recognition of the worthiness which lay in me. I laughed at her, lovingly of course, and I assured her that not I, but the great enterprise, was important, and she replied that I was important to the great enterprise.

When we lay down to sleep, she said to me, "Tell me again how it happened. Tell it all—don't leave anything out."

I began to tell her, starting, of course, with leading my flock toward the mountain. I remember that I got as far as my first glimpse of the burning bush. Then the sequence of things—what He said and what I said in reply—quickly became blurred in my mind. Moreover, the fear I had experienced at the moment when it had all happened began now to grip me in even stronger form, and she felt that I was trembling. "Do not talk, Moses. Close your eyes and sleep!"

I lay still, trying to sleep, but at first I could not. Yet at last a tranquility came over me, and presently I was either fully asleep, or nearly so. Then I felt her tremble, and I roused myself to ask her what had disturbed her. She said, "Gershom."

I said to her, "I will do it."

She seemed still to tremble. I caressed her hair and her cheeks, and I felt the trembling cease. Then, strangely, I felt—may I tell this?—a desire for her, and at the same time I felt that to pursue that desire was inappropriate. I could not form into clear thought the reasons why; I could only feel that it was not seemly so soon. I knew, as I refused myself that which is ordinary among men, that my whole being had been completely permeated by the event of the afternoon.

As I lay there, echoes and recollections of the event came to me. Resolutely I put these from my mind and, instead, I asked myself the question which Jethro had asked me: Would He go to see the Pharaoh, or would I? If I, how would I pass the guards, and traverse the layers of officials? Then I found I had awakened within me echoes of plans I had toyed with on other sleepless nights. I kept telling myself that I must devise not plans, but a plan, a plan which must be carefully conceived, and even more carefully executed. When daylight came I was still without the plan, but now I knew its urgency.

To my surprise, the next day dawned as other days had dawned, and Zipporah fixed me breakfast as on other days. What was changed was not the world outside me, but the world inside. I went, as always, to the sheepfold, and I did my work that day as I did it everyday. Now, though, I did it only as habit, for I knew that I must think through to a plan.

That night Zipporah asked me when I would leave for Egypt. I said to her, "Not for a time. First I must have my plan. Then I must know how I shall carry it out."

"We will not go tomorrow?"

I smiled at her. "Not tomorrow, not next week, not next month."

"No? I have packed our things."

I wanted to tell her that I could not take her. I did not have the heart to say it at that moment. I said, "I will tell you when to pack, beloved."

I was drowsy all that day through, not having slept the night before. Nevertheless, in the evening I went to see Jethro. As we ate some fruit, he said, "In three days you will turn over your flocks to someone—I have not decided yet who."

"Why?" I asked.

"You must be free, first to make your plans, and then free to go."

"As you say."

We sat in silence. He said, "I have given the matter my best thought, Moses." He sighed. "If only I knew Egypt—but I do not. If only I could write easily—I cannot. I make a suggestion to you. After three days you are to go to the oasis of Qilat. Take Zipporah and Gershom with you. There where it is quiet you will be able to think. You will be able to write down your thoughts. I will send parchment rolls with you, and quills and ink. When you come back, perhaps you will read your plans to me."

Three days later we set out with the camel for the long trip to Qilat. As the sun began to set, we came near to an inn. I was at that moment carrying our Gershom on my back, for he was tired and irritable. Zipporah was walking behind us, and behind her was the servant with the camel.

I heard Zipporah cry out. I turned to her, and I took a step to her. She snatched Gershom away from me, and she tore off his clothes. I saw a knife in her hand. She put our boy on the ground, and she raised the knife, not as one stabs, but as one cuts a flowering bush. I called her name, and stepped to her, and took hold of her hand. She pushed me away. I saw that her face was transformed, that terror was written into her eyes and her mouth. In a voice I did not recognize, she said, "Hold his arms, hold him steady." I did not move. "Quick, Moses, before it is too late!"

I thought she had gone mad. I wanted to tear the knife from her hand, to pull her away from our boy. She turned her face to me, pleadingly. "Not for me, Moses. For Gershom. For Him Who is." I bent over our boy, and I held him and she circumcised him, and he whimpered and he bled. She touched the foreskin to my legs. She said, "May you now be free of blemish as your father's legs are free of blemish." She turned to me. "We are mated now in blood."

Gershom was crying. She picked him up, and held him to her,

and I saw his blood begin to stain her dress. I picked up his torn clothes, and gave them to her to cover him. I wanted to carry him, but she shook her head. The terror was gone from her face; instead, beauty greater than ever before suffused her countenance. She held him with one hand, and with the other she took mine. "Quickly," she said, "to the inn. We need warm water. We need to wash him."

I was still gripped in terror, but she was calm.

We came to the inn, and we asked for warm water, and she washed our boy and comforted him.

Only later that night did she speak to me of what had happened. That He had come to slay our little Gershom and only her quick deed had saved him.

Her dress was still bloody, for she had not changed it, but the blood was by now dried. She ran a finger over the stained part of the material. "It is Gershom's blood, Moses. It is your blood, it is my blood. We are mated in his blood. He is a Hebrew, and through this blood I am a Hebrew too. Tell me I am a Hebrew, Moses."

I said, "You are a Hebrew."

Her eyes filled with proud and happy tears. "I am a Hebrew."

I drew her to me and I kissed her.

Had He appeared to her, without my knowing it, near to her though I had been? I thought I would ask the servant what he had seen and what he had heard, but I quickly knew that I would not ask. If I disbelieved her—her so good, so loving, so devoted—must I not think too of disbelieving myself and the burning bush?

Gershom woke up and began to cry, and Zipporah went to him. I stood and watched as she bent over him and caressed him. Then I spoke a silent prayer. "I thank You that You have given me Zipporah."

✳ CHAPTER III

My good friend Caleb assures me that for two quite different reasons our people say little about the plan which I drew up so slowly and laboriously. "We are a God-intoxicated people, Moses, and God-intoxicated people are drunk, and they do not get things straight. It pleases them to exalt His glory, not yours. If that makes you a little jealous of Him—"

"I have not said so, Caleb."

"I am sure you have not." He smiled. He raised his hands in an exaggerated gesture of denial. "I am sure you have not even thought it."

I smiled. "I think that I have thought it."

He laughed. "Who but you would be honest enough to admit it? But you are unjust to our people, at least in this instance. To you and to a handful of us, the plan was very simple, so simple as not to have been a plan at all. You explained it to us in a part of a single night. But our people never knew the whole plan; they knew only where each tribe or clan or family fitted into it. Indeed, what was so good about your plan was that our people were able to fit into the whole thing without ever knowing it."

I said, perhaps still with a little bitterness, "Yet if it had not worked out, they would have blamed me for inadequate preparation—"

"Or for inadequately carrying it out! Of course. Your only real weakness, Moses, is that, modest as you are, you do like some measure of gratitude and of recognition. Or are gratitude and recognition the same thing? You should know better than I"—was he too being a little bitter?—"that a leader of people is not thanked for what goes well, but is cursed for what goes wrong."

Perhaps my plan was in reality a simple one, or at least simple when set down on parchment. Certainly its execution was difficult, not only because of the risks and the omnipresent dangers, but also because of the sheer enormity of the task. Now that we have traversed the fields of Moab and we are encamped near Mount Nebo, no one speaks at all of the way in which, through careful organization, there has been, for the most part, food available for all, and shelter for all, and transport for the infants and for the sickly. We have had these because of the plans which had been drawn up in good detail long in advance.

Yet let me not exaggerate the excellence of the detailed plan, for I, above all, am aware of its notable deficiencies. It is not because what I prepared was wrong. No; I simply did not anticipate everything. I could not.

I mention these things in recollection of the days and the nights of the planning at the quiet oasis of Qilat. There I wrote, and then destroyed what I had written, and I wrote afresh, and then I destroyed it and wrote again.

Let me not burden you with excessive details. Let it suffice to remember the essentials. Our people were mostly in slave camps, but a good many were just outside them—and I myself had not known before my flight how many camps there were, or exactly where they were. I was one person, one solitary individual; I needed associates, a growing number of people to help me. Perhaps some Midianites might come along with me? I would have to look into that. But thereafter I would need to find some secret place or places in Egypt where I could gather some small groups of Hebrews who in some way would manage to escape from the camps or from the nearby huts. Only with the connivance of some Egyptians could I effect such escapes and find such a place. I would either need some money, or else need to find some Egyptians who, without being paid, would be simultaneously trustworthy to me and traitorous to Pharaoh. Could I find these, and where? Our secret place, or places, needed to be obscure enough to escape the notice of the Egyptians, but also impregnable to their attack should they notice them. We needed weapons—spears and shields and bows and arrows—and these would take even more money, or else agile theft.

On the third or fourth day at Qilat, I came to a crux in my planning. Two ways seemed possible. One was to plan that at a prearranged signal, the few outside the camp and the many inside, all secretly armed, would rise in violent revolt, and, through the strength of our arms, overpower the Egyptians, win the pitched battles, and force our way out of Egypt. The second was to assemble saboteurs to make so thorough a shambles of the ordinary life in Egypt that the Pharaoh, however unwillingly, would release us to leave the country.

The first alternative, with the prospect of pitched battles, implied a large measure of bloodshed. Perhaps it was inevitable for some Hebrews to die in whatever form the liberation would take, but surely a plan which necessarily meant extensive bloodshed was inferior to a plan which would reduce or eliminate it.

The fact is that I forced myself to draw up a scheme for a mass uprising even before I drew up my preferred choice of a devastating sabotage. I wrote out both schemes with extreme care, and then I set them aside for a week. During that time, Zipporah and Gershom and I went for enjoyable walks, or, while he played with the Bedouin children, I answered her eager questions about Abraham and Isaac and Jacob and Joseph. Her chief questions I could not answer: How had Judah and Gad and Asher and the other brothers regarded Joseph's Egyptian wife, Asenath? And had Joseph's wife joined the Hebrews as she, Zipporah, had? I could not tell her, for I did not know.

A week later, I reread the two plans, seeking as best I could to find whatever weakness or unclarity might lie in them. It was better, I told myself, for me to discover the flaws than for Jethro to do so.

I found it necessary, or desirable, to rewrite portions of each. But the day came when I was satisfied that our three months at Qilat had been useful, indeed very useful. I told Zipporah that we could leave for Midian the next day.

She nodded. Then her face, as seemed to happen from time to time, reflected some anxiety. "Can we wait, perhaps a week, perhaps ten days? I—I do not want to travel now. It is time for my period—"

"We can wait."

"And," she went on, "if I am with child, as I think I am—please, let us wait."

Ten days later she said we could return to our house. When we came inside the door, she said, "Nothing has happened, Moses! Nothing. We shall have our child."

I embraced her, and I felt her weeping. I said, "You should be happy, Zipporah!"

She said, "Now I cannot go to Egypt with you. You will have to leave me behind."

I said, "I will wait until the baby comes."

"No, no, no! You must not! Our people are in slavery; you must not wait so many months.

Over a period of three days, I read the plans to Jethro, with their alternatives of revolt and uprising, or of sabotage and release. He absorbed not only the substance but also, in large measure, even the exact words I had written. He asked questions, he demanded clarification, he charged me at points with excessive vagueness. When we met on the fourth morning, he startled me by a quiet observation. "I will come a little later to discuss the choice—uprising or sabotage. I have listened with approval to your preparations. But something is not clear to me. Whether you choose uprising or sabotage, in either case your purpose is not only to take the Hebrews out of slavery, but to take them out of Egypt. I ask myself, why? I ask myself, why did the Hebrews go to Egypt? I have learned from you that they went there because of a famine in Canaan. I have learned from you that at that time they were welcomed into Egypt and were given the fertile area of Goshen to settle in. Suppose that they were to become free, and that they could live, if not in Goshen, in one or more desirable provinces in Egypt, in fullest freedom? Why must you take them out of Egypt?"

I said, "He told me to."

"Are you sure you heard Him right?"

"I think that is what I heard."

"If that is what you heard, you cannot disobey. Yet if I were you,

I would want to weigh the issue of freedom in a country against freedom from a country."

"How can I weigh it?"

"Is it that difficult, Moses? I do not think so. Imagine with me, for a moment, that the walls about the camps topple, and the guards disappear, and the Hebrews are able to go wherever they wish and do as they wish. If the Hebrews can find full freedom in Egypt, do they need to leave it?"

I said to him, "I must think this over."

"Yes," he said, "you must think about it."

I went back to my house, considerably puzzled. Certainly, Jethro had raised an important matter. But He had said that I was to bring the people first to the mountain of the burning bush and then lead them to a land of milk and honey.

At first I was unable to bring myself to think about the matter, for I preferred to tell myself that I had not raised the question myself because it was absurd, unreal. I had no option but to do what He commanded. Yet about Jethro's question, I told myself that a people once slaves would never find true freedom among those who had enslaved them. Neither the enslavers nor the once slaved would ever completely shed the ways of the past or the recollections of it. Certainly in those circles in which I had moved in Egypt, there was little awareness of the plight of the Hebrews, and even less sympathy for them. In those circles it seemed to be the view, as I recalled matters, that slave peoples were destined for their lot, perhaps even created for it. In those circles the Egyptians were the free people, the normal people, the gifted people, and those who were not Egyptians were inferior people, abnormal people, despicable people. Surely, so I told myself, there was no prospect, even if the fences fell and our people poured out of the camps, that our people could expect to be treated with reasonable courtesy, and live in dignity, and flourish as Egyptians could flourish.

But was there not a possible other side to the case? My tutors had praised me for my possession of native Egyptian gifts; could not such tutors come to learn that these gifts were not confined to

Egyptians? If, tragically, my brother, Aaron, had been unable to become a doctor, was it not possible that a son, or else a grandson, could do so? Freedom, I told myself, cannot bring instant equality, but where freedom prevailed, equality could follow, sooner or later.

But I had to tell myself that my tutors had praised me only by mistaking me for an Egyptian. My talents, in their eyes, were not individual, not my own, but Egyptian talents. So deeply ingrained in those tutors was the farfetched conviction that all good talents were necessarily Egyptian that they could never change.

Yet, on the other hand, it seemed to me that to believe that Egyptians—tutors or other people—could never change was in its way only a borrowed form of the very evil of the Egyptian ways. To mass together all Egyptians, of the present and the future, was to succumb to what I despised among the Egyptians.

Again, and viewing matters from still another standpoint, I asked myself this question: If Aaron's son, or his grandson, were allowed to become a doctor, would he be a Hebrew doctor or an Egyptian doctor? Oh, one could say that he would be only a doctor, and in that sense neither Egyptian nor Hebrew. But was this true? And would I want Aaron's son or his grandson to be nondescript, and to cease to be a Hebrew?

Then what did it mean to be a Hebrew? Was it only an accident of birth, the accident whereby one animal was a dog and another was a cat? Or did being a Hebrew imply that under some conditions a person could freely make a choice, a choice that could rest on values?

It is now ironical, at least to me, that Jethro had forced me to weigh the issue of freedom in a country and freedom from a country, and he had required me to think through what it meant to be a Hebrew. I told myself that a Hebrew was a person who—but I was not able then to complete the sentence.

I think that I spoke before of Egyptians and their vices. In those days I was perhaps prone to believe that these vices—they were real—were not so much habits which Egyptian society approved of, but rather the characteristics with which Egyptians were born. Yet reared as I was in Egyptian ways, their vices should have been my vices, just as their science and their mathematics were mine. Also, I was sure that Hebrews were finer people than Egyptians, simply by virtue of being Hebrews. Then I remembered the Hebrew slave whom I had saved from the Egyptian, the Hebrew who had scornfully asked me the question that had propelled me into flight. Could he not as easily have been an Egyptian as a Hebrew? Or was he only a harassed person who, in a tense moment, acted out of accord with Hebrew standards?

But what were Hebrew standards? Our father Abraham was an exemplary man. He had generously allowed his nephew Lot to choose the desirable territory of Sodom; he had bravely rescued Lot and the possessions of the king of Sodom when the kings of the East had captured them. To bury his beloved Sarah, he had paid Ephron for the cave of Machpelah, neither seizing it, as he might have, nor accepting it as a gift. He had demonstrated his faith in Him by his willingness to sacrifice his son, our father, Isaac. An exemplary man.

But had not Abraham also sojourned in Egypt? And had he not used the flimsy circumstance that his wife, Sarah, was his half-sister, to let the Pharaoh of that day believe she was only his sister, and not his wife? Abruptly, it startled me to realize that the truth had been concealed—or shall I be candid and speak of a lie? Perhaps in dealing with a Pharaoh, even an exemplary man felt no compunction about a falsehood.

If one could not know from the past what it meant to be a Hebrew, then it was something which the future would need to work out. True it was that Abraham had bequeathed to us his momentous insights; true it was that he had taught us that God is God and that neither man nor an idol is God; true it was that from him we had learned that God alone is infallible and that men, all men, are fallible. Yet from Abraham we had learned only this central principle and no more than that. Just as in mathematics the principle of determining the height of a tree or of a hill was different from designing and building a temple to a given height, so the principle that God is not man, and that God alone can be God, reasonably demanded that one move on to apply the principle to the affairs of man.

These were the things that in a disordered way I pondered over, always asking myself what it meant to be a Hebrew; I did not yet ask myself the question respecting the future, what would it, or could it, mean to be a Hebrew? I was still immersed in the question, should I seek freedom from the country or in the country?

I must be honest. I must remind you that an Egyptian princess had saved my life, and that solicitous Egyptians had reared me, and that Egyptian sages, admirable in their intellect, had taught me. And just as Abraham, born among the Chaldeans, had separated himself from the Chaldeans when the conviction came to him that God was one, and that God was neither a man nor an idol, so I needed to infer that men are all men, and that Chaldeans, of whom Abraham was one, and Egyptians, of whom the princess was one, were people. Accordingly, men were what they were, not because of the parents to whom they were born, but because of the habits and customs of society. A single individual could, like an Egyptian tutor, elect simply to conform to a society, or, like Abraham, use his personal gifts to stand aloof from the society. But men were men, and Egyptians were men, and granted that today Egyptians oppressed the Hebrews, was it not to be envisaged that some day that oppression would end? I felt myself drawn to the goal of freedom in Egypt, not freedom from Egypt.

At the same time, I needed to recall hearing from my mother that He had given the land of Canaan to Abraham for Abraham's seed. But that was a land far away—not as far as other lands, but still far. Moreover, in the generations since Abraham, it had possibly not remained empty (for surely it must have been empty in Abraham's day, for him to have let his nephew Lot freely choose a section and for Abraham to possess what Lot had not chosen). But would it be the same for a whole people to come to a land as it had been for Father Abraham and his small entourage?

And what about the rigor of the journey from Egypt to Canaan? Would it not be better for the Hebrews to gain their freedom in Egypt and to prolong their sojourn there until they would, in the far-distant future, and in an unhurried and orderly way, move on to Canaan? Surely this was better.

I do not assert that I thought profoundly, or in a systematic way. I only remember that that night I was still in the wondrous domain wherein one can think thoughts without needing immediately to act, the domain in which one can spin out speeches to himself on all sides of an issue and remain remote from the need to translate his thoughts into immediate action. Even though I was truly concerned to decide what to do, it was then still possible to carry on the inner debate, whether Hebrews and Egyptians were truly different, or only usual human beings all of whom are the same.

As I have said, I inclined to the view that freedom in Egypt was a sounder goal than freedom from Egypt. But He had spoken. Then by what right did I ponder alternatives at all?

I longed for Him to speak to me again so that I could ask Him and ascertain clearly what He wished. I even spoke to Him, to ask Him if He insisted on our leaving Egypt, but He did not answer. Then I became frightened at the thought that, in even pondering the matter, I was disobeying Him. Why did He not answer? Should He not answer me, as I needed to answer Jethro? Or was it to be His way to speak only when He chose to, not whenever men wanted Him to?

I fell asleep at last and woke in the morning, to hear angry voices outside our house. I arose and walked to the door. Zipporah was there, holding Gershom by the hand. Before her stood a gathering of people, some of them her brothers, and there was shouting and there were shakings of the fists. When I appeared, there were yells of derision, and I heard voices saying, "You stinking Hebrew! You filthy Hebrew!"

It was an ugly moment, and the nasty words could quickly turn into nastier blows, and Zipporah and Gershom—and let me be honest—and I myself might be seriously injured. Especially was I anxious about Zipporah, for she was defiant and even belligerent, and she stood her ground without retreat. Her lips poured noisy scorn on her brothers, and she seemed unconcerned that she might inflame them into open violence. Later, I was struck by the bitter humor of the possibility that I, the future liberator of my people from the Egyptians, myself needed liberation from my wife's people, from people kindred to me.

The arrival of Jethro—someone had run to him to tell him—put a stop, first to the shouting, and then to the assembly itself. It was his presence, not his words, which ended the affair. It was the anger which was clear on his face that cowed his sons and quieted their cohorts. I saw him watch them slink away.

He came into our house. To him and to Zipporah I addressed the single word, "Why?"

Zipporah said, "They are pigs. They are swine."

Jethro shook his head. "They are people. They have dreamed up a story that you, a stranger among us, will take all our wealth away to Egypt, to ransom your people. I know, because they have asked me. They preferred to believe their false fears rather than my truthful words."

"But what will happen now?"

"I undertake to assure you that nothing will happen. I will assemble my sons and make them answerable to me for your safety, this to the point that they will become your guardians."

"Willingly?" I asked. "Or unwillingly?"

"Does it matter?" he asked.

I did not reply to him. Of course it mattered. It mattered very much that these people, before so hospitable, had turned so hostile. It mattered that only the authority of Jethro restrained their hostility. It mattered to me that, after these years in which I had shared their lives, had married among them, had worked with them, was one of them, they could still regard me as a stranger. Were they different from the Egyptians? Only in one respect, that it was the ruler of the Egyptians who had caused the enslavement, carried out by the Egyptian people, while here it was the ruler of the Midianites who was preventing some comparable evil. The difference was in the rulers, not in the people themselves. Jethro suddenly grew even greater in my eyes than before, while the Midianites suddenly became transformed into veritable Egyptians. If Jethro was right—who could quarrel with his wisdom?—the Midianites were people, and they did what unreflective people did. They did, indeed, what my own Hebrews could possibly do, if the way were open for them to do it. Unless my people could be taught differently. Unless they could come to believe that a fear, a suspicion, a hostility to strangers was wrong.

My people now celebrate me as the great lawgiver. Perhaps I have earned their praise. The very earliest law framed itself in my mind long before I learned the need for laws. Let me remind you of how it runs in the code: "You shall not oppress a stranger, for you know the heart of the stranger, for you were strangers in Egypt."

But my uncertainty of the preceding night now disappeared and I no longer had to ask Him. The experience of the morning gave me the answer, both for me and for me to give Jethro. Not freedom in Egypt, but freedom from it. Arduous as a long march to a land of milk and honey might be, surely true freedom was to be gained only in our own land. And, little as I knew of Canaan, it was the land where Abraham, Isaac, and Jacob had dwelled. Canaan was where we would go.

What I did not know then was that in anticipating a law for strangers, I was on the threshold of answering the question, What is a Hebrew? Then I knew only vaguely, as now I know clearly, that a Hebrew, beyond being the offspring of Hebrews, is one who adheres to a law of justice and righteousness, to an obligation to be more than merely a usual person and to be, instead, one who lives by the highest law and the noblest principles. It came to me, even at that early moment, that the greater task before me, beyond freeing my people, was to transform them from slaves into a singular nation of singular persons.

I returned to Jethro to bring the answer to his question. I sat with him, and he saw that I hesitated and that I did not look at him. He said, "I know the answer, Moses." He fell silent. I began to speak, but he silenced me with a gesture. "What happened this morning—will you believe that it brought more pain to me than it did to you?" I turned my eyes to him. "I had thought that I had taught my people better. I had thought that they were better than animals. I had thought that my teachings would guide them, and not the show of my wrath." He sighed. "They are obeying me. Some have slunk in to see me, to speak of their remorse. I fear that this remorse is only their fright of me, their terror that I might punish them. They think they truly are remorseful; they know that I hold them to be cowards, afraid of me. When I pass on, or when they muster the courage to overthrow me, they will repudiate me forever, as this morning they did so briefly. And I had thought that I had brought them beyond this!"

He called for his servant and asked for some fruit, as if he needed this interruption in order to be able to talk with me about my plans. He said, "Will it be uprising or sabotage?"

I did not hesitate. "Sabotage."

"Why?"

"Fewer will die."

He nodded his head. "An uprising could be crushed in one engagement. And those who rise in rebellion must come out into the open and show themselves. This is not the case with sabotage."

"That is how I have reasoned." I went on to review with him the thoughts I had had of deeds which would disrupt the life of Egypt, ruin the commerce, terrorize the people. At times he nodded his head; at times he shook it, forcing me to explain.

He said, "Who will go with you from here?"

I shook my head. "No one."

He frowned. "I will make some inquiries. Perhaps three or four may be willing—"

"I would rather not."

"You must not be foolish, Moses. I will force no one. But if one or two respond— The same with money—do not be foolish. Some you have earned; some is Zipporah's legacy. I shall give you nothing that would not be hers or yours." I said nothing. "I only ask this, that you forgive me for what my people did this morning."

"You were not responsible."

"I did not teach them well enough."

When it was time to say good-by to Zipporah, I steeled myself for her tears, but they never came. To my expressions of my anxiety that I might fail, she replied with a shake of her lovely head and said, "You must trust Him. He called you, and He is sending you. You cannot fail." Then she said, "I do not weep at your going, much as I shall miss you. I rejoice at it, Moses. I rejoice." But when she embraced me, I felt her tremble, and when she called Gershom from his playing, her voice, which was otherwise as true and unwavering as a silver bell, scarcely seemed hers, for it was shrill and even a little harsh. As yet her figure did not show that she was bearing our second child; she looked still like a little girl. She said, "May your God—our God—protect you."

Jethro stood by, silent and brooding. When we embraced each other, he said, "You must teach your people better than I have taught mine." He made a gesture and two men who had been standing some distance away came to us. He put his hand on the shoulder of the one of them who was tall and thin. "This is Elyaqim. He is swift with the knife. He will guard you." Elyaqim smiled. Jethro presented the other, a roly-poly man who seemed old enough to be a young grandfather. "This is Ben Onim. When he was younger, he was a foolhardy spy. He is a carpenter, a smith, and he knows, without the sun or the stars, where east and west and north and south lie. He is not as foolhardy as he once was."

"I do not run as fast as I once did," said Ben Onim.

"He is a cunning man," said Jethro.

I turned to them. "Why do you want to come with me?"

Elyaqim said, "I have a desire to travel."

Ben Onim said, "My wife is a shrew."

Zipporah said, "You buried your wife two years ago."

Ben Onim smiled. "I still hear her scolding me." He threw back his head and laughed. "I am weary of lambs, weary of ewes, weary of sheep, weary of mountains. All my life I have longed to be a ne'er-do-well; this is too good an opportunity to pass by."

The camel was loaded with food, the waterskins were filled. There was a last embrace with both Zipporah and Jethro. Gershom had run off to play; I did not let her call him back.

How much shall I tell? Our journey to Egypt was leisurely, without adventure. At night, around the fire—Elyaqim always gathered the wood, but Ben Onim always built the fire and struck the flints together for the spark—we talked over plans and stratagems. Yet how much shall I tell?

Let me confine myself to things which you may not already know, or which you may know in the wrong way. Let me select two such, as examples. I now hear from Caleb that my brother, Aaron, came forth from the camp to meet me, that He had bidden him to do so. Perhaps He did. But Aaron and I met only after we had already been in Egypt for a month. Here is how it was. I had bought fresh Egyptian clothes, first a moderately priced uniform of a minor official, and then, wearing this uniform, I bought an elegant garment. As I had done in the days before my flight, I now made my way into the camp where Aaron had been, disdainfully passing the guards. Nothing there had changed. I walked to the work compound, saw Aaron from the distance, and I promptly left, for it was sufficient at the moment for me to know where he was. That night Ben Onim and I worked out our plan for freeing Aaron. It was simplicity itself, like a game that children play. (Indeed, were it not that the stakes were the freedom of our people, and were it not for the constant danger, the whole experience in Egypt might well have seemed a series of children's deeds.) The next day I returned to the camp and to the work compound, and I asked for the officer in charge. He was a young man, and belligerent. I said, "Was it you, or your predecessor, who has complained about the Hebrew, Aaron ben Amram?"

He said, "Not I. This is a new assignment for me."

"I am sent to interrogate him. Bring him here."

For a moment the officer looked as though he would demand some written form from me; I, of course, had one all prepared. But as I expected, my arrogance overwhelmed him, and he had Aaron brought into the hut. Indeed, he lingered there until I haughtily dismissed him. I said to Aaron, "You are to keep quiet and not to respond to what I say. I am your brother, Moses."

A cry almost escaped his lips. "I cannot believe it."

I suppose that I had changed some. Indeed, if I had changed as much as he, it was not surprising that, not expecting me, he had not recognized me, for it was only that I was looking for him that enabled me to recognize him. His scraggly hair, obviously neglected, had mostly turned gray. He walked with a limp, as if he had either been injured or was not well. He was thin, emaciated. His eyes, though, were what were the most changed, for they lacked all sparkle, as if he had completely forgotten what it meant to hope.

"Hush! We have only a moment now. My story is that I am taking you out of the camp, to the district authority. Outside the camp there is a cart we will get into. All the way to the cart you are to whine and beg my mercy. I will cuff you once or twice, and you are to scream."

I called the officer. "I am taking him to the district authority. Strike him from your roll."

The officer hesitated. I remembered some of the words from Midian, and I snarled at Aaron, "You stinking Hebrew!" I cuffed him, shouted to him that he was to come with me, and I pulled him out of the hut. He whined; perhaps I had cuffed him too hard. The officer looked on and grinned.

Ben Onim was waiting in the cart as we passed through the gate, Aaron all the while shouting, "Mercy! Mercy!" As we got into the cart, I saw Elyaqim loitering across the open place, whittling on a piece of wood; it was his way of having his knife ready.

Back at the inn—how carefully we entered it!—Aaron and I embraced. We talked as he bathed and put on the Egyptian clothes, those of a minor official, which I had myself worn at first. I said, "We will talk later. Where is Miriam?"

"I don't know. She has not been in my camp."

We left that inn and made our way to another one, which I had visited the day before and had paid for the four of us, for us two and Elyaqim and Ben Onim. When we got out of the cart, Ben Onim drove it off, to return it to the man from whom he had hired it.

The plan had worked, then, very easily. I knew, though, that it had been easy only because the Egyptians had absolutely no reason to suspect that the servile Hebrews were up to something.

In a few days, Aaron was more like the man I remembered. He told me that he was now a widower; he did not know where his four sons, Eleazar, Nadab, Abihu, and Ithamar, were. He was still fearful; indeed, his fearfulness tended to communicate itself to Elyaqim, Ben Onim, and me. His disposition to talk, to talk ceaselessly, I ascribed in part to his fear and in part to the recency of his release.

The second matter I would comment on is the narratives which I have heard about my audiences with the Pharaoh. I have questioned Caleb about the narratives, for it passes my understanding how these accounts could be transmitted from narrator to auditor without raising a thousand questions. The basic story, as the people tell it, has no rival for its utter simplicity. I simply went to Pharaoh and spoke to him!

It is as if Pharaoh had no court or courtiers, no bodyguards, no soldiers, no royalty to be the buffer between him and his suppliants. It was as though I, Moses, went to him in the way that I would go to a vendor of figs at his stall in the gate of a city.

And most ridiculous of all is the supposition that I simply entered Egypt and promptly betook myself to the palace and walked in casually, even jauntily. It was, of course, not like that at all.

I saw the Pharaoh, but almost two years after we had come to Egypt. I saw him only after the official heralds proclaimed publicly that the Pharaoh would admit me to the palace and guarantee my safety. (Of course, I did not go to the palace.)

In that period of two years, there was no dearth of incident, no dearth of further planning. Especially was there no lack of meetings, some long and tedious, made longer and more tedious by Aaron and by his multitudinous suggestions. The difficulty with him was that half of what he suggested was worth considering, and, indeed, reflected an ingenuity that all the others of us lacked. The half not worth considering was worthless merely because it was devoid of any realism.

Progressively our meetings grew larger, that is, more and more people were at them, and progressively we had difficulty in finding a place at which to meet.

I will not tax you with all the details. We had been in Egypt for a few months, but did very little. Elyaqim and Ben Onim were progressing in their learning of Egyptian. Elyaqim spoke it better than Ben Onim, for he was younger, and the muscles in his tongue had not become hardened and unpliable, as was the case with Ben Onim, but Ben Onim understood it somewhat better than Elyaqim.

Every night the three of us went each to a different tavern, leaving Aaron behind us, for we did not trust his discretion for this task. A typical procedure was what happened with the Egyptian, Tat-Rin. In a tavern, when Tat-Rin and the others had drunk their wine, the conversation turned, as was normal, to the throne, to the cost of food, and, sometimes, to the Hebrews. I was alert for some voice to speak out a dissatisfaction with conditions, or to say a word of sympathy for the Hebrews. Sober men would have guarded their tongues, but wine might loosen them. Tat-Rin spoke one night of the Hebrews, but not with any particular sympathy. "The Pharaoh uses those miserable slaves, yes, but for what? To build buildings he does not need and storehouses for what he alone owns, he and no one else. And meanwhile poor people lack houses, and craftsmen lack jobs."

A voice spoke up. "Be careful what you say, Tat-Rin."

Tat-Rin looked at the speaker with contempt, as if he was sharpening his tongue before using it on the speaker. Then some fear seemed to overcome him, and he kept his silence for a moment. But somewhat later he said, "This land is a land only for the rich. And I am a poor man, a tutor to the stupid sons of the moderately rich. I know how the wealthy live, and I know that I will never live like them."

The same voice as before spoke up. "Do not utter treason, Tat-Rin."

"I have said nothing treasonable. I have not said a word about the Pharaoh." He picked up his wine goblet and drained it. "The Pharaoh is a model of magnanimity. He is high above all men in wisdom, in kindliness, and in understanding, as befits a man who is divine and immortal!" He turned to the man who had rebuked him. "Were my words treason?"

A chorus of noes, mostly mocking, answered his question. I noticed that two men spat, and I marked them as well as I could, for perhaps they too merited inquiring into.

Two nights later, again at the tavern, Tat-Rin spoke out his discontent. I was asking myself if he were something more than only a malcontent. A third time we went to the tavern. The conviction came to me that Tat-Rin was more than a malcontent.

When he left the tavern, I left too. He lurched about, half-drunk. It was I who arranged that we bump into each other. The test was now what sort of response he would make, for if he was disposed to revile me, he was too bitter for me to use. I helped him to his feet. He said, "Wine and my legs were not meant for mating; I shall arrange a divorce for them."

I put my arm around him. "I will guide you to your home."

We walked together. He pointed to a hut which even in the moonlight was clearly a hovel. "That," he said, "is my palace. The palace of a useless man, a tutor who teaches at the lowest rates."

"You should raise your rates."

"I have no royal shield, and I have never had the money to buy one."

"Perhaps if there was some official to whom you gave a gift—"

He laughed. "My record at bribery is without blemish. Four times I have paid a bribe, each time amassing the amount needed with difficulty, and each time the official who took it was seized by an admirable fit of repentance, timed, felicitously, for when the money had already gone from my hand into his pocket. Court officials are not immune from bribery, but only from living up to the deals they have made." He invited me into his hut.

I said, "It is late."

He made a gesture expressing his indifference. "Who cares what the hour is."

I went into the hut with him, for I considered him no more than half-drunk. "How do others come to be royally approved tutors?"

"They are the poor relatives of the rich. I chose for my parents poor people, bereft of any rich relatives. Twice, twice mind you, I was near to having a rich patron, but each time there was an occasion for me to grovel, and because I knew exactly how to grovel, I did so rather poorly, for I groveled with my words, but exhibited my contempt in my face. Our Egypt is a stinkhole for all but royalty, the nobility and the rich!"

I said, "You are right." Then I said, "I too want to leave."

He said, "I want to go east, across Canaan, across the crescent, and all the way to Chaldea. Maybe there I can find some situation—" He fell silent. Then his head began to droop on his chest, and presently he had trouble keeping his eyes open.

I said, "Shall I help you to bed?"

"First I must urinate." He took my arm, and I led him outside. "I water Egypt better than does the Nile." I guided him back to the door, saw him go inside, and returned to the inn where we were staying.

For the next five days, Elyaqim followed Tat-Rin wherever he went, so that we could know where he did his tutoring, whether for small and unimportant businessmen, or for the very rich and the high nobility. Tat-Rin had told the truth: he was a tutor to people of no great consequence.

We learned everything that we could about him. He was married to a seamstress. They had no children; indeed, they were living apart, for the wife had the reputation of taking lover after lover, and she was then living with a soldier. Tat-Rin was known as an honest man, a bright man, and a luckless man, one who might have risen in the social scale if only some single opportunity had chanced to come his way. His drinking worried me; yet it was said of him that he never completely lost control of his tongue, for though it wagged, it did so only as he ordained that it should.

A month later, after seeing him several times, I brought him to my room in the inn. I poured a goblet of wine. I said, "I have something to discuss with you. Something important. Something private. There will be this one goblet, and after it no more."

He said, "I am not a slave to wine."

"One glass will not affect either of us." He picked up the goblet. I went on. "I am a Hebrew."

He put down the goblet. "I do not believe you."

"Why not?"

"You are not in a camp. You speak perfect Egyptian. You carry yourself like a free man."

"Does a man in our evil Egypt proclaim that he is a Hebrew when he is not?"

He said, "Your name, Moses—it is a good Egyptian name."

"It was given to me here in Egypt."

"This is incredible! Not that I do not believe you. But this is incredible!"

I said, "It is my intention to bring freedom to the Hebrews. To bring them out of Egypt, to the land of Canaan."

He laughed. "It cannot be done. It cannot."

"I shall do it."

"How?"

"I have plans. And the Hebrew God will help me."

Tat-Rin snorted. "You say God. Not gods. You have only one? We have many. Is your Hebrew God more powerful than our Egyptian aggregate? I believe in none of them, neither in ours nor in yours."

I did not respond to these words. I said, "I have made plans. They will work out. And when once we reach Canaan, you will be able to go on, and to make your way to Chaldea."

He snapped at me. "In return for what?"

"The help you will give me."

He seemed to think about the matter. "What kind of help?"

"I need two dozen people like you. You are number one. You will help me find twenty-three more."

"Where will I find them?"

"Where I found you. In the taverns."

"Why should I get into something like this?"

"Because you want to leave Egypt."

He narrowed his eyes and looked at me. "I will need to consult my wife."

I replied without hesitation. "Where? At your hut, or at the hut of the soldier she is living with?"

"How do you know about her?"

"Because I know a great deal about you. Enough to think, or at least to hope, that you will join me."

He moistened his lips. "Suppose—suppose that I say yes and, tomorrow or the next day, bring the police here to take you into custody?"

I shrugged my shoulders. "I have known that I must run some risks. I run as few as possible. You are, of course, a risk."

He thought for a moment. Then, to my gratification, he said, "I know only one person now."

I said, "I will be grateful for the one."

I noted that he went on without hesitation. "The man is a sandal-maker. He is a person who likes to say no when all other people say yes." He smiled. "He is quarrelsome. His shop is near the western gate. His name is Nephros."

I said, "I do not like quarrelsome people. What would he do for us?"

Tat-Rin frowned. "I do not know. This I can say, he is a man of great physical power. Immense arms, immense legs. I think, but I am not sure, that he is also a man of courage. I have heard him say, not in a tavern or in some public place but only to me, in the privacy of his shop, that slavery is an abomination." Tat-Rin frowned. Then he spoke very quietly. "Some people sing one and the same song; others pursue one and the same pleasure, like fishing. Nephros is a man with only one sentence on his tongue: 'Slavery is an abomination.'"

"Shall I go to him, or will you?"

"I have not fully decided that I am with you."

"I see." I tried to put some contempt into my voice. "Then your words in the tavern—they were only a half-drunk's silliness?"

"Not at all!" He had raised his voice. "I do not yet believe you are a Hebrew! You may be only a policeman. Prove to me you are a Hebrew."

"How shall I prove it?"

"Are you circumcised? Show me."

Without hesitation, I showed him. "Now do you believe me?"

"Almost. I need more proof."

I went to the door and called out, "Aaron." I turned to Tat-Rin. "Aaron is my brother. Tell me to ask him to do something, and I will say it to him in Hebrew."

He said, "Tell him to lift up this goblet of wine and to pour it over your head."

Aaron came in. I said to him in Hebrew, "Lift up the goblet of wine and pour it over my head, and do so silently and without delay." Aaron's face showed that he was puzzled. Nevertheless, he picked up the goblet and he poured it over me. I looked at Tat-Rin.

"A shame to waste that wine!" he said. He turned to Aaron and said, "Do you understand any Egyptian?"

"I understand Egyptian."

"Tell me who your people are."

"We are Hebrews."

I motioned to Aaron to leave. Slowly, I dried my head and my face. I said to Tat-Rin, "Well?"

"Now I will drink a goblet of wine." I poured it for him. He picked it up and brought it to his lips, as if to sip it. "I will myself go to Nephros." He drank the wine. "I will go to him tomorrow. I will return here tomorrow night." I walked to the door with him. He said, "Do only you Hebrews circumcise?"

"Our father Abraham had many descendants. Many desert people circumcise."

He smiled. "Had you said that it is only you Hebrews, I would not be going to Nephros tomorrow."

When he had gone, Elyaqim came out from behind the curtain; he had not yet put his knife back into its shield. "I took it out," he said, "when he mentioned going to the police tomorrow." He poured himself a goblet of wine. "I have never had wine poured over my head; only oil."

I wanted to ask his opinion, to have him tell me whether he thought we could trust Tat-Rin. Something within restrained me. Only later did I understand what that was; it was my unwillingness to give even Elyaqim the impression that I was uncertain. I must speak of this again.

Aaron came in, expostulating. "How could you let wine be poured over your head?"

"It was necessary."

"But me—why did you ask me to do it? Am I a servant or a slave? You should have asked Elyaqim."

I looked at him, annoyed. "If you are ready to wield a knife as Elyaqim does, you can become my knifeman. Please go to sleep, Aaron!"

He was offended; I did not care. He did not leave; instead, he sat down with us, sulking. I was tempted to tell him again to go to bed; I did not. A little later Ben Onim came in. "Tat-Rin did not go to the tavern; he went directly to his home. He urinated at the side of his house and went in. He lit his lamp, I waited until he blew it out, and then I came back."

"Good," I said. I turned to Elyaqim. "You will follow him tomorrow all day."

Toward dusk the next day, Elyaqim came in. "Tat-Rin has been to the usual homes where he has students. But before noon he went to the shop of the cobbler, Nephros. They ate their meal together."

"Good. Eat some food, Elyaqim, and then go back to Tat-Rin. Follow him. If he goes to the tavern, he must meet with an accident."

"Yes. But why?"

"Because he should not go to the tavern. He and Nephros should come here."

They came.

That is how we began, first with Tat-Rin and then with Nephros. Slowly we gathered more people. Slowly these people helped me learn where the Hebrew camps were and what tribes were in which of them.

I must speak of the Egyptians who joined with us. I must do so, for it appears that our people have transmitted no clear recollection of them and what they did. They say nothing more than that a mixed group, a large one, left Egypt with us; this is a great injustice.

The names of two of them deserve our deep homage. Qurmene, a short, squat man, had a boat on the Nile, and he eked out a living ferrying passengers across the river. At times he used to take rich people on the river, people who enjoyed fishing for sport, and Qurmene knew the best places to fish. He was constantly in difficulty with tax collectors, alleging that they overcharged him and that they kept the excess for themselves. Qurmene knew the ways of water, and the perils in marshes, and the deception provided by the vegetation that grows where land and water are together.

It was through Qurmene that we added the other man, named Anquru. A most worthy human being! Anquru had at times in the past gone fishing with Qurmene. Anquru was a lesser nobleman, a wealthy merchant who dealt in grains. He had large holdings of land, and his peasants—he kept no slaves—were the beneficiaries of his kindness. When first I met him, his bitterness both repelled me and also surprised me, for the reports about him spoke of him as benign. Only later did I learn what had changed him and why he had reponded to Qurmene's proposal to join us. Anquru had gone with his wife to a castle near Memphis, invited there by a cousin of a cousin of a cousin, a nobleman. The Pharaoh had been there; Anquru's wife was beautiful, and the Pharaoh had demanded a night with her. Anquru had indignantly said no. He was put to long and acute torture, and he finally gave in. He was carried back to his room and prepared himself, through his tears, to tell his wife that she must go to the Pharaoh. At the door of the room he insisted on being set on his feet. He first leaned against the door to muster the strength to go in. Then he entered. The room was dark. He groped for the lamp and went out again, calling for a servant to light the lamp. The servant came, but was quaking so that he could not get the lamp lit. "Call someone else!" said Anquru. "Only I am here," said the servant. "We were all sent away, and the Pharaoh's bodyguards took our places." The lamp was finally lit, and Anquru went into the room. He heard a faint moan, and he went to the bed.

He never described what he saw. He would begin to, and then break down. She had been raped, raped by the Pharaoh. Then, in shame, she had stabbed herself. She had died before the dawn.

Anquru's noble relative was only slightly horrified. And he found fault with Anquru: why had Anquru refused the Pharaoh? And why had his wife caused herself to be raped, when, merely by gracious acquiescence, the Pharaoh could have enjoyed her, and she, the Pharaoh?

Anquru had shouted that he would avenge himself on the Pharaoh. But the other nobility, including the high nobility, spoke to him ceaselessly, advising him to be quiet, to realize that he could do nothing to the Pharaoh; they even berated him for having let himself undergo torture. And they outraged him when they spoke of his wife as foolish, as childish, as culpable in not gladly complying with the Pharaoh's wishes, and in preposterously killing herself.

Out of Anquru's ill fortune came our good. His estates were large, and there was ample room for us to meet, and even room for us to stay. There were huge storehouses where we could assemble the supplies that we would need.

There was both the general danger there, and the special. The general, that we would be discovered; the special, that the Pharaoh, having wronged Anquru, would proceed to confiscate his property. But Anquru, after joining us, did two things. He went to his kinsman to beg him to carry his apologies to the Pharaoh, and the kinsman, taking Anquru to be fully in earnest, congratulated him for this prudent step. The other thing was Anquru's assembling all his male peasants, this before we began to gather at his estate. He said, "If you work for me, know that I may be in jeopardy, and you may be in jeopardy through me. Any of you who wish to leave, I will give some money to, to move on elsewhere. I beg you not to stay with me unless you are willing to be in the same great jeopardy I am in." A dozen peasants left; the great majority stayed, and those who stayed were of unreserved loyalty.

Perhaps we would have been able to manage without Anquru, for it was urgent that we manage. We might have found another way and his wise counsel elsewhere. But with him, and with his estates, we had a place to bring the representatives from all the tribes. We brought these men in and out of the slave camps.

And slowly, we began to make our plans for an act of sabotage, debating which of several projected acts should come first. Two concerns seemed paramount, that the act we select must hurt Egypt, and that it must be the kind of act which would frighten as well as harm. And all the while that we discussed the choice, there was the growing anxiety for us that it was inevitable that at some stage, whether in the first action, or the second, or later, the Egyptians would become acutely aware of us and begin to take their countermeasures. Indeed, as our group grew larger, the likelihood became all the more probable that an Egyptian policeman, somehow roused to suspicion, would worm his way in among us. Our very first action, then, needed the advantage of surprise that the later ones would lack, and therefore the first one had to be chosen carefully, and it could not be allowed to fail. Moreover, the Egyptians, from the lowliest beggar to the Pharaoh himself, would need to know that it was we who had done it, while at the same time, we would have to retain our concealment intact.

The most acute debate was over a related question. There were those, Aaron among them, who believed that one single, massive action would bring Pharaoh to release us, and we needed to plan not only for such an action, but for our possible immediate release. I thought the latter unlikely, but it was not necessary for me to express it, for both Anquru and Tat-Rin did so, and Ben Onim supported them, all of them contending that Pharaoh would not release the Hebrews after only one action, and, even if he promised to do so, he was not to be believed.

These discussions and debates were occasionally acrimonious, especially when a Hebrew opinion was countered by one from one of our Egyptians. Our Hebrews were suspicious, and some even hostile to these Egyptians who had joined us; the Egyptians from time to time were a little scornful of the Hebrews, especially Tat-Rin. Anquru, though, was always courteous.

To two men, one a Hebrew and one an Egyptian, I owe, from that stage of planning, a debt beyond paying. The Hebrew representative of the camp tribe of Judah was the man who subsequently became my closest friend, Caleb ben Jephunneh. He it was primarily who, through his good humor and his wit, closed the gap between our Egyptians and the Hebrews. How likable he was then!—just as he is now, hurt though I believe he is.

The other man was the cobbler Nephros. Here was a man who was vulgar, whose speech betrayed his lack of schooling, and whose understanding was at times limited. Yet he it was who in some way worked a change in our Egyptians by his speeches, for he was not an outsider helping us. No, he was a part of us. Our quest for freedom became his quest. Through him our Egyptians were embracing not the cause of freedom for others, but for themselves. Even Anquru, who was a man of extensive property, caught the spirit of the poor sandalmaker Nephros.

I must mention one distasteful matter: One of the group wondered about our women, our widows and spinsters. Should we not have in our group someone who, at the right time, would be our link to these single women? It seemed reasonable, and I said so, and immediately Aaron proposed the name of my sister, Miriam; she was a spinster. To my dismay, her name brought forth an immediate assent, only because she was my sister. Could I say that I did not want her when the others spoke with such warmth about her?

I had not yet seen her. I had told myself that it was stupid to run the risk involved in my going into the camp where we learned she was simply to see her. The truth is that I did not want to see her. Oh, I wanted her freed from slavery. But I did not want to see her.

You must believe me that I do not ascribe to that time the feeling which an incident that happened much later elicited. I assure you that this is not the case. At any rate, against my better judgment, I agreed for Miriam to be spirited out of her camp. I saw her at

Anquru's estate. She threw her arms around me in great affection, and I tried to return the warmth of her greeting.

The men who brought her to me had told her about our enterprise. Her words were so earnest, and her affection so deep, as she asked how I was, and where I had been, and said how well I looked and how proud she was of me. "You are not married, are you, Moses?"

"Yes, I am married."

"To a Hebrew woman?"

"When I was a fugitive, I married a Midianite woman. We have two children, a son whom I know, and another child who was to be born after I left Midian."

"It is good to see you," she said. "I am proud of you. I wish our parents had survived to be proud of you."

But when she left me, I saw her spit. Was it my Midianite wife?

It was I who made the decision that our first act would be to poison the Nile. The decision in part was due to our having among our Egyptians a chemist and dye man. It was he who made the red poison. The Hebrews in our group helped Nephros carry out the pouring of the vats of red poison into the river, doing so by night, over a period of a week. Slowly the fish in the river died, and gradually the river came to be more and more red, and at last it was a deep red. We then sent the Hebrews back into the camps, to alert our people that Pharaoh might possibly free us. We sent the Egyptians into taverns all along the river; even Anquru, who was not used to frequenting the cheap taverns, insisted on going too. At the taverns they were to tell people that it was the Hebrews who had poisoned the river.

But that is not exactly right. What our Egyptians whispered in the taverns was that Moses the Hebrew had been sent by the God of the Hebrews to poison the river, and that the Hebrew God was punishing the Egyptians for the enslavement. How quickly the whispers grew on other lips into frightened shouts!

What a calamity this poisoning was to Egypt! And how quickly the word spread from tavern to tavern, and from tavern to market place, that the God of the Hebrews was working vengeance on the Egyptians.

I too visited taverns and market places, and I too heard people speak in great terror of Moses the Hebrew, of Moses the great magician. Of Him they spoke nothing.

Then the Nile began to lose its redness, so we needed to pour the last of our vats of poison into the river. There came from the Egyptians a renewed clamor as loud as we could have wished. Then, of a morning, royal heralds walked around the cities, proclaiming that the Pharaoh wished to confer with Moses the Hebrew. The heralds continued all the day and into the night.

One of the heralds was brought to me, in the dark of the night, at the point of Elyaqim's knife, his eyes securely bandaged. I said to him, "Tell your superior to tell his superior, and let the word go up to Pharaoh, that Moses will confer with him. Let the Pharaoh come with one bodyguard, and one only, to the Temple of Re in Memphis at midnight, two nights after tonight. If more than one bodyguard comes, Moses will not appear."

The herald was sent away. Two nights later our Egyptians were stationed along the way to the temple, to give the signal if more than one bodyguard accompanied the Pharaoh and, indeed, to resolve the doubt that some of us had that he would appear at all.

The three of us, Aaron, Anquru, and I, received the affirmative signal that the Pharaoh was making his way to the temple, and we walked to the building, I fearful, Aaron shaking, and Anquru silent and angry. Anquru's face was completely covered. The Pharaoh and his bodyguard stood before the temple, the bodyguard carrying a torch.

I spoke first. "Let your bodyguard bring the torch before you so that we can look at your face and see that you are the Pharaoh." The Pharaoh spoke, and the bodyguard moved. The sight of the face filled me with a mixture of terror and hatred. I waited for Anquru's hate-filled words: "It is the Pharaoh." Anquru turned and walked away.

I have shortened things considerably, but I think I have now said enough. Yet, I came to the Pharaoh, but only after a long and torturous series of incidents, and only after plans and schemes and perils and anxieties.

The Pharaoh said, with all his majesty, "What is the meaning of these outrages?"

I did not quail. "The Hebrews are to be free."

"They are my slaves," said the Pharaoh.

Then Aaron spoke up. "The God of our fathers has appeared to us. He commands us to make a three-day journey into the desert to worship Him."

I could scarcely believe my ears. I became as furious at Aaron at that moment as I was at the Pharaoh. Instead of demanding our full freedom, he was asking for some brief surcease, as if we were under some necessity to bargain away our full rights for something considerably less. Or else, this three-day journey was Aaron's idea of a ruse, whereby we would turn the desert journey into a permanent flight. I shook my head; it was not going to be done that way, not at all. We were not going to petition the Pharaoh for some tiny favor; we were going to gain what we were entitled to, not as a gift from him, but as our right.

The fury in me kept me from fully following the words that then passed between Aaron and the Pharaoh, words that seemed to suppose that we were asking only for the right to go out into the desert to worship Him—I remember that at that moment it crossed my mind that I knew nothing of how to worship Him, for I had never heard a word of how He wanted to be worshiped.

Then words came to my tongue, and I shouted at both of them, "No! No! No! We Hebrews shall be free! Our demand is freedom, full freedom, nothing less than full freedom!"

Aaron tugged at my sleeve, and roughly I pushed his hand away.

The Pharaoh snarled at me, "This trick of yours with the blood in the Nile—my magicians can do these things. And they can find a remedy for what you have done."

If he thought it was blood, that was fine; it was not blood, it was red poison. I said, very quietly, "This is only the first of the plagues we bring onto Egypt. There will be more."

"I will not give up my possessions. You Hebrews are mine."

"We are not yours, we are the people of our God."

"I do not know Him. You are mine."

I said, "You will free my people."

He said, "I shall not."

"Then you and your people will suffer even more." I turned and walked away, and after a moment, Aaron followed me.

The next night, when we met at the estate of Anquru, we were a smaller group, for representatives of three of our tribes did not appear. The reason was clear; the Egyptians had already taken enough measures so that the ease with which we had before spirited the tribal representatives from the camp was gone. However, for as many as nine of the twelve tribes to be represented was gratifying.

But it was a dismal evening, for some of us who were there were discouraged, discouraged because they wanted immediate success and therefore concluded that we had failed, for the plague of "blood" had not overwhelmed Pharaoh. Worse than that, the cruelties in some of the camps had already increased. Indeed, the Pharaoh had issued an edict that the materials for the bricks would no longer be supplied, and the Hebrews would have to gather the clay and the straw themselves; nevertheless, the same quantity of bricks was to be demanded as before.

I remember vividly the words of the man from the tribe of Zebulon, words which Caleb tells me that our people later put into the mouth of Pharaoh: "Why, Moses, have you come to disturb the people? All you have done is make things worse. Let things alone. We can live through it, and maybe everything will get better."

Caleb said, "They will get better. Tomorrow they will feed us roasted tongues of hummingbirds."

Yet others besides the man from Zebulon spoke in discouragement. Indeed, the turn of the meeting was this, that I, in coming to Egypt, had brought some damage to our people.

Anquru spoke up. "Never once has Moses promised you that one single action will bring the freedom. Never once. We sat and we talked about what we would do first, because we knew we would have to do a second thing, and a third, and a fourth."

One of the Hebrews said, "You are not in one of the camps to be beaten as we are."

Nephros said, "I am here to be killed, if need be, in order for you to be free."

A quiet young man spoke up, a man who had not spoken, as far as I could remember, at any of our earlier meetings. I did not at that moment recall his name; I knew only that he was from the tribe of Ephraim. He said, "We are not here to discuss abandoning our goal. We will not abandon it, ever. We have only one thing to talk about: what do we do next?" This young man was Joshua bin Nun. He was then perhaps twenty or twenty-one. One saw immediately that he was a very intense young man. Even to this day I have never seen Joshua smile. I have also never seen him diverted from our cause, never seen him relax his efforts, never seen him rest. I was to come to know that he was bright, and understanding, and vigorous. Increasingly, I was to grow in my respect for him.

But I was not won to him as I was to Caleb. I was never to be amused by him as I was to be by Caleb. Indeed, let me say it, that Joshua is, and always was, for all the warmth of his fervor, a cold man, a distant man, and Caleb was, and is, a warm, hearty man. Let me say further that I love Caleb, love him as I have loved only one other man, my father-in-law, Jethro. Joshua I have never loved; I have only deeply admired him and deeply respected him. And my admiration and respect, for reasons you will hear, brought me heartache, and I am not sure that this heartache is gone.

The discussion went on, and, of course, many spoke up, but not Aaron. He was silent, and he was angry at me, and I was angry at him. We had had only one conversation, a brief one, when we had returned to the estate. I said to him, "In the future, we must plan together what we say, so that we say the same thing."

His reply to me had been an outburst of resentment, as if I had humiliated him and as if his strategy of wheedling the Pharaoh was better than mine of making a direct demand. He went on to say that if only I had abstained from challenging the Pharaoh, he, Aaron, with his fluent tongue, would have succeeded in persuading the Pharaoh to release us for a three-day march.

Possibly Aaron could have done this. Yet my own conviction was that Aaron was deluding himself, both about his eloquence and about the Pharaoh's tractability. As Aaron rehearsed to me what he would have said to Pharaoh, if I had permitted him to speak, his words seemed both plausible, and at the same time implausible, and I was led to wonder if my brilliant brother was susceptible to self-deception.

The acts of sabotage, according to Caleb, totaled ten, and our people speak of them as the plagues which He visited on the Egyptians. I myself never counted the acts. Let me say, though, that some were actions that we "conspirators" carried out, carefully and methodically. Some, though, were boons that must have come from Him: the lice, the boils, the locusts, the darkness. It was we, though, who unleashed the abundance of scorpions whom our people speak of as frogs.

It was we, not He, who carried out the reluctant, climactic task of the murder of the first-born. It was gentle Anquru who resolutely administered the poison to the Pharaoh's own son; it was Nephros who was prepared to poison the Pharaoh who was himself a first-born. However garbled is the account of the plagues, with respect to their sequence and the manner in which they came about, there is no purpose in now trying to arrange them in true order; indeed, I have forgotten it.

But I cannot forget the preparations which we made for our flight. We assembled food; we assembled transport; again and again we went over the plans for the time when the moment of release would come.

It was our plan that it would come at night, on a night when a full moon would give us the light we would need. The Pharaoh, at his capitulation, might give the orders for us to be freed the next day, at dawn, but, no, we would not wait that long. That very night was to be it, the night in which our people would need to be alert, to be awake and watchful for the exact moment when the news would come. Because we were constantly distrustful, we enjoined our people to mark the lintels of the doors of our Hebrew hovels with lamb's blood—something I remembered from Midian—so that we could thereby distinguish our people from the Egyptians.

Early that night we distributed our large cache of swords and spears and bows and arrows among our people, just in case that, at the last minute, we should need to fight our way to freedom.

The night previous to our release, He at last spoke to me. He spoke to me as I lay in my bed, sleepless. My anxiety could not have been more acute than it was, and my fear of failure was making my heart beat as though it was struggling to be released from its prison in my breast. He said, "Tomorrow night I shall visit judgment on the Egyptians. Their houses will know death, but your houses I will pass over. I shall pass among the Egyptians as a destroyer." I needed His reassurance. I alerted all our people to be ready.

I lament that more Egyptian first-born were killed than needed to be. So concerned were we to make the Pharaoh capitulate that understandably we were too efficient, too relentless. By nightfall, the first of the deaths were reported to Pharaoh; by midevening the Pharaoh-to-be was dead. An hour later, after nightfall, the Pharaoh gave the word that the Hebrews were to be released. At midnight, the camps began to empty.

Days later I heard some of the accounts. Some of our people, in their bitterness, ransacked the homes of the Egyptians to gather up whatever treasures they could. It pains me to hear from Caleb that our people speak of "borrowing" from the Egyptians the treasures they took; I would rather admit that they seized them or stole them or simply confiscated them.

I say that I have heard these accounts since I did not witness what went on, for Aaron and I—yes, Aaron, because I remembered He had told me that Aaron was to be associated with me—Aaron and I were where we could quickly visit the Pharaoh at his summons and observe him give the written orders for our release.

Perhaps you wonder how the orders reached all the camps. We had, of course, prepared likenesses of them in advance, and we had our couriers on horses ready to ride into the camps with them. If you ask the question, could we not also have arranged a false release, then the answer is that we contemplated this, but only as an extreme measure. An authentic release meant that there would be no immediate opposition from the Egyptians; an inauthentic one was fraught with attendant dangers. Our intention was to reduce the risks to the vanishing point.

The Pharaoh, thoroughly terrorized, signed the orders. We forced his own officers to convey them, under our guard, to all the camps. Like the waters of the Nile, our people streamed out of the camps and the huts. They met our men, who stood with torches and banners, and told our people where the tribes were to assemble for the march.

There was confusion, of course, the confusion of joy. Some things went wrong; most did not. The Egyptians who saw us were perplexed and so thoroughly cowed that not one of them, so I have heard, lifted a finger to hinder us.

The camps and the huts were emptied. The march—what a long march it became!—began. In charge was Qurmene, the fisherman; he it was who led us eastward across the desert to the Sea of Reeds, and he it was who picked out the marshy area where we were to cross the sea and leave Egypt.

In those days, I was unaware of something that Caleb has since told me, something which both amuses me and, I must confess, irritates me. It is a fact that at the height of some of the plagues, the Pharaoh agreed to our release and promptly, when each plague began to subside, changed his mind. As our people tell it, this change of mind came about because He had hardened Pharaoh's heart. If one were to accept this, it would mean that at the same time that He sent me to Pharaoh to obtain our release, He so arranged matters that I would not get it. This absurdity amuses me. The irritation of which I have spoken stems from the implication, for if He was influencing the Pharaoh to abstain from releasing us, then reasonably our enslavement at the Pharaoh's hands was also a result of His influence. The Pharaoh, thereby, would seem free of all personal responsibility for what he had done and was doing; indeed the Pharaoh was acting not out of choice but out of the compulsion which He had put upon him. Now, it is well and good to ascribe to Him the control of what happens in the affairs of men, but to suppose that this control extends to the point that man has neither choice nor direct responsibility is something I could not and cannot accept. Even in those days in Egypt, I found myself wondering about these things, and at times I floundered in a confusing dilemma. On the one hand, unless I believed that He was in some way guiding what I was doing, I could have only limited confidence in some successful outcome. I can say that the massive problems, and the recurring refusals by Pharaoh to release us, could possibly have deterred me, and possibly even have impelled me at this or that point to desist, unless I believed in His guidance. On the other hand, all along the way, I, and those with me, faced decision after decision, with terrible responsibility hinging on each. To what end were our sharp debates and our marked differences of judgment and painful progression toward settled conclusions, if in effect He, and not we, were deciding? If He alone decided, then we were thinking in vain, discussing in vain, deluding ourselves that decisions confronted us for us to weigh. If He alone decided, then of what use was it for a man to have a mind, a capacity to reason, an inner sense of having weighed this factor and that factor and ultimately of having come to a conclusion?

I did not know at that time to what extent this important matter of man and decision would come to be related to issues which arose later. The situation then was this, that we Hebrews had been living in slave camps, subject to the rules of the Egyptians and to the whims with which cruel officials applied the rules. Now came our release, not only from slavery, but from Egyptian rules, indeed from all rules. Whereby were we now to be governed? As I say, I do not now remember the extent to which I pondered this matter, but I can say that it did pass through my mind.

Still another comment is necessary. We needed to flee as quickly as possible before the Pharaoh, again changing his mind, could muster the troops and the armaments to cut off our escape from Egypt. I gather from Caleb that, as our people now tell it, the Egyptians drove us out! This is, I must say, utterly absurd! They did not drive us out; undeviatingly, they attempted to retain us and to constrain us.

Indeed, our first great crisis was the belated Egyptian pursuit of us, to keep us prisoners in the land. Had not Qurmene carefully plotted our journey and meticulously guided us to our crossing, we would have escaped from the camps only to be trapped at the sea, and then would have been brought back into an even more horrible enslavement. When the change of heart came over the Pharaoh, and he pursued us with his horses and chariots, he nearly overtook us. Indeed, Qurmene so led us that the Egyptians must have thought us confused and bewildered. But so mad had the Pharaoh become that he lost all discretion and began to give preposterous orders to his commanders.

When we were at the sea, preparing slowly to make our way across the marshes, from our rear came the disturbing word that the Egyptians, in full pursuit, were closing in on us.

I confess that momentarily I lost heart. The wind was blowing and black clouds were hanging low; I had a presentiment of disaster, to the point that, pushed now beyond endurance, I cried out to Him, "Rescue us! Rescue us!"

He answered me calmly and clear. "Why do you shout to Me! Speak to the children of Israel and have them move on."

The east wind was blowing the waters away, so as to provide us with some passage. Qurmene was there—blessed Qurmene! A cart here and a cart there became stuck in the soft soil, but Qurmene had made provision. Nephros had his crews, and his own powerful arms, to free the carts and to enable them to move forward.

Without that east wind I fear we would never have managed a

rapid crossing. Somehow, the wind seemed constantly to be shifting its direction, but mostly it retained its gusts from the east; one had the feeling of two walls of water enclosing a dry road. We crossed the sea, and then the Egyptians, driven on by the insane Pharaoh, recklessly followed us. Their heavy chariots became mired in the loose soil, and the shifting winds suddenly obliterated the roadbed. Their chariots could move neither backward nor forward. The men, dressed in their heavy armor, found themselves engulfed in what had become a deep chasm. The horses panicked and pulled broken chariot onto mired chariot, with the harnesses holding the horses fast, so that the waters began to overwhelm the sturdy animals. The Egyptian army was destroyed, completely destroyed.

I confess that I was grateful for their destruction. In part, it was a proper recompense for their past cruelties, and for their pursuit of us. In part, it was not I or we who had destroyed them, but their own imprudence. In part, it was that saving wind.

How had that wind appeared so fortuitously? Later, Tat-Rin explained it as a lucky coincidence, and he gently smiled at me when I declared that He had brought it, brought it just when we needed it. I think that Tat-Rin was never persuaded by my belief.

I believed, and I still believe, that He provided the wind that split the sea. I believe this; I cannot prove it. Indeed, if I could prove it, I would no longer need to believe, for if one can prove, he is no longer believing; he knows. One believes only when one does not know.

When we were across and safe, I prayed to Him, and I thanked Him for our deliverance. Those Hebrews near me I led in prayer.

But from the distance I heard the sound of singing and of drums and tambourines. I went toward the sound. There was Miriam, dancing in wild abandon, glorying in the death of the Egyptians.

I cannot say now whether the slight distaste I had for my sister awakened in me a distaste for her vindictive pleasure, or whether her vindictive pleasure evoked an increased distaste for her. To my mind, to rejoice at our escape was quite different from her unreserved delight in the death of the Egyptian soldiers.

Moreover, it was He who created all things, and the Egyptians too were His creatures. How could we rejoice at the death of His creatures!

I thought that I would stop the dance, but I saw that it was too frenzied for me, or for anyone, to stop. I walked away, beset by a disgust that almost destroyed my joy at our freedom.

Then I told myself that I was being too harsh, that I must expect even our Hebrews to do the human thing of celebrating the destruction of our enemies.

My thoughts turned to Zipporah, and to Jethro, and to Gershom. And to the baby that Zipporah was to have given birth to. Before, on the occasions when I thought of them, I felt a little guilt, for my heart and my mind should rather have concentrated only on our escape from slavery. Now, though, I could think of them and wonder how soon I could see them, for now, so I thought, the worst was behind me. Now we were free, and now we could make our way calmly and steadily to the Promised Land.

Now, so I believed, all would go well.

✳ CHAPTER IV

About some minor matters there are differences in recollection; my own may be no better than that of others. For example, it is remembered by some that, even before we left Egypt, and even before our flight to the sea and the Pharaoh's pursuit of us, He enjoined us to celebrate annually in the month of Abib our wondrous redemption from slavery. My own recollection, on the other hand, is that this injunction came only after we had made the crossing to safety. I can, of course, be wrong. But it scarcely makes any difference whether it was before or after, for the essential requirement was that we needed to celebrate it so that our people would never forget. And I am satisfied, at least up to the present, that our people have set freedom as the very cornerstone of our collective being, as they should. Indeed, since it was He who sent me, and He who saved us at the sea, it is He who is the source of our freedom.

Yet, nevertheless, there were those of us who in various ways did our part in the release, so that the celebration of our freedom has needed to recall the part that man played. Otherwise the celebration would be only of Him, and we could easily forget that His divine deed was helped by our human efforts.

I recall very vividly, however, the discussion, indeed the disputes, with my brother, Aaron, about the celebration. These were never over the question of celebrating our freedom, but how. My own thought was perhaps too little imaginative. There was a tangible element, that is, the specific time when we were released, the happy spring season of Abib. Surely we ought to set aside some days in that season when we would recount the glorious story to ourselves and to our children. Yet Aaron, with his more vivid imagination, was overflowing with many additional ideas about how to celebrate. To put it simply—his presentation was scarcely simple—he proposed that, in the season of Abib, we should both repeat those things which we had done in Egypt, and even add to them. In Egypt we had smeared lamb's blood on the lintels of our hovels; even now that we were free, we should do so every year in commemoration of the great event. Moreover, according to him, each household should take a lamb, a year old, without blemish, and slay it at evening, and roast the meat. Along with the meat, we should now eat cakes of unleavened bread, made of dough which, because of our haste, could not be allowed the time to rise; also, we should eat bitter herbs to recall the bitterness of the enslavement. Aaron, indeed, proposed that we should eat this Passover meal with our loins girded, and our shoes on our feet, and our staffs in our hands, as if we were prepared to travel.

I am no longer sure why I did not take to his suggestions, even though I remember very clearly the reason which I then gave him. I said to him that his proposals seemed so complex and elaborate that our people would be so preoccupied with doing all these things they would forget the freedom itself. When I now ask myself why I then argued in this way, I explain to myself that somehow or other I have had a personal aversion to acts which have seemed to me in any way artificial. To dress up for a journey when one knows that one is not going to travel the slightest bit, seemed a little silly. I could readily understand that in Egypt we needed to smear the lamb's blood on our doorposts for the specific purpose of distinguishing our abodes from those of the Egyptians. But to slay the lambs as he proposed seemed useless to me and unnecessary. Moreover, the Midianites, as you may remember, had done almost the same sort of thing, though with quite a different meaning, and it seemed to me that if the actions were the same, the differing explanations were very secondary.

There is perhaps no great importance in this specific difference wherein I irritated Aaron. Beyond that difference there had arisen a separation between him and me by now much deeper than the level of the disputes that we had. My own concern, so it seemed to me in my arrogance, was with the tremendous issue that men must be free, and his concern, so I thought, was with lambs and dough and herbs and clothes.

Since he was fluent, and annoyed with me, he attacked my opinion with considerable eloquence. "You understand freedom, Moses, but you do not understand people. Freedom is not a tree you see, or an apple you can bite into and taste. People will forget freedom, unless there are things to see, and things to do, and things to taste. You think you will preserve the thought of freedom simply because the idea is important. I tell you it can be forgotten, and even perish. It can perish, unless you give the people both the thought of freedom and also the way to remember the thought."

I said, quietly, "Our people cannot possibly ever forget the thought of freedom."

He said to me, "You do not know people. They will forget. You make the mistake of thinking that because you will not forget, the people will not forget. You are wrong."

I said, "You speak in behalf of these things because you like them. I speak against them because I do not."

He became furious at me. "You do me injustice. I speak of these things because I know people. I was in the camp and you were not. You do not have bitter memories to forget, but I do. You do not understand that our people want to forget the ugly things that went on in the camps, and you do not understand that as soon as they forget the misery of the camps, they will forget about freedom too."

I could see some rightness in his words, for certainly I myself had tended to forget the minor distresses I had experienced in Midian, and I remembered that in Midian I had been able mostly to forget those happenings in Egypt which had led me to flee. Nevertheless, I could not help believing that my brother, Aaron, by his very nature inclined to things like the dressing up for a journey he would not go on, and he could revel in what seemed to me a preposterous slaughter of lambs.

We had these disputes, and I think that each of us was aware that there was a growing rift between us. And it somehow seemed absurd that, having gained our freedom with so much difficulty, we should now be laboriously quarreling about the proper way to celebrate it. I think, too, that I was irked by the frequency with which he would tell me that I did not know people, but perhaps I was irked, not so much by the frequency, as by the anxiety that he might be right. I, of course, finally gave in to Aaron, but not out of the conviction that he was completely right; I did so only to keep a genuine separation from developing between us. I do not remember thinking through this matter of the rift; I gave it only passing thought.

I mention this matter of the observance of our freedom, though the issue is long since passed, only as the prelude to recording a different matter, again in terms of a rift. I make no pretense of false modesty, for I know that at that time it was I who was the leader in all that we did. Perhaps in recounting the events in Egypt, much as I have spoken of myself, I have given insufficient emphasis to what I personally did, that is, to the way in which it was I who had to make the uncertain and perilous decisions. I stress these things for the reason that as I now met with the tribal representatives, I began to notice a subtle shift. In Egypt, I felt acutely how dependent on me everyone seemed to be: whether Caleb, or Joshua, or Ben Onim, or Elyaqim, or the noble Egyptians who were joined with us. Although people spoke their ideas and at times challenged mine, there was always some sense that all revolved about me, and that, until I spoke the final words, they were uncertain or even floundering in indecision.

Before, we had all come to be of one mind no matter how much we disagreed. But now that we were safe across the Sea of Reeds, that older sense of dependency on me or of deferring to me appeared to be changing. I noticed it, for example, in my own cousin, Korah, who represented our tribe of Levi. Korah seemed to me to take special pleasure at our council meetings in opposing me. At that early time he did so somewhat guardedly, but not so guardedly that I did not notice it. I was able to catch, in the nuances of his voice, his feeling that now that we were safe, my wisdom was no longer better than anyone else's. It is too much to say that, at the time, Korah was challenging me, and certainly he did not then seem intent on supplanting me. Perhaps I should have suspected that; I did not. Again, irritating to me though Aaron was,

I never considered that he had any thought but of acquiescing in my leadership. No, Aaron never seemed to me to be trying to reduce me while raising himself.

I can say in all honesty that, in those days, I had no deep inner feeling of concern for my role as the leader. Perhaps I am not clear. I mean this: to me it had been more important for our people to escape from Egypt than for me to be the leader in their escape. It was more important that they should in time be led to Canaan, and then into Canaan, than that I should be the one to lead them. Yet on the other hand, I cannot deny that I was finding some gratification in my being the leader.

At no time did I take to myself some special title. When, as happened, people asked me what they should call me, I responded, "Simply call me Moses." I know that our people have spoken of me as the Man of God; surely, though, this is no title in the way that the word "prince" or "king" is a title. But I know now, as I possibly did not know then, that I did want to lead, that it was important to me to lead. I did not want to be called Leader, but I did want to be the leader. I wanted to lead, though, simply because I had a vision of what I wanted my people to become. Yet how easy it is to lead when there is danger, or when there is a purpose like freedom, which can unify people! And how different things were to soon become, now that we were free and out of the old danger and not faced with any imminent new ones!

There was time now for me to begin longing to see my Zipporah and Gershom and the other child. I could not go to Midian, for I did not think I could leave our people. Elyaqim was willing to take a message to my Zipporah, and I was prepared to send him on his way. To my surprise and my joy, he said to me, "I will carry the message. But I will return."

"By all means come back."

"Of course, I will come back."

I said, "By all means, Elyaqim."

Then he said, "Wherever you go, Moses, I will go."

His words brought gratification to me. That gratification would have been greater if I only had perceived a bit more clearly the slight dissent from my leadership which had by then begun.

Warmed as I was by Elyaqim's words of affection for me, or at least by his confidence in me, I then began to discern, though very dimly, that there was something which I wanted from him that was far beyond any personal loyalty. It was for an Elyaqim, and for my own people, to be loyal, not to me, but to the conviction I had come to, that our people, as Hebrews, needed to become a very special people. For me this was already a necessity and not a luxury. And this seemed to me to mean something more than a journey to a distant land of our own.

But there was this long journey to make, and it was in no way to be an easy one. Our first destination was, of course, in accord with His command to me at the time of the burning bush that I was to bring our people to the sacred mountain, Sinai, which lay quite far to the south. Any journey toward it had the virtue of leading us directly away from whatever Egyptian forces might have been gathered on the east coast of the Sea of Reeds.

As we traveled, we passed through or near some villages; there Shallum ben Malqishalem, our manager of supply, was able to buy replenishment of our flour and our fresh vegetables.

At night, if one looked south from our camp, one could see in the distant sky the reflection of the fires of the volcanoes; indeed, there were times when in the daytime we could see pillars of smoke in the south. I have learned from Caleb that our people have made these sporadic sights into daily ones, and that they now relate that we were led at night by a pillar of fire and in the day by the clouds of smoke. Let them think so; there is no harm in it. But we had our regular scouts, the chief of whom was Joshua bin Nun, who went ahead of us to look over the route which we were to follow.

That our people tell little of the inordinate toil of the travel itself does not surprise me. After all, those who now survive to remember it were the very young among them. Besides, there is little interest among people in the mundane matters of how we arranged for food and shelter, and most of all for water, for matters of greater import arose. Before the Exodus, we made our travel plans; often I had reason to be vexed when the arrangements, made so carefully, broke down through the carelessness of some one person, or through the negligence of some other. But the alertness which had prevailed among us in Egypt could no longer be maintained now that we were making our leisurely journey to the mountain. When something went wrong, our people were not averse to complaining to the tribal representatives, and these in turn were not averse to complaining to me, often as if it was I and I alone who had been careless or negligent.

But, also, there were times when the unexpected became a debilitating experience. For example, our scouts had pointed our way to the oasis of Marah, and they had described glowingly the abundance of the wells of water and the greenness of the trees there. By this time our water supply had begun to run low, and even what was left in the waterskins had lost the freshness which one wants. Our columns moved on, and the oasis of Marah came into our view. To my dismay, the orderliness of our march promptly disappeared. First individuals and then clusters of people rushed headlong to the wells.

Our scouts had seen the wells and had gone right to them; to this day I cannot believe, despite what they told me, that they ever tasted the water. Now, when our people drew up the buckets, and took deep draughts, they found the water salty and bitter, undrinkable like the water of the sea. There arose an immediate clamor from our people who, angry at the water, directed their anger at me. I remember hating looks and ugly words. In the midst of this minor unpleasantness, Ben Onim came to me, to suggest that we cut down some of the trees of the oasis and throw them into the well; they would partially cover up the taste of the water and render it drinkable. I quickly gave instructions to do as he suggested. The trees were cut down, thrown into the wells, and the water lost enough of its bitterness to be drinkable. While the people were drinking and complaining and disdainfully filling their waterskins, young Joshua bin Nun came to me. Not too far away was still another oasis, Elim, with no less than twelve wells and eighty palm trees—how well I remember Joshua's precise report—and perhaps the water at Elim would be sweet. I said to him, "Ride there and taste the water, and ride back."

As I waited for him, I observed the chaos at the wells of Marah. People piled upon people, and people pushed people, and those who were pushed, pushed back, and here and there fights broke out, both between people of different tribes and between our loyal Egyptians and the Hebrews, and, indeed, even between people of the same tribe.

It was clear to me that if our people were to approach the wells at Elim in some orderly way, then everyone would get his due of water, and in ample time. The milling about only delayed things, and it needlessly could give rise to petty conflicts and to occasional fights. I saw that I had been myself negligent in that I had not prepared a plan for what to do at an oasis. Indeed, I had scarcely thought of, or thought out, any system of over-all organization of our people, having contented myself with tribal representatives. I think that I assumed—wrongly—that the representatives would organize the tribes from within.

As I stood and watched the milling about and the confusion, and as I heard the shouts of some and the angry retorts of others, I became aware of how deficient my planning had been. The truth is that I had planned primarily how to get us out of Egypt; I had envisaged transport and food, but I had not planned in any depth for our march across the wilderness. There was no doubt that our people needed some procedures or rules; otherwise, we would have recurrent chaos, or worse, at every oasis we came to.

In the midafternoon, Joshua returned with the encouraging word that the waters at Elim were sweet and cool. From the top of the hill I watched our people at the well, mulling over in my mind a half-formed intention of trying to quiet the people, and of mustering some words to speak to them, of giving them some rules right there and then.

I felt keenly that I should come before them and speak to them, that I should, at this first instance of their restiveness, talk to them about orderliness, about co-operation, about rules. Then it occurred to me that I must move them as quickly as possible to Elim, and only after they would have drunk the refreshing waters, would it be possible for me to get them to listen attentively to a speech. Yet even as I began to ponder what I would say to them, and when I would say it, the disturbing recognition came to me that I was thinking almost as much about my personal leadership of my people as I was about the people I was leading and that was why I wanted to make a speech. The fear arose in me, even then, that I would so intertwine the concern for my people with a concern for myself and my leadership, I would come to the point of not seeing the difference.

I rehearsed in my mind an orderly speech in which I would tell them how we could all drink at an oasis in an orderly way. But at Elim I made no speech to the people. I only watched them, and I made the speech to myself. Even so, the words did not come easily, for the reason that I felt I must be exact. I thought of consulting my brother, Aaron, who would surely have a torrent of words at his command, but I was apprehensive that Aaron would teach me to say what I did not have in mind, or else he would lead me into an abundance of words which said nothing. So, I made no speech to all the people. Instead, I summoned the tribal representatives and told them that we needed to be orderly in our drawing water from an oasis; I said only that, and no more than that. They all agreed.

When we came to the oasis of Elim, all there went smoothly, so smoothly that I made a mistake. I inferred from the smoothness at Elim that the confusion and minor altercations at Marah had been an exception. I attributed the disorders at Marah to the combination of the thirst and the disappointment. Surely I was seeing at Elim the innate orderliness of our people.

But maybe I did not make my speech at Elim for a different reason. Maybe it was because I had little confidence in what a mere speech would accomplish. How often, at our various council meetings, words had been multiplied almost beyond the point of endurance before a decision was reached, and how seldom were many words needed once a decision was made. As I wandered about at

Elim, I saw Caleb ben Jephunneh and I called to him; he came to me and we walked together. I told him about my having contemplated making a speech, and of deciding not to. He grinned at me. "You are wise not to, Moses." He kicked at a stone, looked at me and said, "The time to make a speech, Moses, is when you have nothing to say."

Now, all appeared to be well, for Elim was orderly as Marah had not been, and I concluded that a people who could come to restrain themselves needed no imposed restraints. And possibly because I did not yet adequately notice the incipient dissent from my leadership, I did not connect that dissent to the disorder at Marah; or maybe the two were not connected.

If I have given an impression that we moved quickly from Marah and to Elim, that is, of course, not the case. I no longer remember how long it took; it was weeks, not days. We were a huge assembly of people, and our travel was always cumbersome.

We moved slowly but steadily. When we went beyond Elim, reports began to come to me that our people were becoming weary, that they wanted to rest, that we must break our march and pause to rest.

To me this seemed strange, for I had thought that at Elim we had thoroughly refreshed ourselves. I do not know why I was reluctant to interrupt our march, for there was no specific urgency to speed to the sacred mountain. Yet somehow I had the intuition that a pause would not be prudent or useful.

I sought out Caleb, and I put the matter before him. He shrugged his shoulders. "Our people are weary. That means that they are beginning to grumble. If we continue to move, they will continue to grumble all the more. If we pause, they will find renewed strength to grumble. You must decide in which way they will grumble the less."

"They grumble because they are weary, Caleb."

"They are weary. They grumble because people grumble."

"But what do they grumble about?"

"It does not matter. They will discover their excuse to grumble after they have begun to grumble."

These words of Caleb troubled me, perhaps more than they
should have. I confess that his certainty that our people would
grumble had not occurred to me. I was weary, too, but had no
impulse to grumble. All seemed to me to be proceeding well, and
I could see nothing worth complaining about. Why should they
grumble and I not? Why, I asked myself, this difference? Apart
from the superficial answer that I knew more clearly what we had
to do than they did, I could not give myself an answer.

Then Joshua bin Nun came to me and I welcomed the sight of
him, for surely, in his typical manner, he would cast aside the unimportant and never be diverted from the important. Joshua could
tell me if the weariness and the grumbling needed to be taken
seriously, or could be ignored. I spoke to him as I had spoken to
Caleb. He gave me an answer which was different and which
frightened me. "They are weary, but not so weary that they need
rest. They will grumble, but you need not at this time be disturbed
by it. Something else, though, must be considered."

"What is that?"

"We are about to leave Shur and enter into the Wilderness of
Sin. Shur is a place which is settled, it is where the native people
have their small settlements. When I have been out scouting our
route, I have noticed that the nearer we come to the Wilderness of
Sin, the more we have seen guards and sentries and weapons in the
villages. I have asked questions and received answers. The Wilderness of Sin is full of bands of marauders. We must be prepared for
those who might attack us."

"Why in the world should anyone attack us?"

He shrugged his shoulders. "Perhaps out of fear of us. Perhaps
because they think we are trespassing over their land—"

"But this land is worthless."

"True. But it is theirs. Or maybe they think that we have
treasures which they would like to own."

I was silent, for I needed to think. Then I said, "When we were
leaving Egypt, we had our armed fighting men. We assigned them
to protect our rear. We trained them for that. Should we bring
them together again?"

Joshua said, "We need to reassemble them, but not only to guard our rear. We need to protect our advance and our flanks."

Then I shook my head. "Why should we need an army? We are a peaceful people. We armed ourselves against the Egyptians because we were compelled to. Why should we form an army when we have no enemy?"

"I only repeat that the people of the villages speak of bands of marauders."

I had traveled through these lands on my flight from Egypt and therefore I could not credit what he said. I had been welcomed with food and shelter everywhere I had come, and no one had harmed me, or ever threatened me. No one had stolen from me— I had nothing to steal!—and when I had been sent on my way, it was always with a skin of water and loaves of bread and cheese. Why should this Wilderness of friendly people suddenly turn into an area of foes? And why, having faced the reality of fear in Egypt, did I need here to conjure up an unreal fear?

I said to Joshua, "I will consider the matter."

He said, "In the meantime, shall I alert our guards? Shall I assemble our fighters? Or at least their captains?"

I did not answer him. I said, "I am still uncertain whether we should press on, or encamp and rest."

He said, "I think we should rest."

So we encamped. Can I say that we rested? Hardly. At Elim we had filled all our waterskins, so in our present encampment we knew no thirst. But I, or someone else—not one, but many—had somehow done something wrong, for I had thought that our food was, if not plenteous, at least sufficient.

I usually ate with Aaron and his sons. Sometimes Miriam, unbidden, joined us. Aaron's appetite was always good, and mine never. Miriam was a small eater too, for she could seldom sit still. Aaron had been tall and thin when we had been in Egypt; one could not now call him fat, but he had put on weight. Miriam was as thin as before, and her voice seemed to me to be a little less shrill than it had been. Now, though, as the three of us, Aaron,

Miriam, and I, sat on the ground, one of the cooks of our tribe of Levi brought us a battered tray of food. Miriam said to him harshly, "Is that all?"

He looked at me, not at her. "That is all." He walked away.

She arose from the ground and overtook him. "Why is that all?"

"Because that is all that was given me."

"But why?"

"Because our supplies are low."

She came back to Aaron and me. She spoke to me, not to him. "Why are our supplies low?"

I said, "I do not know."

She raised her voice. "But you ought to know. You are the leader, you ought to know." She sat down. "This is not enough for the three of us."

I said, "It is not for three. It is for you and Aaron." I rose from the ground.

She said, "It is not enough for two."

I was angry, angry that there was so little food, angry that she had spoken to me as she had. I saw our cook a little distance away and I went to him. "Where are the supply carts? Take me there." I followed him as he walked among the Levites, and then across the encampment of the Reubenites, and to a place where the carts were assembled in a neat circle. Some of the people there seemed to know me, some did not. I said, "I must see Shallum ben Malqishalem." One of the men made a gesture with his hand, and I went in the direction he indicated, beyond the carts. Some men were seated on the ground, and I saw the back of the head, the shoulders, and the brawny back of Shallum. As I approached him, I called him by name. He turned his face to me. I saw a red welt on his right cheek, and his left eye was closed. "Shallum," I said, "what has happened to you?" He slowly rose; I looked at the other men, and they all had bruises and scabs on their faces, and some on their arms. Shallum was on his feet. I went to him and I said, a second time, "What has happened to you?"

"We have had a little trouble."

"What kind?"

He scowled. "The food. We have had thieves. And burglars."

I immediately remembered what Joshua bin Nun had been saying. "Desert marauders?"

He shook his head. "Our brother Hebrews. The tribes of Dan and of Simon and of Issachar."

"The tribes! Shallum, I cannot believe it!"

He felt his face. "Not the entire tribes. People from the three. They have been coming in the middle of the night, half of their band to fight us and the other half to steal food during the fighting."

I was too shocked to speak right away. Finally I said, "Have they stolen much, Shallum?"

"Enough."

I said, "Why have you not told me?"

"We were sitting here talking about telling you." He looked around. "I think we can manage now."

"But how?"

"More guards. More weapons."

I was heartsick. "And have our supplies become low?"

He said, "It has been long since we replenished them."

"I thought you were doing it as we went along."

"Sometimes I have been able to buy. But never enough to keep up with the amount that we must distribute. Constantly our supplies have been decreasing. Four days ago, the thefts began. We have barely enough for three days."

"Why did we encamp if we were so nearly out of food?"

One of the men near him said, "Why did you not consult us before you decided to encamp?"

"Because I did not know about the food. I should have been told."

Shallum said sharply, "I should have been asked." He came to me, put his face against mine, and shouted, so that my ears began to ring, "I should have been asked!"

I am afraid that many ugly things to say came to the tip of my tongue. I said none of these, but spoke very quietly, "Yes, you should have been asked."

Again he shouted, "I should have been asked!"

I did not know what further quiet word to say. I did not move away from him. Slowly he moved away from me. I remained motionless.

Then he spoke, in a lower voice. "We are ready for them if they return tonight."

I turned around and walked away. That Shallum had been somewhat nasty to me was scarcely as important as that our own people had been stealing our supplies, and I was disheartened by both. Curiously, it seemed to me easily possible to forgive our people, but not Shallum. I was furious at him, eager to hurt him, in need of some retaliation, and I was furious at myself for having answered him so quietly. I was the leader—should he have spoken to me as he did?

Certainly I had to do something about the thefts. I—we—could not tolerate them. I went over in my mind the names of the representatives of Dan, Reuben, and Issachar. I should send for them, so I said to myself, and give each of them a private scolding and a stern warning. But what kind of a warning? And could not each of them speak to me as Shallum had spoken, as if I were not the leader and were not vested with some authority? But with what authority was I vested? Oh, He had sent me, and they had received me. But at no time had they asked me to be their leader, and at no time had they made me any open suggestion that they commended my leadership.

Angry as I was, I became aware that I was hungry, and satisfying as it had been to make the gesture of giving my food to Aaron and Miriam, I began to be tormented at being hungry. Yet I was certain that, hungry as I was, I had absolutely no wish to eat. Rather, the matter of Shallum and the thefts, and my anxiety about how the tribal representatives would respond to my chiding, combined to unsettle me. Then for a moment, I wanted to hurry back to Shallum, to scold him without mercy—indeed, to strike him; for another moment I wanted to gather all the people and publicly denounce the tribes from which the thieves had come, to the point that the nine other tribes would fall upon these three, and damage them. Yet, fully angry as I was, I saw no virtue in such actions. Indeed, I found myself asking myself why for a second time I had begun to toy with the thought of making a speech to all the people. Was it because I had some need to put myself before them, to set myself as their undoubted leader and have them so acknowledge me, whether they wished it or not?

At that very moment, Aaron came to me. "I must talk to you, Moses." I did not reply to him. He said again, "I must talk to you, Moses."

I said, gruffly, "What about?"

He said, "I have been thinking about my duties."

"What about them?"

"They are not clear to me."

I snapped at him. "They are not clear to me either."

He seemed to ignore my reply. "It occurs to me that I should be given some kind of title, an important one."

I must relate that at these words of his, I laughed, laughed in my bitterness, as though it was all funny. He turned away from me, red in the face, and began to stride toward the camp of us Levites. I called to him, "Aaron, come here." He continued to stride away. I shouted, "Aaron, come here." He took three steps and stopped. He did not turn around but remained where he was, motionless. I said, less loud, but still loud enough for him to hear, "Aaron, you are to come to me." I wondered if he would.

For a moment he continued to remain motionless. Then he turned slowly and he came to me. I motioned to the ground, and first I sat, and then slowly he sat down. I said, "Thieves from three tribes, Dan, Reuben, and Issachar, have been stealing our supplies. What shall I do about this?"

"Punish them! Punish them!" I could tell from his voice that he was angry at me, rather than at the thieves.

"How, Aaron? And who is to do the punishing?"

He did not answer. He only said, "Punish them! Punish them!"

I said, "Our supplies of food are low."

He said, "I want a title, an important one."

"Tell me what your duties are."

"It is for you to tell me."

I said, "You are right, Aaron: I do not know people. I do not know Hebrews who would steal food from the common supply. I do not know managers of supply who keep information from me and who then upbraid me for not having it; and I do not know you who demand a title. I want the council of tribal representatives assembled immediately. Please do so at once."

He arose and shuffled off.

The first person to come was my cousin Korah, the representative of the Levites. His greeting to me again seemed less than cordial, but I preferred not to notice. When next Caleb came, the warmth of his greeting to me emphasized how cold Korah had been. He said, "You seem to be worried, Moses."

I nodded. "There are things to worry about."

"Naturally." He sat on the ground. "My tribe of Judah has not yet become weary of resting. I am weary of it."

"We shall move soon."

"May I have a private word with you, Moses?"

Korah said, "You may speak. I am not listening."

Caleb snorted, "And I am not sitting!" Korah, who had been standing, walked a few paces away.

I said, softly, "What is on your mind, Caleb?"

"Our Egyptians. Without them we would still be in Egypt. They came with us. Are they part of us, or are they not?"

I said, "They are part of us."

"Who represents them at this meeting?"

I said, "I have been remiss. I should have invited one of them. I think it should be Anquru."

"May I go and bring him?"

"Please do, Caleb." He rose and started to walk away. I said, "Thank you, Caleb."

Korah saw him go, and he returned to where I was. "I see no reason for secrets."

I said, "It was nothing secret. It was simply a private word."

He said, "There is no reason why all of us should not know everything."

"I repeat, there are no secrets."

"Then why did I have to move away?"

"Because he was chiding me and preferred to do so in private."

He glared at me. I knew nothing to do but to glare back at him. Presently some of the others arrived, the men from Asher, Naphtali, Gad, and Reuben. I motioned for them to sit down. Next came the man from Benjamin, and Manasseh, and Zebulun. Then Joshua bin Nun from Ephraim came. By a curious coincidence, the representatives of Dan, Issachar, and Simeon were not there yet. I wondered if I should begin without them and without Caleb, who had not returned. I decided to wait. Besides, Aaron too had not returned.

The representatives of Dan, Issachar, and Simeon straggled in. I greeted them, trying to conceal my spite at them. I made up my mind: I would denounce the tribes as the first matter I would bring up. Caleb and Anquru then arrived. It was Caleb, not I, who introduced Anquru to the tribal representatives. The man from Dan said to me, "Who is this man, and what is his tribe?"

I said, "You know his name is Anquru. He is by birth a nobleman. He is the leader of the Egyptians, who are part of us."

The man from Dan said, "They are with us. They are not part of us."

Anquru said, in Egyptian, "What did he say?"

I replied, "He asked who you are. I said you are the leader of the Egyptians, who are part of us." I said in Hebrew to the man from Dan, "They are both with us, and part of us!" I looked around at the representatives. They all kept silent.

It occurred to me that the man from Dan had made it a little awkward to begin now with the denunciation of Dan, Simeon, and Issachar. I noticed that Aaron was still not back, but I saw no reason to wait for him. I said, "I wish for Joshua bin Nun to tell us what he has told me."

Joshua rose. He spoke slowly and clearly. The Wilderness of Sin was the home of marauders, he said; we needed to regroup our fighting men. It was something which could not wait.

On no faces did I see any alarm. All nodded their heads. Then one man spoke up and said, "We must train for more than defense. We must be ready for offense." I alone shook my head; the others all nodded, including Caleb and Joshua.

I said, "We need only to protect ourselves. We will attack no one."

Anquru said, "I do not understand." I translated into Egyptian what had been said. Anquru said, "It is not enough to defend ourselves. We must be ready to carry the fight on to those who would fight us." I put into Hebrew what he had said. I added, "Perhaps we should indeed prepare for offense. But only as a part of our defense. We are not going to attack anybody. We are a people of peace."

I said this quite belligerently, hoping that my way of saying it would set matters straight. No one commented. I went on. "We are a people of peace. We are a kindly people."

Just at that moment, Aaron returned, a huge smile on his face. "Moses! Moses! Good news!"

"What, Aaron?"

"Miriam. Miriam and Hur ben Caleb ben Hezron of the tribe of Judah . . ."

"Later, Aaron," I said. I motioned to him to sit down. I spoke, then, of the disorders of Marah, and I said that I wondered if the tribes were well enough organized from within, and I said that I thought that it was urgent for this to be done and, I added, to be done soon. No one opposed what I had said; I thought, though, that I detected some kind of indifference. I went on, "This matter of inner discipline is important. We have had a repeated nasty incident. . . ."

Aaron interrupted me. "Pardon me, Moses. Let me speak." He arose. "To Moses and me the information has come about thefts of food from our supply carts." There were comments of indignation. "We know exactly which tribes are guilty. We could name them. We prefer not to. We prefer for each tribe concerned to handle the matter as it sees fit. If the tribes concerned do not handle the matter, then we shall have to make this the concern of all of us."

I have shortened Aaron's speech, and I have not reflected his eloquence, for I lack the ability. How he spoke! How he held them entranced!

He, of course, weakened what I would myself have said, for I would have named the names and would have been direct and blunt; how powerful, though, was this weakened statement of his!

Perhaps Aaron's was the better way. He offended no one; he was a petitioner for their favor, not their leader telling them what was expected, or even demanded. Yes, perhaps his was the better way. Time would tell, when once our supplies would have been replenished and when we would know whether the thefts continued or not.

Aaron had spoken as I knew I could never speak. And when he had finished, he looked at me with a flush of triumph on his face, and I knew that however extravagantly I would praise him, it would scarcely be praise enough.

There seemed to be no more to say or do, and I was prepared for the meeting to end and for them to leave and to return, each to his tribe. One of the men—I think it was the man from Reuben —asked, "How serious has the theft of food been?"

I said, "We cannot permit it."

"Of course not; I agree with that. I am asking something different. Are we in danger of running out of food?"

"I have just been to the supply manager. We have enough for three days."

"Three days!" There was a murmur among the men, a murmur of discontent. A number of people spoke at the same time, and I could not hear any single voice; all I could notice was that the tone of the voices was disapproving.

Then one voice stood out above the rest. I did not know which person it was who spoke; somehow I seem to remember that, at the time, I was sure that it was either the Danite, or the Issacharite, or the Simeonite. The speaker was lost to me, but not the words which were spoken, for these I shall never forget: "Did you bring us into the Wilderness to kill us all off from hunger?"

What was I to say to these horrible words? Everyone became

silent. They had all heard the man; they all turned to me, waiting for me to speak, for me to reply.

I knew what to say; perhaps I did not know how to say it, or perhaps I had the sudden desperate hope that my eloquent brother would speak and save me the need. I discovered then—I was to rediscover later—that there were times when eloquent Aaron contrived to be silent.

Everyone was still and unmoving, like the people in the pictures which the Egyptians loved to paint. They were not going to move until I spoke.

At last I found my voice. "We have finished our business; you may go."

The first person to stir was Joshua. He arose. "We must assemble our guards and prepare them." He walked away. Slowly they arose one by one, most of them nodding to me before leaving; Korah, I noticed, did not nod.

The last to leave was Caleb. He came to me. For once there seemed to be no twinkle in his eye. He shook his head. "You made a mistake in Egypt, Moses. You brought us all out. There are some you should have left behind." I nodded my head. Caleb shook his head again. He walked off.

I turned to Aaron. I expected him to make some comment, to speak some word to ease the hurt which I felt. There was an expression of eagerness on his face. I waited for him to speak. Then I said, "You were very eloquent, Aaron."

He beamed at me. "Yes, I thought so myself." He said nothing about the hurt to me.

Quite a bit later, Joshua returned to me. "I have done something without your consent. I have suggested to Shallum that he cut all the rations in half."

"And he will?"

"He demands that you yourself give him the instruction."

"Did you Ephraimites receive reduced portions tonight?"

"They were reduced."

"And he will cut the reduction in half?"

"No one will perish from hunger. We can replenish our supplies in a week—if we break our encampment tomorrow."

"We shall move tomorrow, Joshua. Thank you."

I made my way to Shallum, and I confirmed what Joshua had said. Shallum grunted. I hoped that he was saying yes.

✳ CHAPTER V

I do not know how long it had been since I had had a sleepless night. Perhaps had I not been hungry, I might have slept. I did not sleep that night.

I should like to believe that I can now sort out my thoughts. I must admit, though, that possibly I ascribe to that night thoughts which came to me only later. But this is certain, that that night, I kept hearing over and over again the words, "Did you bring us into the Wilderness to kill us all off from hunger?"

If, as Aaron had said, I did not know people, then maybe I had begun to learn. To learn that Danites, and Issacharites, and Simeonites would steal for themselves food that belonged to all of us. That Shallum could be readily offended, and Miriam demand her due of food, and that the man from Dan could say that our Egyptians were not part of us, and that Aaron required a title—and an important one. And all were Hebrews.

On the other hand, there was young Joshua, quiet, efficient, and, so far as I knew, without any selfish streak in him—if only he would sometimes smile. And there was pleasant Caleb, levelheaded and always dependable. These too were Hebrews. Everyone was different from everyone else, so what was it that they all had in common? They ate, they digested, they egested. They were born, most of them had procreated or would procreate, and all would die. What did they have in common?

Then it seemed to me that what they had in common began with what they lacked, what each one of them lacked: the three tribes lacked enough food, as did Miriam, and Aaron lacked some inner satisfaction, and Shallum lacked the measure of attention from me which he wanted. And when a person lacked a thing, he needed to try to get it. The way by which he would try would be different in one person from another, and in one situation from another. But men would try to get what they lacked. If it was food or money, they would steal; if position, they would interpose themselves as Aaron had done in making his speech; if recognition, they would become nasty, as Shallum had become nasty.

And men would even kill, as I, Moses, had killed.

Why did this all suddenly seem new to me? Was it that, raised as I was as the perpetual student, I had thought too much about studies and too little about people?

And what was it that my mother Jochebed had said? I tried to recall something she had told me. At first all I could remember was that it had to do with Noah. Then I remembered: it was the story of the rainbow. It was that He had put the rainbow in the sky so that men would know that never again would He destroy mankind. And He had said that this was so, even though man's inclination from his very youth was evil. Man's inclination from his very youth was evil.

I wondered passingly then, and I have wondered from time to time since, about the meaning of that sentence. In Noah's time, because men had become so wicked, He had destroyed all but Noah and his family. Perhaps the meaning of the sentence was this, that man, once he ceased to be a baby, simply and naturally became prone to evil; the promise in His rainbow meant only that He would not destroy man.

But did that not mean that men would not destroy each other, and therefore themselves? If man, once he passed beyond babyhood into youth, became prone to evil, then what could prevent him, who was prone to evil, from actually doing evil?

And what was evil? I had killed an Egyptian; was that an evil? Was it evil to kill an evil person? And who was to decide what person was evil, and what person was not? Perhaps a king. But what if the king was himself evil, like the Pharaoh of Egypt?

The Pharaoh was the guardian of Egyptian law, and I suppose he even issued new laws; I had broken Egyptian law. But was the enslavement of our people a legal enslavement, planned and carried out in accordance with Egyptian law? If so, the laws, like a

person, could be evil. But laws in themselves could not keep a
person from doing evil, unless the laws themselves were free of
evil, and unless those who obeyed them became, in some way,
immune from evil. Perhaps just laws, carried out in a just way,
could keep a people from doing evil.

We Hebrews had no laws, we had no lawgiver, we had no ruler
to carry out the laws. We were a shapeless people, merely a collection of tribes, plus our Egyptian associates. In Egypt, I had
come to believe that we Hebrews must become a special people.
Surely between the time when we were still a shapeless people, and
the future when we could possibly become a very special people,
something decisive, something of tremendous consequence would
have to take place.

If I give the impression that in one single night I analyzed, in all
its import and ramifications, that which I later caused to ensue,
that is clearly wrong. That night I had only begun to think, and
that night I came to no solution. Indeed, I spent most of the night
in bitterness at the taunt thrown up to me, "Did you bring us into
the Wilderness to kill us all off from hunger?" How dismal, yet
good, it felt to remind myself of the ingratitude of our people for
all I had done, for in reminding myself, I could tell myself that I
was different, that I was better, that I was holier than they! Yet
how could I believe that I was not prone to evil, if it was true
that all men were prone to evil? I could not believe it, but I could
luxuriate in our people's ingratitude to the point of almost believing
it.

Moreover, I could not let myself forget that we were not yet in
our safe land of milk and honey, immune from all discord and
danger. No; the question of our food was a real question. And the
desert marauders were apparently a real danger. And Aaron had
said something to me about Miriam and Hur, and in his gloating
over the speech he had made, he had forgotten it; and in my hurt
at the taunt, I too had forgotten it.

I did not ask myself how serious was the feeling behind the
hateful taunt. I did not ask myself, as I might have, if open re-

bellion against my leadership could ever take place. Perhaps I did not want to face the possibility.

The sequel to the decision to move on was a murmur of protest from our people at the need to break our encampment.

I saw Aaron just long enough to learn that Miriam and Hur ben Caleb ben Hezron of the tribe of Judah had decided to be married. I was pleased; perhaps she would move her abode to the Judahites. She did. I liked everything about him, though I wondered what he could have seen in Miriam. Remember, though, that I am extremely biased.

We moved on southward, slowly, of course. I sent Shallum and some of his people ahead to find a village where they could replenish our supplies; one of Joshua's scouts went with them, for Joshua himself was busy with our guards. I suppose I say guards because I do not like to say soldiers, even though that was exactly what they were.

Shallum and his associates left early in the morning. Late in the afternoon I began to wonder when they would return and how much food they would bring with them. They did not return in the afternoon, nor in the evening, nor in the night. The next morning I sent for Joshua. "Shallum and his men have not returned. Take some guards and go look for them."

Miriam brought Hur to me in the early afternoon. She was happy, and she was without an unpleasant word to me. She was most affectionate, and it troubled me that she obviously loved me and that I did not love her. I had never spoken to her about the obnoxious dancing she had done; I tried the best I could to show great happiness at her happiness. It was not hard to be friendly to Hur, for he was a pleasant, though gruff, person, and he gave an impression of strength and reliability. When next we would encamp, they would, in the presence of the tribes of Levi and Judah, publicly proclaim themselves man and wife. I supposed that we could have some kind of family celebration too, and that Aaron's four sons would all join with us. Perhaps Aaron's grandson Phinehas, the son of Eleazar, would come too. I wished desperately that my Zipporah and my Gershom and the younger child could be present.

Aaron came up, as Hur and Miriam and I were trudging onward. He told Hur and Miriam of his speech at the meeting, and I spoke enthusiastically about it. I said, "If ever a speech is needed to our people, you will be the one to make it, Aaron."

He nodded. "Naturally. I am the second in command."

Startled though I was, I did not dispute with him. Oh, I should have. I should have there and then made it clear that the command was a matter of ability, not a matter of being the leader's brother. I did not say that; at that time it did not seem important. I can say, though, that I thought it.

There was no second in command. Not yet. I had not thought about it. If I had thought about it, I could not then have decided between two people, Caleb and Joshua. How different they were! Joshua was cold, efficient, brave; he was young. Caleb was brave, warm, wise—was he efficient? As efficient as Joshua? I did not know. I only knew that Caleb was a man whom one loved. He was younger than I, but older than Joshua.

I was impatient for Shallum to return, or for Joshua to come to me with some news of him. The hours dragged on, and neither came. Not until after sundown, toward the end of the twilight, when we were ready for the one-night encampment. It was Joshua who came; it was just light enough for me to see that his face was dark with fury. "Moses!" he called to me. "Moses!" He ran to me. He took my arm and led me aside so we could be alone. "Shallum is dead. So are all his men. All of them. Dead by the sword."

"When, where, Joshua?"

"They are dead, outside a village. A village without people, with corpses and burnt houses all around. The marauders."

I felt weak, to the point where I might even have fallen over, had Joshua not held my arm. I repeated what he had said: "Shallum and his men dead!"

"We buried them where they lay."

"And the food?"

Joshua shook his head. "Not a spoonful of flour was left in the village."

I have the feeling that over and over again I have spoken of my anger, as if that was my only response to each and every event. Perhaps you remember that Jethro had told me that there was anger in me, but I think that he meant it in the sense of its depth in me, not something which came to the surface no matter how slight the provocation was. I had not denied, surely not to myself, that an unfathomed anger resided within me, and resided there without my awareness. I think, though, that my anger, before I determined on our liberation, was infrequent. Once, though, that I embarked on the liberation, I have had to mention my anger often only because of the particular events which stirred it. I think, though, that anger and leadership must necessarily go hand in hand, for the leader is beset by an abundance of adversities and some quantity of people whose frailties, whether of negligence or of ambition, rub on him, or grieve him, or startle him unpleasantly. To be a leader is to be always potentially angry, especially if the leader cares about what happens, cares even beyond the thwarting of his personal will. For a leader to disguise his anger is often useful, but for him to control it is even more urgent. And for him to restrict his anger, whether it is concealed or not, so that it is never out of proportion to what has made him angry, is the heaviest obligation of all.

There are different kinds of anger: anger accompanied by disgust, as at the burglary of our supplies; or anger accompanied by chagrin, as when the Midianites gathered about the hut where Zipporah and I lived. There is no end to the kinds of anger.

But that Shallum and his company had been killed brought a new kind of anger to me. Anger deepened by a stirring within me to vengeance.

It was intensified by dismay, the dismay of an unpleasant surprise. Along with the dismay there came a fear, for the Wilderness marauders now loomed as a reality, as a threat which before I had not taken seriously. Questions came to my mind. Who were they, and how strong were they? If they attacked us, would we be able to repel them? And, above all, what would happen within the hearts and minds of our people if their ongoing anxiety for food were forced to give way to a heightened anxiety for their lives? And if the marauders were to slay some of us, how much more tellingly our people might taunt me with having brought them to the Wilderness to die!

This latter thought went through my mind and it added to my anger. Along with my grief, there burned also the fury that Shallum and his companions had set out peacefully to find food, food they would not have stolen, but would have bought. Why kill peaceful emissaries? And why had He allowed these men of ours, bent on a necessary and quiet mission, to be killed so cruelly? Why? Was He putting us, putting me, to some test?

We were without food, and I was worried; there were marauders about and I was frightened. And my fright increased my anger.

The distribution of half rations spurred a wane of hostile murmuring. The danger from the marauders spurred a half panic among us.

This was the worst period of time I went through.

The hunger was growing. Then my Midianite friend, Ben Onim, came to see me. "Why are we hungry, Moses? There is food all around us."

"Food all around us? Where is it?"

"There is manna here, Moses."

How our people expand the story of the manna! As they tell it, they had clamored for food, and in response, He had rained the manna on them, to test them as to whether or not they would walk in accordance with His revelation or not. On the sixth day, as they tell it, He rained a double portion, so that they would not need to gather any manna on the Sabbath day.

I confess that Caleb has almost succeeded in confusing me with these stories. Nevertheless, I remember very, very well. His version (citing, of course, what our people say) somehow or other brings some quail into his account; when I tell him that the quail came at another time, he shakes his head; our people put the quail together with the manna, he says with his smile. And he tells me how the people used an *omer* to measure the amount each man gathered, and that each person gathered exactly the amount he needed, not more and not less. Wonderful! And finally, according to Caleb, I am supposed to have instructed Aaron to put an omer of manna in a jar, to preserve it and—here I am still quoting Caleb—to put it before the *Testimony* for a memorial.

Bless our people! The Testimony came later. The matter of not leaving any manna over—I do not remember and I do not grasp it. Perhaps it is their way of saying that He who provides food provides it every single day, a wondrous idea which, of course, absolves man of a need to provide for the future.

As to the manna—our people liked the pun, *manna*, "what is it?"—it came so fortuitously that I cannot help but believe that He sent it. I am grateful to Ben Onim for telling us what it was: insects would leave a deposit on the leaves of the tamarisk tree, and the deposit would fall to the ground where, as the day wore on, the sun would melt it, unless it were gathered very early in the morning—and he had assured us the deposit was both edible and tasty, "like wafers in honey." Ben Onim knew all about it; at no time did he say that He had sent it!

There is more that our people tell of the manna: that He especially created it at the time He had created the world so that it would be ready for us at the right moment. That its taste so varied that to a sucking child it tasted like a mother's milk, and to an adult, like fowl or fruit, depending on what food the adult had an appetite for. Marvelous food! It sustained us in our need! But it was not so tasty that we Hebrews did not in time grow weary of it and complain!

I have spoken so long about these various accounts, for I must assert that once I learned from Ben Onim that the manna would keep us from starving, and after I praised Him for providing it, I dismissed the matter of food from my mind, for I was preoccupied with other matters, my grief at the death of Shallum and his associates and my anxiety about the marauders. Especially was I anxious about the mood of our people, for I could not help but wonder what would happen should an attack come, and should the marauders succeed in overrunning our soldiers at some perimeter. Would our people riot, as they had at Marah, and impede the rest of our soldiers from their military task? Or, would they so flee in panic that a handful of marauders would pursue and annihilate them?

We were a people without any discipline. Our suffering in Egypt, and the necessities of our flight, had welded us together for a while, but clearly we were becoming looser and looser. The tribes were themselves scarcely units, but were themselves divided into clans and families. The unity and cohesion which had persisted was only what remained over from the watch night of our freedom. As for me, I was their leader, yet not chosen by them, but put over them. I ruled by my intelligence, or by my lack of it, and by my concern. But my rule was that by a man, not rule by law.

We had no law. We had had Egyptian law, but we were freed of Egypt. Abraham, Isaac, and Jacob had left us no law. When Jacob and his sons had come to Egypt, they numbered no more than seventy people. Perhaps they might then have devised some laws, but so warmly had the Pharaoh of the time welcomed them to Egypt that they simply accustomed themselves to Egyptian law. So we had no laws.

To be ruled by a man, benevolent as I think I was, and possibly actually was, is not the same as to be ruled by law, for a man can become angry, or frightened, or drunk with his power, and then injustice is born, and grows. What our people needed was law. Worthy law. Just law. Benign law. Law which they would respect and therefore observe. It seemed to me that in the interval between that moment when we needed the manna to sustain us, and the future moment when we would enter Canaan, our people needed to be changed from an undisciplined people into a disciplined one, from a people led by me, Moses, into a people led by law.

I began to regret that though as a student I had had the opportunity to study law, I then had not been interested. In retrospect, my disinterest had been an error. We needed law; we needed a lawgiver.

Fed by the manna, we were able to move on. Our people's minds were on their bellies, while mine was on the marauders and on our people and law.

Their hunger was now somewhat alleviated so that it was time therefore for their thirst to discomfit them again. I concede that they were justified in being discomfited. Not alone were they thirsty, but so were the flocks and herds. At that juncture our scouts informed us that we were nearing the double oasis at Rephidim. We pressed on. To my annoyance, when we arrived there, our people again broke their ranks; to my chagrin, no water bubbled up from the springs, for the oasis was all dried out.

A large group of our people gathered around me, and they reviled me, and at least with their words, they threatened my life so that I had every reason to be afraid of what they might do to me.

How well I remember some of the shouts: "If you cannot get us to water, let somebody lead us who can." Again, "Let us get rid of Moses!" And, "You and your family have plenty to drink, haven't you?"

If I say I was frightened, I speak only part of the truth. I was indeed almost in actual terror. I did not answer the shouters, not even when some of them jostled against me and shouted in my very ears. Beyond the near-terror, I was in despair, for the very simplest of reasons: I had not the least idea of what to say or do. And I was their leader!

Then there was a shout from the distance, a shout as of joy, or at least of relief. Three or four of the men gathered around me had picked up large stones to throw at me; the shout grew louder, and the word "Water!" was clearly audible.

Caleb tells me now that the water came at Rephidim because I smote a rock with my rod. The only smiting that took place there was what people intended for me. What happened was that Ben Onim had begun to dig with his shovel and pick, and he broke a crust of limestone near the springs so that a stream of water promptly gushed forth.

Let there be no mistake: there were people ready to kill me. And more of them, if not ready to kill me, were over and against me, and, indeed, I was over and against them. How painful it was that they were my people, whom I wanted to be a special people. Indeed, I needed for them to be that. Yet they were little different at Rephidim from their sheep and cattle; if different, it was only that the sheep and cattle were tame, but my people had become wild.

But you must ask: had not the scouts gone on to Rephidim and examined the springs there? The answer is no. Joshua proposed this; I said no, for I did not want another incident like that involving Shallum.

Was I not wrong in overruling him on the scouts? In retrospect, yes. In prospect, it seemed the prudent thing to do. Perhaps a better leader than I would have been omniscient, as I was not, and would have known the future, as I did not. I had to make a decision, and, unhappily, I made the wrong one. How could I know in advance what was the right one? How I longed for omniscience!

I sought out Ben Onim to thank him. He smiled. "You did not live in Midian with us long enough to learn all the tricks of the desert, Moses."

Ben Onim is still remembered by Caleb, but not by our people. They prefer to remember Rephidim in terms of me and of my magical rod. Since the oasis at Rephidim is double, they give two names to the place, Massah and Meribah: Meribah, I understand, for they certainly *quarreled* with me; Massah, according to Caleb, comes from the view they now hold that they were *testing* Him. Let them think so; it was I, though, whom they were testing. Indeed, I was so shaken by their near-assault on me that, now that we had a source of water, I thought it well for us to encamp for four days. A leader learns that what he intends for one purpose comes to be interpreted as having a different one. We encamped simply so as to be near the water supply for a bit.

All the while we had been steadily moving toward the sacred mountain, Sinai, and the terrain had become somewhat hilly. With the marauders always on my mind, I conferred with Joshua quite often. He had become, without any title such as Aaron demanded, our military commander. He had been mustering our soldiers and training them, and he it was who suggested how our people should be allocated for the encampment at Rephidim.

Near this oasis there is a plateau, marked by a peak high enough for a person on it to see all around him and to be seen. The plateau rose above some hills which were not as steep as one might wish, but steep enough to afford a better defense than flat ground would provide.

We deployed our sentries around our encampment, so that by the second day we felt secure. Indeed, that morning, Miriam and Hur proposed that they be married. At twilight, in the presence of a good many Levites and Judahites, they stood before Aaron and me, and they spoke words of pledge to each other. Then Hur said, "Tell us now, Moses, that we are man and wife." I spoke the words. Hur kissed Miriam, and I was about to do the same. Aaron, though, audibly cleared his throat. "As the oldest brother, I too must speak."

He spoke beautifully. Perhaps a bit too long. Nevertheless, it was quite beautiful. And he ended up by saying that their marriage was a valid one for the reason that I, Moses, had approved it. Then I kissed Miriam, wondering what it was that Aaron had meant. Then some singing began, and some dancing; it was a joyful moment, and, at the time, I was very happy for Miriam.

When the festivities, such as they were—there was no banquet, as I had heard there had been at weddings in the early days in Egypt—began to die down, I asked Aaron what he had meant.

"Oh, it was something that came to me on the spur of the moment. Surely when a man and woman marry, they should do more than simply proclaim publicly that they are married. They should

have some public approval. And you are our leader." Then he repeated. "It came to me on the spur of the moment." He smiled. "I
have, of course, been doing some thinking."

I said, as I knew he wanted me to, "What about, Aaron?"

"About our people. About people."

"What about them?"

"What they need."

"And what do they need?"

"Something more than food and water and shelter."

I said, "I have thought so too."

He said, "They need purpose and obligation, and memorials and
symbols." I began to interrupt him, but, with a gesture, he waved
me silent. He went on, "They need what the Egyptians have and
we have never had. They need priests."

I suppressed an inclination to snort. Keeping from my voice the
disapproval which I felt, I said, "What for?"

He answered at length. I will not try to reproduce even in reduced compass what he said. Let it suffice that we needed priests,
and we especially needed a high priest. And when I asked him
what kind of a person the high priest would be, he said, as I expected him to: a man of intelligence, of quick mind, of fluent
tongue. I said, gently, "A man like you, Aaron?"

He pretended to hesitate. "Possibly."

I said, "It is something to think about." I was dissembling; I did
not need to think about it to be against it. I had seen Egyptian
priests; I had watched them; I had attended Egyptian worship.
Rubbish!

When I was alone, I asked myself why Aaron had made the proposal—that is, beyond his obvious belief in the merit of his suggestion. Was he proposing a priesthood, or himself as a high priest?
Was this so because, now that we were out of Egypt and on our
march, he personally figured less and less in our plans? It was
Caleb or Joshua, not Aaron, whom I consulted. Was Aaron offended? And did he recognize that in meeting the burdens of our
march, he was no match for Caleb or Joshua, or for Ben Onim? Did

he therefore need some outlet, some important title that would sound as if he were second in command—when he was not?

I felt sorry for Aaron. To propose so preposterous a thing! Poor Aaron! So brilliant of mind, so well-intentioned, and so impractical!

Impractical, of course, in comparison with practical me.

On our third day, a dispute broke out between some people of the tribe of Ephraim and some of the tribe of Dan. For a very simple reason I do not now recall what this dispute was about; I soon became lost in an abundance of them. This first one was brought to me, and, acting as a judge as I had observed Jethro do, I settled the matter, apparently to the satisfaction of all. Within a half day there began to gather before me a host of people, some from the same tribes, some from different tribes, demanding that I judge between the conflicting parties. I spent almost all of the day settling one affair after another.

How well I settled these disputes is not for me to say. But I, whom four days earlier our people were prepared to assault or even kill, abruptly emerged as the judge whose verdict was eagerly sought. As I gave a decision, there were those who cheered at my words and those who departed downcast or sullen. I remember that many people gathered about to listen to the litigation, and Caleb was among them. He remembers something he said to me which I too remember. Forgive my immodesty for quoting his praise of me. It is what he added to the praise that made me remember his words and now prompts me to record them. "You are an excellent judge, Moses, clearheaded and fair-minded. There can be only one result of the fame which you will acquire by tomorrow morning; our people will discover endless bases for litigation." He clapped me on the shoulder. "You should have discouraged them by an outrageous decision or two!"

We walked together to the edge of the plateau. We could see our sentries scanning the horizon. I said, "Caleb, will the marauders come?"

He did not smile. "The better question is, will we be able to drive them off when they come?"

"You really think that?" He nodded. "Why?" I asked.

"Because we are in the Wilderness, where no one owns the land. When the land is not owned, no property of any kind is owned. The marauders will try to take away from us what we have, as if it is ownerless."

I said, "I am frightened, Caleb."

He said, "That young man from the tribe of Ephraim—Joshua bin Nun—impresses me greatly, Moses. Were it not for him, I would be even more frightened. You should name him our general, Moses."

"I have come to rely on him very much."

"You show a sound judgment, Moses." He leaned against a rock. "Let me ask a question. Do not be pained by it; I ask it of myself, more than I do of you. This is the question: What lies ahead, Moses?"

I said, "We are traveling to the land He has promised to us through Abraham."

"That I understand. But even so, what lies ahead is hidden at least from me. We will some day enter into Canaan, as you have said. But what kind of people will we be when we are ready to enter, and what kind of people will we be when we are settled in that land?"

"Have you some thought, Caleb?"

"Nothing that deserves the word thought. Only an unclear idea, or maybe a distant hope. Some stray wish that I do not think I myself understand."

I said, "Tell me, Caleb."

"I am not sure that I can. I can try." He leaned forward. "From my mother I have heard the story of Abraham. I have often asked myself, why do we reckon our history from him? He had a father, he had a grandfather. Why from him, not them? I know the answer: Abraham went away from Ur of the Chaldees—a prosperous city—because he could not be part of the falseness of the place. He could not worship a piece of wood or a piece of stone. So he left. He left both because of what he could not believe and because of what he had come to believe. Otherwise, he would have stayed there and that is where we would be if he had stayed there. And we would be Chaldeans, not Hebrews. Then what is a Hebrew?" He stopped speaking, as if he was waiting for me to say something. Only with difficulty did I restrain myself. I did not want to say to him that I too had had such thoughts. I did not want those thoughts to influence his; I wanted his thoughts as his very own. He moistened his lips. "A Hebrew is a man who lives by truth. Abraham separated himself from falsehood. We Hebrews are a people who must always be separated from falsehood. Unless we are a unique people, as Abraham was a unique man, we are nothing."

I took hold of his hand and I held it tight, but I turned my eyes away from him, for I did not want him to see how full of tears they had become. I said, "Unless we are a unique people, we are nothing." Then I looked at him, indifferent to whether or not he would see my tears, and I saw that Caleb, the man who always joked and laughed, was weeping as I was weeping.

We embraced each other, holding each other fast. Then we released each other.

He took a step away. "Meanwhile," he said, "our people of truth includes, at least in the tribe of Judah, a splendid collection of liars!" He laughed, and as he moved away from me, I heard him continue to laugh.

How good it was to discover that his vision was kindred to mine! And if the two of us, without consulting each other, could have the same vision, then there must be dozens upon dozens of us Hebrews who had received the legacy of Abraham.

To my knowledge, then, Caleb had the vision. And in the council of the representatives of the tribes, it was his voice that so often spoke the words of sound sense, and it was to him that often the others looked. Surely here was a man who, if something happened to me, could succeed me.

He was a man who joked. Was it because, beyond all the rest of us, even beyond me, he was of such serious purpose that he needed the relief of joking?

It seemed clear to me that day that while Joshua bin Nun was virtually the second in command, the man who would some day succeed me was Caleb. Joshua was a good military man; Caleb was a man with a vision.

I sought out Tat-Rin, the Egyptian. After we had greeted each other, I said to him, "I need some information." He waited for me to continue. I said, "Tat-Rin, what makes law law?"

"A tyrant with enough power. That is what makes law law."

"No, that does not make law, that makes tyranny."

"I have known no law which was not tyranny."

I shook my head. "You must have studied about law in those ages when there was a benevolent Pharaoh."

"Law is what a ruler wishes. Tyrannical or benevolent, law is the will of a ruler."

"Are you saying that there is no such thing as law in its own right?"

"I know of lying scholars who speak sometimes of law as a result of the experience of a community of people. These are not laws; they are customs or wishes. And customs or wishes are not law."

"And is there no law independent of some ruler or the customs of people?"

"How could there be?"

"Maybe you confuse law and law enforcement."

"Without enforcement there is no law."

"But Egyptian Pharaohs and Egyptian scholars often speak of ancient law. Of law so old that it lasts beyond the lifetime of the Pharaoh who has decreed it."

"These inherited laws are a convenience. When they become inconvenient, they are changed or abandoned. If you wish to delude yourself into believing that there is some real difference between law and law enforcement, you may do so. I see no difference. The true law is what is enforced."

"But even a Pharaoh has been known to obey a law inherited from the ancient past."

"This is solely a matter of appearances. Also, why should one bother to promulgate a new law if there is an old useful one around?"

"Why do you think that an old law can be useful?"

"Because society is molded by old people, so that what is ancient receives an eminence it is not entitled to. So ancient law appears wise and just. The opposite is the truth. Ancient law and injustice go hand in hand."

"Are there no ancient laws that are just?"

"No, because laws which are possibly just are the laws that became abrogated."

I shook my head. "I think you give one-sided answers, Tat-Rin. I should never describe as law what we have known from the present Pharaoh. But I believe there is such a thing as law."

He shrugged his shoulders. "Shall I repeat my denial? What can I say that I have not already said?"

"You can do this: you can concede, if only for the moment, and only for the sake of argument, that there is such a thing as law in its own right, free from contamination by men. Can you try to do that?"

"I am willing to try."

"If there were such a thing as law in its own right, what would make it law?"

"Strictly for the sake of argument, I could suggest that human experience, especially self-protection, turns common sense into useful law. But I have not observed that society, either over a period of time or in a single short interval, is marked by common sense. Therefore, you can eliminate human experience as a source of law. A second possibility is the fraud of all our Pharaohs: they pretend to believe that they are themselves gods, or else the gods' representatives on earth. They imply thereby that their decrees are not their own, but are the gods'. This is sheer deception. The Pharaohs are men, not gods. This is the case simply because there are no gods."

I said, "I do not believe in gods. I believe in a God."

"I will not risk offending you, Moses. I am silent."

"Please speak."

"We Egyptians possess many gods. As I have thought it out, to believe in many gods is to believe in none."

"Then, like us, you can believe in one God."

"To believe in one God is simply to concentrate an abundance of silliness into a single enormity, no less silly."

"What makes it silly?"

"I have heard how you Hebrews think. You think like this: Creation is a reality, and therefore there must be a Creator. Is that right?"

I said, "What is wrong with this argument?"

"Simply this: if creation proves God, one is arguing from an effect back to an antecedent cause. If that is right, then one must ask about this God, of what antecedent cause is He an effect? If there is an antecedent cause, this God is no god. And when once one asks the necessary question about antecedent cause, the entire idea of a God stands out as preposterous."

"God," I said, "is the uncreated Creator."

"That," he replied, "is a beautiful sentiment. It has a single deficiency; it is utter nonsense." I was silent. He went on, "Is that not so?"

"I do not know."

"But I do. The words themselves are nonsense; the idea behind the words is nonsense."

I said, "But how do you know they are nonsense?"

"I have spoken with Hebrews. They unite in telling me that a He, whatever that is, exists. I say, prove it. They tell me that He did this or that. I say, prove it. They become tongue-tied. I say, tell me what He is? They stammer." He leaned toward me. "One cannot ask these questions without asking questions about how things began. I mean, how they began at the first beginnings. You Hebrews start after the first beginnings, but you think you are starting right with them. No, you start with He Who is. I ask, how did your He Who is come to be He Who is? You Hebrews never answer that." He leaned back. "I am no smarter than you Hebrews. But I keep pushing my mind back to the very beginnings, as far back as a man can push his mind. At times I admit nothing makes sense except to imagine a He like yours. But all sense disappears whenever I push my mind back further and further. Nothing makes sense except to imagine some He, and yet it is still nonsense to imagine Him."

I said, "I confess that I have never thought about these things. I was reared in the belief that He exists, so I never asked, does He? And besides, He spoke to me, and He sent me to Egypt—"

"I consider you a worthy man, Moses. But that that He of yours spoke to you, and sent you to Egypt—forgive me for doubting. Oh, I do not say you are lying. I say only that somehow you became deluded. Fortunately, it has been in a worthy cause. But that does not alter the delusion."

"He spoke to me," I said, softly but firmly.

"Then let Him speak to me, too." He looked directly at me. "I have heard enough about this that I have given it a good measure of thought, Moses. My conclusion is that you Hebrews use your delusion for a worthy purpose. That is the principal way in which you differ from the Egyptians. I admire you Hebrews. I am honored to be with you for the present, until I journey eastward to Chaldea. But I wonder if you Hebrews, too, may not some day turn your delusion into something unworthy."

"How, for example?" I asked.

He said, "I do not know. But suppose that one of you is as ambitious for power as the Pharaoh, and makes a public proclamation that He has spoken to him and appointed him to be your emperor. And suppose he were to go on to say that to disobey the emperor is to disobey Him. Would that not be a disaster?"

"I am afraid so."

"And what is to stop any wicked lunatic from saying that He has spoken to him? Privately, of course, so that he cannot prove it, and he cannot disprove it. What you Hebrews believe is worthy, but it is also potentially very dangerous."

"Then where is law, Tat-Rin? And how can men live without laws?"

"I do not know. There are, of course, laws that are bad, and laws that are good. But even good laws can become bad, as when laws

become mechanical and rigid. Can men live without laws? I suppose not. But I would rather trust a good man who rules with justice than I would a book of rules."

"But a good man can turn wicked."

"I spoke of my preference. I spoke of something bad, and of another thing less bad. I did not speak of a good."

The conversation left me discouraged, not so much because Tat-
Rin seemed to me one-sided, as that he seemed to me not to be
wholly wrong, even though I did not think at all that he was right.
I kept asking myself what the flaws were in what he had said, but
I found it difficult to pick these out. Several things seemed to me
clear. Our necessity was not so much for laws as for good laws, just
ones. One might even go further and say that what we needed was
not law so much as justice, and that justice was the true goal, with
laws only a possible means to justice.

But what was justice? And how could men be sure what justice
was?

Or, to say the same thing in a different way, there was something beyond laws that was needed: Teaching, and example, and
encouragement, and exhortation.

I do not assert by any means that I understood my confusions as
clearly then as I think that I understood them later in retrospect.
Before I spoke to Tat-Rin, I was persuaded that our needs were
simple. After I spoke to him, it all seemed very complex, and difficult to accomplish, or even impossible.

But if I understood Tat-Rin, despite my confusion at that time, I
then remembered Aaron and his saying that we needed priests, and
I again dismissed that as preposterous. But even as I dismissed it, I
began to be troubled that maybe it was not.

It was the next morning, at dawn, that the marauders struck.
They rode on camels, brandishing swords. They made a double onslaught, from the east and south of the plateau. They struck suddenly, but our sentinels managed to give a signal. I ran to the peak,
to station myself there. Joshua bin Nun was already there, with a
dozen or so couriers. Together we looked to the east and the south,

and we saw the ferocity of the attack. Joshua left me to go to the east where the fiercer battle was.

It was our good fortune that our encampment was on the plateau, and that the sides were steep, and the camels could ascend the slopes only with difficulty. Aaron and Miriam's husband, Hur, joined me. I said to them, "Aaron, look to the north, and Hur, look to the west; perhaps they will attack from there too."

To the east and the south, our men were managing to withstand the assault. Then I, not Aaron, saw a column appear on the north. I raised my arm and pointed northward, saying to Hur, "Send two couriers to the northern perimeter to alert our people, and one courier to the east to inform Joshua."

Then Hur himself saw still another column approaching from the west. I looked to the east; Joshua seemed to be looking to me. I pointed to the west and to the north. As I pointed, I saw our two couriers reach Joshua. Joshua waved to me; he strode toward the north and I followed him with my eyes. And, deliberately ignoring my friend Tat-Rin and his unbelief, I prayed to Him that we might be saved from the foe.

It is of little consequence that now our people blend strange things together. We repulsed the foe that day, and we won a victory. Our people, however, tell that when my arms were raised, our soldiers gained, and when I lowered them, they began to lose. So long was the battle, as they tell it, that my arms became tired, and when I sat on a rock to rest, Aaron and Hur held up my arms. Perhaps our people derived this from my raising my arms in prayer to Him. They also remember something I do not, that after the victory, I built an altar to Him, something which never happened. Without His help, it might have been a defeat, not a victory, but I built no altar. We were camped at Rephidim because of the water; our people, though, say that we encamped there because of the plateau, for I foresaw the attack on us and sagaciously chose the high ground from which to repulse the foe.

We lost a few men in the battle. In the next days, I learned their names; now I have forgotten them. These men, then, have become nameless, except possibly to their families, and all this was long ago. We won a victory, but its price was too high. These dead could have said to me in truth that I had brought them out of Egypt to die in the Wilderness. To die in the Wilderness—not that I had slain them; it was others who had done that.

It came to me acutely that when I had been young, the enslavement of our people never had made a sharp impact on me. When I went to visit the camp, I left the ease of the palace, but I always returned to it from the camp. I think that I had felt that the enslavement was some kind of exception, an unpleasant disturbance in the midst of a living that was pleasant and exciting in a good sense. There were no problems in that pleasant living. I know, too, that I thought, later, that once we would have left the slave camps behind and would be a free people, living would naturally be pleasant and exciting and devoid of problems. Now I began to wonder if even free people ever found living pleasant and easy. Adam and Eve, even in their paradise, had not found it so. When they were driven out, it was to go into an even greater lack of ease. Men would eat bread only by the sweat of their brow, and women would go through great pain in bearing children. And worst of all, back in the early time when the world numbered only four people, Adam and Eve and their two sons, there were already enough people in the world for Cain, in a fit of jealousy, to have slain his brother Abel.

Men killed. Men were jealous. The inclination of man was evil, from his youth onward. That is how men were, and are. That was why the marauders had slain that good man Shallum. That was why they had made their foray against us and killed and wounded some of us.

Some day we would reach the Promised Land. If Adam and Eve could go astray in paradise, would not our own people go astray in the land of milk and honey? If Aaron was right that I did not know people, he must have meant that I did not know all there was to know about people; surely, though, I knew about the evil in man.

Later in the day, Joshua brought to me three of the marauders who had been taken prisoner. Their language was like ours and like the Midianite, though a little different from each. I turned to the oldest of the three, and I spoke only one word: "Why?" He gave no answer. I repeated the word, "Why?" Again he gave no answer. Then I spoke to him as if I were about to strike him; indeed, I shouted, "We are peaceful people. Why did you attack us?" The man to his right said, "You are passing through our land." I said, "This land belongs to no one. It is wilderness; only nomads live here."

He answered, "It is our land. Whatever belongs to passers-by belongs to us."

"You kill and you steal. Is that your way of life?"

"It is our land."

I tried to talk to them further so that I would understand, but it was futile. Killing and stealing were their ordinary pursuits and neither by my words nor by anyone else's would they ever be moved to consider these wrong. I walked away; then I came back and said to Joshua, "Who are these people?"

He said, "They are the clan of Amalek. And Amalek was the grandson of Esau, the son of our father Isaac and the brother of our father Jacob. They are related to us."

"Related?" I thought I remembered that there had been hostility between Jacob and Esau, but they had become reconciled. "Did the Amalekites attack us because of Jacob? Or would they have attacked us anyway?"

Joshua said, "I do not understand your question."

I had thought my question clear. "I will ask it in a different way: Do the Amalekites attack everybody? Or did they pick us out to attack?"

"They attack everybody they think they can plunder."

In my mind I considered three peoples: Egyptians, Midianites, and Amalekites. Perhaps among the Amalekites there were counterparts of Zipporah and Jethro, or counterparts of our noble

Egyptians. Here were three peoples whose common bent was to hate and damage peoples who were different. Was this the way of all peoples, and was our people's way the same—unless they were taught better?

And as we moved through the Wilderness would there be other Amalekites who would assault us? Surely such a possibility was a reality.

But perhaps this hostility on the part of the peoples kindred to us Hebrews (to distinguish them from the Egyptians) existed because they were desert nomads, people of no great wealth, people whose food was limited, and whose learning and knowledge were primitive. In Canaan, when we reached there, could not all be different? Canaan was a land flowing in milk and honey. Our fathers, Abraham, Isaac, and Jacob, according to all I had heard, had no problems with the Canaanites; no one had assaulted them. Only with the coastal peoples, the Philistines, were there problems. Their king, Abimelech, had had lecherous designs on our matriarchs Sarah and Rebekkah. There had been some trouble with the Shechemites, but only because Shechem ben Hamor had raped Jacob's daughter Dinah; and, I must say, our people have always condemned her brothers Simeon and Levi for the outrage they had perpetrated on the Shechemites when Shechem tried to make decent amends.

I wished, then, that I knew more about Canaan. I thought even in those early times that it would be well to send a deputation into Canaan to see what the conditions were. I had no reason to suppose that civilized Canaan would be anything but favorable.

But the Wilderness was different. People like the Amalekites probably existed in different part of the Wilderness, and I had every expectation that the Wilderness would be a place of danger to our people, in contradiction of the hospitality I had myself experienced as a lonely fugitive. We needed to quit the Wilderness as soon as possible. The name Amalek has become among us the term for those of our enemies who have no reason to be enemies. Amalek and the Wilderness were one.

We tarried a few more days at Rephidim, and then we moved on toward the sacred mountain Sinai, planning to encamp in its vicinity.

He had instructed me to bring our people there. He had said no more than that our people should worship Him at the mountain. He had not said how.

How does a man worship? By now our people know. When first we encamped in clear sight of the mountain, we did not know.

I remembered some of the worship of the Egyptians, though I never really understood it. Their worship arose from their beliefs. They have a peculiar one that, after the death of a person, whether king or even a commoner, his soul lives on and becomes divine; this sort of thing is silly, and the best way to keep from believing that the soul becomes divine is not to believe that the soul lives on. The Egyptians have a great many sacred days; they have a profusion of gods and an endless assortment of sacred animals, some which they eat, and some not. Some of them like to slay a sacred bull and scatter the pieces in different parts of Egypt. But the main reason that I do not understand Egyptian religion is that it changes from place to place. It changes from one side of the Nile River to the other! Surely there was nothing I could learn from the Egyptian religion.

As to the Midianites, I know that for the watch night of our freedom in Egypt, I had borrowed from their spring festival of the young lambs. Yet I had used only the matter of smearing blood on the lintel, to distinguish our houses from the Egyptian. I suppose there were other facets of the worship of the Midianites, but I either had not noticed them or, if I had, I did not remember them. I rejected the Egyptian and knew little of the Midianite, and the result was that I, the great leader, was bringing our people to the sacred mountain to worship Him, without knowing how!

Obviously one could pray, as on occasion I had. One could speak to Him, or ask His help, when there was danger. But if there was no danger, or if I wanted nothing, then what would I say in a prayer? I discovered then, as never before, what it meant to be heavy of tongue. Surely my brother, Aaron, would have no difficulty in speaking to Him, in praying.

Yet if I were now to consult Aaron, I would hear again his preposterous suggestion that we needed priests and, especially, that we needed a high priest, him.

I faced an uncertainty, and I knew no way to banish it.

✳ CHAPTER VI

Before us in the distance there loomed the lofty mountain. From its peak one saw in the daytime an endless ascent of smoke. At night, the peak was aflame and the sky was red. Our people had learned from one another that this was His sacred mountain, but instead of rejoicing, they were fearful. From time to time, the report came to me about how fearful our people were. And they wanted quickly to finish whatever was necessary at the mountain and to go away from it. I was not fearful; I could not think of Him as something to fear.

To my joy, Elyaqim returned, and not alone! My lovely Zipporah was with him, and so too were my first-born, Gershom, a handsome lad, and my sweet second child—Zipporah had named him Eliezer, "God is my Helper"—and my father-in-law, Jethro.

Neither, then, nor even now, has it been possible to describe my exultation. I can say only that my unreserved joy approached the high moment as when we had found ourselves safe across the Sea of Reeds. Aaron came to me, and I presented my family to him, and he made a flowing speech of welcome, to which Jethro replied with dignity. As he was speaking, Miriam and Hur came to us. She greeted the children with some affection, she was somewhat courteous to Jethro. To Zipporah she was unspeakably rude. "You are not a Hebrew," she said. "How could my brother have married you, you Wilderness woman!"

In all my life I have never seen as pitiable an expression as that which replaced the friendly smile on Zipporah's face. She burst into tears, and she ran from the tent.

"Get out!" I shouted to Miriam. "Get out, stay out, and never return!" I did not wait for her to leave, but I too ran from the tent. Zipporah was running in the midst of the tents, and people stared at her and they stared at me. Then she fell, and I came to

her. She was crying; she was beating the ground with her hands.
I bent over, I knelt by her, and I stroked her hair, and I spoke
the words of my love to her. Then she grew silent and limp, as
if she had fainted. I picked her up in my arms, as I had picked up
the injured lamb. I carried her to my tent. Only Jethro and my
children were left. Had Aaron and Hur thought that I had sent
them away too? I did not care.

I laid her on the bedding, and I stroked her cheeks and her
arms. I turned to the children. "Stay here with your mother. Your
grandfather and I must speak."

Jethro and I walked away from the tent. He said to me, "I know
your hurt, Moses. It is greater even than Zipporah's."

I said, "I have done His bidding. My task for my people is over.
May I and my family return to our home with you?"

His handsome face darkened. "Wherever I am, you are welcome." He shook his head, "I have no home, Moses. My children
have turned me out."

"Turned you out? Because of Zipporah and me?"

"Because I did not teach them the rules of the good life well
enough."

"This is incredible."

"It is a reality. I am neither the first, nor the last father, or chief,
to whom this happens."

"But for me to be the cause of it—"

"You are not the cause. You have provided only the occasion."

"But your own sons— How can this be, Jethro?"

"I have a double bitterness. That it happened to me. That my
own sons did it. But it is not unheard of among men, Moses."

"Did they truly cast you out? Did they drive you away by
force?"

He smiled, bitterly. "Perhaps they did not cast me out. Perhaps
they caused me to cast myself out."

I was pained for him. But my thoughts turned to myself. I could
not go to Midian. I could not stay with my people. No, I could
not stay. I said, "I will not let Zipporah stay here to be in-
sulted—"

"Where will you go, Moses?"

"It does not matter, Jethro."

He shook his head. "I do not underestimate Zipporah's sorrow, nor yours. But your sister is not all the Hebrews. You are very angry, Moses. A wise man makes no decision in the midst of his anger."

"We are outcasts, Jethro, both of us."

"They have not cast you out, Moses."

"I am casting myself out." I said this in all honesty, believing it to be a final word, one which could never be recalled.

He said, calmly. "Our situations are not at all the same, Moses. When your anger subsides, I will venture a suggestion to you."

"Make it now."

"The time is not appropriate."

"Make it now, please, Jethro."

He shrugged his shoulders. "You have associates. Summon them. Put before them your intention to leave. Let them discuss. Let them, not you, make the decision."

"I will consider it." We began to walk to my tent. I said, "I regret that there is no fresh fruit to offer you."

"I appreciate your remembering my tiny pleasures."

We returned to the tent. The reunion with my beloved Zipporah was all but ruined. I remembered an expression our people use: "It turned to ashes in his mouth." The reunion for which I had so earnestly longed would henceforth and forever be like the memory of a loathsome disease. An infection from my sister, Miriam.

I summoned Joshua. "I wish to convene our council. Only this time, do not invite Anquru. But tell him of the meeting, and of my wish to speak to him later, to explain why he is not summoned."

The representatives began to assemble. As we waited for the last of them to appear, I looked at them. On the faces of most of them I could read neither hostility nor warmth, except for Caleb and for my cousin Korah. Caleb was smiling, joking with those who sat beside him; Korah sat silent, frowning, possibly glowering. Then Aaron arrived. He motioned to me to step away from our circle. I followed him. I waited for him to speak. He did not face me. He said, "You have been cruel to our sister, Miriam." I turned around and walked away from him. He followed and took hold of my arm. "You forget all that Miriam has been through."

"And you forget it is my wife to whom she spoke!"

"But Miriam is your sister and Zipporah is a woman—" He stopped.

I said, "And Zipporah is a woman of the Wilderness?"

"Miriam is your flesh and blood."

I said, "Have you anything more to say, Aaron?" He did not answer. I said, "And it is you, not I, who understand people!"

I walked back to the gathering of the representatives, Aaron following me and trying to speak to me. I stood before them, and they became silent. I said, "I put before you a matter. Today my wife has joined me, with our two sons. My wife is a descendant of Abraham, through his wife, Keturah. Abraham has many descendants, so her descent from Abraham is unimportant. She is not a descendant of Isaac nor of Jacob. Yet she is my wife, and she remains my wife. Perhaps to some of you it is unacceptable that I, your leader, should have a wife not of our people. In the future there must come a time when I will no longer be your leader. Perhaps, now that my wife has joined me and now that you know that she has joined me, the future can become the present. I have gathered you to ask one question: Shall I remain your leader? I seek your answer. I name Caleb ben Jephunneh to conduct your discussion. Through him, I can learn your will."

I started to walk away. Korah spoke up. "One moment. I have known about your wife; I gave it no thought. Now I will think about it. But another matter concerns me." He rose. "We are greatly in your debt for having led us to freedom. No one else could have done so. But in the Wilderness there are things which have gone wrong. Perhaps in the Wilderness, another person could keep things from going wrong."

I said, "That is, of course, possible. You may discuss that too, if you wish. It is the other matter of my wife who was not born a Hebrew which I summoned you to discuss." I strode out, and I could hear Korah's voice speaking as I walked away.

In looking back, I keep marveling how, in a few short hours, so much had changed. The sacred mountain still sent its smoke into the sky. Earlier in the day, I had been engrossed with the question, how shall we worship Him? Even more important, I had it in the forefront of my mind that our people needed just and worthy laws, and I had not yet come to an understanding of what it meant to have such laws. And now, instead of my vision of a special people whom I would lead into the land of Canaan, there was every prospect that within the hour I would have no people. No matter; there are occasions when a man must risk his position, or his wealth, or his safety, or anything that he holds precious, on behalf of something which he holds more precious than all of these.

The hours went by, and I waited and waited, distressed, uncertain, angry. As the sun was beginning to set, Joshua came to me. "Would you return to our gathering, Moses?" I followed him.

Caleb was standing before them. "Moses, we have had a very earnest discussion, and therefore much which is foolish has been spoken. Nevertheless, good sense has prevailed. And we have at last spoken this good sense with almost a single voice. Moses, we rejoice with you that your wife and children have been reunited with you. We ask you to extend to them our warm welcome." He smiled at me. "We can now return each to his tribe, until you, our leader, summon us again." I heard a chorus of approving voices. One by one the representatives departed. Only Aaron remained.

He said to me, "It was almost a single voice."

I said, "You are my brother; you should not have been present for their discussion."

"No one told me not to."

"You should have known this without being told."

"But I needed to be sure that no one spoke of you unjustly."

I said, "I am sure that you spoke eloquently on my behalf."

"I was doing so, until Caleb interrupted me. Moses, there was one voice against you. It was—"

I broke in. "I do not need to know."

"But you do. It was Korah. He spoke against you. With vehemence."

"If only one spoke against me, I am very gratified."

"About Miriam, Moses—"

"Let me be, Aaron!"

When I spoke to Anquru and when he had heard me out, he said, "You were right; I did not belong at the council."

"I am curious. Do our people often remind you Egyptians that you are not Hebrews?"

"Often? I would not say often. Rather, from time to time."

"And when it happens, how do you feel, and what do you say?"

"How I feel and what I say depends on who it is who has spoken. Sometimes I speak with irony. I say, remember that we who are with you are the Egyptians who enslaved you, and who did nothing to free you; in fact, we are not really here with you, but we are still in Egypt, living in luxury out of your toil."

"But how do you feel?"

"Offended. Until I remember that it was my people who enslaved yours. I do not hold myself responsible for what my people did. But I am ashamed. And that shame wipes out my feeling of offense."

I said, "Now that I am still their leader, I make a promise to you. The promise that I shall teach our people that they must not bar Egyptians from the assembly of the Hebrews, for you Egyptians who are with us are our brothers. Perhaps it will take a generation or two. But you are already part of us, Anquru."

I hoped to spend the evening with my family. There awaited me a long line of litigants and I listened to a few cases, and I made my decisions. Then, thoroughly weary, I asked the many remaining to return the next morning.

At last I was alone with poor, unhappy Zipporah. I told her about the council of representatives, I told her of my conversation with Anquru. As I spoke, she interrupted with sobs. And as I spoke what words of comfort I could, her fatigue carried her off to sleep.

In the morning, she smiled the smile I remembered. I had a few words too with Jethro about the meeting of the council. I invited him to be present at the litigation to come before me, as in Midian he had invited me. He came and sat silent but attentive. Late in the afternoon, I finished the last of the cases.

I expected Jethro to make some comment on how I had conducted the various litigations. He said nothing about it. Instead, he said, "It is a wondrous thing, Moses, that you have been able to bring your people out of slavery. Though I encouraged you, I had reason for doubts. Now I have no reason to doubt. Blessed is He who saved you from Egypt! Surely He is the greatest of the gods—"

"We believe He is the only God."

"That is what I mean, Moses! Would you allow me a privilege? Can you obtain a lamb for me? I should like to offer it as a holocaust to Him."

I think that under other circumstances I would have tried gently to dissuade Jethro, for I had no interest in animal sacrifice. I had, of course, never witnessed any, for I made no effort to attend such laughable exercises in Egypt, or in Midian. I must make it clear that I found Jethro's wish touching, and I would have acquiesced simply in order to please him. But most of all I wanted to witness this form of worship, to learn how I would respond to it.

So, at one and the same time, I sent a messenger to purchase a lamb from one of the flocks, and I summoned Aaron and told him of Jethro's intention. Aaron brightened up. "We must invite our leading Levites to be present. And we must all break bread with Jethro."

It was at sundown that the sacrifice took place. A small altar of stones was prepared, and its fire was kindled. Ben Onim and Elyaqim helped Jethro hold the lamb. If it is possible to slaughter an animal in a kindly way, Jethro did so, but I found it uncomfortable to watch. The body of the lamb was prepared, and then it was put on the hot flame, and it was completely burned up, the while Jethro repeated again and again, "Blessed are You, O God, Who have brought your people out of Egypt." At one of the repetitions, I heard Aaron's voice join with Jethro in the words, "Blessed are You, O God, Who have brought *our* people out of Egypt." Then our elders, even Korah, joined in the words. They moved about the altar, forming an unconscious circle, and as they moved, they seemed to sway, and presently the swaying turned into a slow dance. Then they spoke faster, and some began to chant the words and to sing them, and they danced faster and faster. The sun set, and still the fire burnt, and the odor of the roasting lamb —not the odor, the stench!—distressed me, but I alone was distressed. The dancers' faces were lit up both by the fire and by passion and zeal, and the dancers seemed to me to have become something quite different from normal men. Then Korah shouted something, exactly what I do not know, and the dancers stepped back from the altar while Korah approached it, dancing quickly; then all but Korah sat on the ground, and Korah whirled about, rapidly and gracefully, and all the while the chanting of "Blessed are You" continued. Then Korah sank to the earth, either dizzy or exhausted, I do not know which. He lay for a moment, and then crawled to the side of the circle.

Aaron slowly approached the altar. His dancing was slow, almost no more than a walk, but his face shone with a radiance beyond all the others. He danced with dignity, with his head erect and his shoulders thrown back, with his arms slowly rising and falling as he moved around the altar. The chanting ceased, and Aaron danced on in silence, until at last he raised his hands as if to quiet those who were already quiet. In a voice of strange beauty, he alone chanted Jethro's words, "Blessed are You, O God," slowly, lingering over every syllable. He finished his singing; he ended his dancing. He spoke: "Now we break bread together and eat."

I was torn, for this was all foolishness to me. Surely He did not want animal sacrifice, and surely He did not need people to dance before an altar. Or to sing, "Blessed are You." Yet if perhaps He did not need these things, was it the people who needed them?

And, quite beyond these questions, was not Aaron my brother a most impressive figure? And did not his resonant voice cut right into a person's heart?

Had I been wrong about all this?

I had noticed that when we were on the march, there were only a small number of litigants who came before me. Whenever we encamped, the number grew. The longer we encamped, the greater grew the number. I wondered if leisure made disputes increase.

My mind was on the sacred mountain, and what we should need to do in obedience of His command that we come here. I hoped that He would speak to me and tell me. I knew our people were becoming impatient, yet I knew nothing else to do but to wait. And the number of those who came before me for litigation constantly grew.

After a few days, Jethro rebuked me, gently. "You are doing an unwise thing, Moses. Your burden is too great for one man. You must designate judges throughout the tribes."

I said, "And by what law will they judge?"

He replied, as if I had asked an almost silly question, "By His law, of course."

His law! I remembered my conversation with Tat-Rin, the conversation which had so discouraged me. What to Tat-Rin was utter nonsense was to my father-in-law, Jethro, a simple fact. Could the objection of Tat-Rin be met in any way? His assertion was that kings, in their own interest, proclaimed that their laws were divine. Could there not be divine laws free from the self-interest of the king, or the leader, or any man? Could there not be in truth divine laws, laws which came from God? A Tat-Rin could disbelieve, yet his disbelief would not alter the reality.

But if our laws were to come from God, then they needed truly to come from Him. If they came from only me, they were my laws, not His. And they could not come from Him unless He would in some way provide them.

One thing became certain to me: He needed to provide them in the hearing of all the people, not in my hearing alone. Unless, and until that should happen, one could not speak of His laws.

It was no great chore to follow Jethro's advice and to appoint judges. I did so, but I cautioned them, as prudently and subtly as I could, that, so far, they had only their common sense to go by.

We Hebrews had judges even before we had laws! And what could be more preposterous!

The next day, the smoke ceased to arise from the mountain, and that night the peak was not aflame and the sky was not red. I have tried to remember if these stopped all in one day; perhaps it was over several days. But, no matter. What could the cessation mean but that He was ready to speak to me?

For two days all was quiet on the mountain, making me certain that soon He was to do something, or say something, though just what I had no idea. I summoned the tribal representatives. I told them of His words to me at the time of the burning bush, of His command that I go to Egypt and bring our people in their freedom to this sacred mountain. I told them that the quiet that had descended on the mountain, timed so wondrously to our being there, surely meant He was to speak to us.

They listened to me attentively, and, so I imagine, apprehensively. I could see on the faces of some of them reflections of their fright, for men in general seem to be afraid of God. Someone spoke, and there was a common nodding of the heads. The voice of that man trembled. "We will do whatever you say, Moses."

Then Aaron spoke up. "If there are to be sacrifices, you must name someone priest to be in charge of them."

I tried to keep from my voice the annoyance which I felt. "We are all priests, Aaron, a kingdom of priests, all of us holy people."

Aaron glowered at me, and I turned my eyes away from him. My words had been spontaneous, of course, yet they had arisen from what had evidently become a conviction within me ever since Aaron had first spoken to me about priests and sacrifices. Only later, as I thought over the words I had used to answer him, did I recall that I had not replied at all to his supposition that sacrifices would be desired or needed.

Then someone proposed that I assemble all the people—as many as could gather in one place—and speak to them as I had spoken to the representatives. I gave my assent. Late that afternoon the huge assembly took place at the foot of the mountain. In the morning I had been aware of an air of fear among the tribal representatives, but when all the people were gathered, there was something that hovered over us far beyond mere fear, something kindred to terror, as if my people were poised to flee from the place, should some single alarming incident occur. They were more eager for the assembly to end than pleased to be gathered.

I spoke briefly, in words like those I had spoken to the representatives. Then it dawned on me that in some way my words must surely strike them as incomplete and unsatisfying, for the people seemed to want me to tell them exactly what was going to happen, and it was this that I myself did not know. I felt that I must say something, yet I could not say anything false. What I said, mustering my words without having thought out what to say, was that the important thing was for everything to be prepared, and that all the people, especially the men, needed preparation. I told them to wash their clothes, and themselves, and to be ready; I told the men not to touch their women. I told them to await a signal, and to stay off the mountain until they heard it. I was improvising; perhaps if I had known what I was going to say, I would have said something totally different. But I think that what I said was almost perfect for the occasion, for I was telling the people what would keep them reasonably busy doing, or, in the case of not touching their women, not doing. As they dispersed, Aaron came to me: "Are there to be sacrifices, Moses?"

"Only if He asks for them."

Immediately he began to protest. Fortunately, someone intervened, the representative of the tribe of Naphtali. "Be assured, O Moses, that all that He commands we will do." I replied to him in words that I have forgotten; my chief recollection is that he saved me from having to discuss sacrifices with my brother, Aaron.

The two days passed in such complete quiet and inactivity that I began to become anxious and even worried that they might stretch into four, or eight, or endless days. It was not that I doubted that He would speak to us, but only that I did not know when and how He would speak. On the night after the second day, I began to be beside myself with worry that still another day of endless waiting would confront us, and I prayed to Him, both silently and out loud. Indeed, so passionately did I pray that Zipporah was momentarily awakened, but on my reassurance that all was well, she fell asleep again.

I recall that for a time I was diverted from the oppressive anxiety by wondering about my having told the men not to touch a woman. I myself, of course, abided by that. I remembered that the night after the burning bush I had also abstained from touching my beloved Zipporah. I kept wondering why I associated not touching a woman with the events of the highest sanctity. I tried to recollect whether or not I heard that any such association and practice existed among the Egyptians or the Midianites, but I could remember none. Was this something, instead, that I had myself devised? I did not know. Curiously, I remembered exactly the opposite, for it was said that among some peoples—so Egyptian scholars reported—that the sanctuaries had an array of sacred prostitutes, carefully chosen for the honor. At the time of the spring sacred days, it was believed that the deity needed to be implored for the vegetation to be renewed, so that the sacred prostitutes invited the male worshipers to intercourse at the height of their dance-worship, believing that just as the man sent his seed into the woman, so the god sent his seed into the earth, so that it became pregnant and bore the fruits, becoming Mother Earth.

Some even thought that the acts of intercourse compelled the deity to unite with the earth; I could not believe in a deity whom man could compel. I wondered if some aversion had arisen in me to the accounts of sacred prostitution I had heard and only dimly remembered, and that my aversion had pushed me to want the sacred moments completely free of such abominable things.

There were, of course, prostitutes in Egypt—not sacred ones!—for I had been accosted a time or two, without, of course, responding. It seemed to me vile for a woman to let a man use her body for a sum of money, and even more vile for the man to hire the woman. But I knew that this went on in Egypt as, so far as I knew, it did not go on among the Midianites. Perhaps among Wilderness people there was no prostitution, but prosperity in the cities of Egypt seems to have brought it about. The prosperous Egyptians had a special bent for seductions and infidelities, and prostitution, and I hated their ways.

To think about these things interrupted the anxiety I was going through, and in that way relieved it somewhat. I think, too, that I was half asleep when I thought about these things. Perhaps I even dozed off. But all too soon my wakefulness returned, and, unable to rest or be still, I walked out of the tent, and paced back and forth. It seemed to me that it must be time for the dawn, but it was still dark in the east. After a long while I returned to my tent, lay down, and tried to sleep. I heard a sound, a low sound, kindred to thunder. I ran out of my tent, and looked to the east. The dawn had indeed begun, but smoke was rising from the mountain, blotting out the sky above the peak. Suddenly there came a very loud sound. Smoke gushed forth from the mountain in a huge black stream, forming a cloud above the mountain. From this cloud of black smoke there was fire reflected, like flashes of lightning. The noise from the mountain was sharp and loud like the thunder which comes right with lightning. All about me people were stirring from their tents, some simply to look out through the portals, and others coming out from them in fear. A voice called out to me, "Is it He Who is doing this?"

I said, "Let the signal be sounded. Let the trumpet blow. He is about to speak to us."

From nearby I heard the sound of a trumpet, a long blast, and throughout our encampment I heard the echo of other trumpets picking up the signal.

The smoke had become even thicker over the mountain, and the rumble even louder. The people gathered about me, and I walked in the direction of the mountain, the people following me, without anyone rushing ahead of me. I reached the incline above them. The mountain ceased to make its terrifying sound, though the smoke still poured forth in its abundance. We all stopped, and we listened, but the silence continued. Then there came an even louder roar from the mountain, and my ears seemed ready to split, and this almost unbearable sound continued.

I heard His voice in the midst of the sound. I heard it clearly. I understood the words. I heard them, I absorbed them. I learned them, and later I wrote them. Later I had our people all learn them. All of us at the foot of the mountain heard Him speak those Ten Words: I am He Who brought you out of the land of Egypt out of the house of bondage. You shall have no gods besides Me. You shall make no graven image or statue of anything found on earth; you shall not bow down to these. You shall not swear falsely when you invoke My name. Remember the Sabbath and keep it holy. Honor your father and mother. Do not kill, commit adultery, steal, testify falsely against your neighbor, or covet what belongs to him, his wife or his slaves or his animals.

I heard this clearly, clearly and unmistakably. Our people heard this—but, regrettably—not as clearly, and not as unmistakably. They knew, all of them, that they were hearing His voice, but they were in deep terror, so that many of them told me later that they had heard His voice but could not distinguish His words. Of Tat-Rin and some of our Egyptians, I shall speak later.

Some of the people were so frightened that they fainted, and some from the fringes of the crowd took to their heels. I stood above them, calm, happy, satisfied. When a silence intervened, a voice called out, "You speak to us, Moses. Let Him not speak to us, or we shall all die of fright."

I said, "There is nothing to fear. He has told you what sins to avoid—"

"Let Him speak to you, and you to us."

Then others took up the cry, "Let Him speak to you." The assembly seemed to melt, to fade away, as if people could not stay where they were, but needed to hurry off. Presently I was all alone.

When I hear the account from Caleb, I tell him that since he was present, he must know that our people have mixed things up a bit, and they now tell things which simply do not fit together. I shall mention some of these. What impresses me, though, is that despite the differences and the contradictions, what they tell both is sensible and also accords in general with what happened. Is it important that they do not remember exactly, and they give different versions of the events, sometimes confusing what happened then with what happened a little later? For example, they tell this, that when subsequently I went up the mountain, I went alone, and also that Aaron, and his sons Nadab and Abihu, and seventy elders accompanied me toward the peak, but that I alone ascended to it. Again, they tell that Joshua went up with me, though I alone went up to the peak. These details seem to me not to matter at all. What is important is that our people at the foot of the mountain heard His voice, and that I understood His words, and that I taught our people to know those words.

Ten words. A list of laws, short enough for even a child to learn, to remember. The essence of a list that could be longer, or of lists more complicated. The Ten Words were enough for ordinary people.

We already had our judges; now we had our laws. Laws which He gave to us. Laws which I heard in joy and satisfaction, though our people heard them in fear and terror.

After midday, the sounds abated, though they did not cease. I walked among the tents, throughout all the encampments, omitting not a single tribe. Wherever I went, people told me that they had heard Him, but invariably, though, they asked me what He had said, for many of them had not understood His words. So often that day did I repeat the Ten Words that whether I cited them correctly or not, they achieved a fixed form in my mind, and I was able to speak them without hesitation. I wondered that almost no one besides me had heard all the Ten Words clearly, but they insisted with a single voice that they had heard Him, that I attributed their lack of grasping His words to their fright.

Part of the time Aaron walked with me. After the third or fourth time, he, rather than I, answered the questioners, speaking the Ten Words exactly as I had spoken them. I did not ask Aaron if he remembered the words from hearing Him, or me; I knew intuitively that he would not have wanted me to ask that question, for Aaron was truthful and would not have enjoyed admitting that he too had not grasped all the words.

We walked among the Egyptians too. Most of them had been as frightened as the Hebrews. I wanted them to tell me how wondrous it was that He had spoken to us, and even to them. To my deep disappointment, no one spoke this way, not even my good friends Anquru and Nephros. In truth, I was more than disappointed, I was saddened for a moment, and for a passing instant angry. Here and there some Egyptian mentioned hearing the sound. Tat-Rin said to me, "I did not grasp the words, Moses. Perhaps I do not speak Hebrew well enough." His voice carried his customary irony.

I did not linger in the Egyptian camp. Perhaps it was because Aaron said that he needed to speak to me privately. We turned toward the encampment of the Levites, and at dusk we sat before my tent. A great weariness had come over me. Aaron began to speak, to tell me that there was something urgently needed. I tried to follow what he said, but I interrupted him. "Can we speak early tomorrow morning, Aaron? I am so tired and sleepy that I can scarcely hear you."

For a half moment he seemed offended. Then he said, "Until early tomorrow morning."

Sleep did not entirely elude me. Yet the refreshment which I wanted, and needed, did not seem to come to me. Zipporah sat by my bed, stroking my head.

I dozed off. I dreamed that I was at a meeting of the council of representatives, and that Anquru was speaking: "Now that Moses had received the laws for us, we must make him king. Kings are lawgivers, and Moses must become our king."

In the dream I remembered the words of Tat-Rin, that Egyptian kings falsely declared that they were gods and that their laws had come from the gods. Were I to become king, I said to the council in the dream, someone would say some day of me too that I presented my people with my own laws which I lied about, saying that they were from Him. How could people believe my words, free of all doubt? By my refusing to become king!

The Ten Words were not mine; they were His. They must never be thought of as mine. Always they are His.

CHAPTER VII

In the morning, Aaron said to me, "Now that He has spoken to us, and given us His law, we need to worship Him, to thank Him." I nodded my head. "We shall assemble the people, and offer an animal sacrifice to Him, a lamb or a kid. As Jethro did."

"I see no necessity," I said, "to offer an animal sacrifice."

"But you agreed that we must worship Him and thank Him."

"It is the animal sacrifice which I see no need for."

Aaron threw up his hands in despair. "How else shall we worship Him?"

I said, "We can speak; we can pray."

"That is no worship. That is merely words."

I said, "I think He understands words."

He was exasperated. "Of course He does. I did not say that! But the people—they will not understand what it means just to speak and to do nothing more."

"I have a higher regard for the intelligence of our people than you have."

He turned and walked away from me, very angry. "You persist in not understanding. Yesterday He spoke to us, and gave us a law. I know the Ten Words. Perhaps others know them. How will our people know how important those Ten Words are?"

"They know that He gave them."

"But they have to do something, or to see something, to make the Ten Words a part of them."

I said, "No."

He shook his finger at me. "Then I warn you, they will forget those Words, or they will ignore them. The Words are His, not theirs. The Words must become theirs."

"I do not see how a sacrifice will make His Words theirs."

"Because the sacrifice will teach them that the Words are theirs."

His eyes filled with tears. "Listen to me, Moses! I understand these things better than you do. So far, what has happened is only that He has given us the Words, but we have not yet told Him that they are ours. He gave them, He commanded them. It is for us now to say that we accept the Words."

I fell silent, and I imagine he thought that I was considering what he had said. Perhaps in a sense that was so, but in reality I was struck by something he had not directly said. Yes, He had commanded those words; I it was who had grasped those words from out the overwhelming sound. Suppose an evil outcome were to ensue and that people would think that the words were mine, not His, and that I had decreed them, in much the same way that Egyptian kings decreed their laws? Would it not be wise for our people to be persuaded to these Words as their own, and gladly say so, and say so of their own conviction? The Words would then be theirs as well as His. Or, to go further, suppose we were to make an agreement with Him, a contract, a covenant, as men in Egypt and, I suppose, elsewhere did when they made a business arrangement? A contract between our people and Him! Not between a ruler and his subjects, but almost as if we and He were partners!

I said, "I am not sure that I agree with you. Suppose I did? How would you arrange matters?"

His face began to glow, and a cascade of words came from out of his mouth. These I no longer remember exactly, but the main suggestion I do, and clearly. The twelve tribes, so he proposed, were to be assembled, each around a tall pillar, yet around me on all sides, and I would be standing by an altar which would be built. Each of the tribes at its pillar would offer a sacrifice, gathering the blood of the slain animal in basins, bring the basins to me. Half of the blood I would throw on the altar. I would have before me the Ten Words in writing, and I would read them to the people. I would ask, Do you accept them, or do you not? Hopefully, the people would say yes. Then I would throw half of the blood where the people nearest to me were standing, and even on them, and then I would pronounce the covenant as sealed in the blood of the animal.

I wondered, as he spoke, if he was devising his plan as he went along, for he spoke rapidly, even getting out of breath. I did not like his plan, not one bit. Especially did I not like the part that he had designed for me to play. Indeed, I said to him, "Should I be the one to throw the blood? Could you not possibly do so?"

Promptly he said, "Of course I can do it. And do it well!" Then his face clouded over. "I can see myself doing it. But the people do not really know me. Not yet. Maybe some day they will. They know you. You must do this yourself." I think that I could have persuaded him to do it. Yet the reason he had given for my doing it seemed to me very sound. I had to take note of my brother Aaron's integrity, for if he had said that he would do it, I would have felt bound to let him—assuming that I agreed with the whole thing.

I said that I had to think things over. He replied, "Do not wait too long, for preparations must be made, and those take time."

"I will give you my answer at noon." I was reluctant, most reluctant. I had no inclination for the kind of elaborate ceremony that he proposed. Especially did I not like the throwing of the blood, throwing it on people near me. Yet I felt myself more and more inclined to follow his suggestion, though still fearful that something might go awry, and the whole thing could end up in a useless or even ridiculous way. It occurred to me to seek out my friend Caleb and to ask him his opinion.

I repeated to Caleb as reliably as I could what Aaron had suggested. I explained to him why, against my usual attitude, I was inclined to say yes. He said, "I must admit that I would myself never have thought of anything like this. But Aaron may understand people from a standpoint that I do not. What do we lose, Moses, if we do this?"

"It may turn out to be something some people might laugh at. Especially our Egyptians."

"I will take Tat-Rin for a long walk during the ceremony," Caleb said. "In that way you will not throw the blood at me."

I said, "Shall I summon the council and consult them?"

He nodded. "Summon them, but do not ask them, tell them."

When the council assembled, I did as Caleb suggested, and I was pleased to notice how the heads nodded in agreement. But my cousin Korah of the tribe of Levi arose. "I favor very much what you have told us. It is my opinion, however, that if you are to read the Ten Words to us, someone else should throw the blood. I think this is an honor you could give to another person."

Caleb said, "To you, Korah?"

Korah said, "And why not?"

Caleb said, "Why not?"

Then the representative of Benjamin arose. "It must be Moses and not Korah. We of the tribe of Benjamin acknowledge Moses as our ruler—"

I interrupted. "I am not your ruler."

"You are our leader, and Korah is not. If someone besides you is to throw the blood, let it be someone who is not from the tribe of Levi as you and Korah are, but someone from another tribe."

Then many people wanted to speak, and to wrangle, and it seemed clear that there was sentiment that someone other than me should throw the blood, but no possible agreement on who it should be. The discussion waxed warm, and then hot, and Korah arose to speak too often and too long, and I could see that Aaron was wetting his lips as if he too was going to speak. I managed to quiet them all, and I said, "The reading of the Words and the throwing of the blood are not really separate things. Therefore I think—indeed, I decide—that I shall do both." Only Korah disagreed with me; he tried again to speak, but there were many, especially the man from Benjamin, who shouted to him to sit down and be quiet. I said that the meeting was over; a few came to me to applaud the arrangements I had described, but I saw Korah walk away, his anger and disappointment clearly reflected in his face.

We held the ceremony the next morning. My part was both easy and difficult. The reading of the Ten Words came very naturally to me, the throwing of the blood did not. I think that my voice broke when I spoke some words which I had prepared: "This is the blood of the covenant which God has made with you according to the Ten Words." I remember clearly how a feeling of solemnity seemed to grip all the people, even me, and I think that I was almost moved to tears when the people repeated after me, "All that He has spoken, we will do and will obey." I wish that I could say that it was the ceremony which moved me; perhaps it was. I believe, though, that it was the fervor with which our people repeated that sentence so important to me, "We will do and will obey." The Ten Words were now theirs.

But something I had not expected took place. When all seemed over, Aaron arose and began to dance majestically about the altar. Other Levites gathered around to watch him, and then they too danced, and gradually the dancing became general. The solemnity was not only not broken by the dancing, but the fervor of it all rose in pitch and intensity.

Aaron had been right; I had been wrong. He had understood the people's hearts better than I.

I was left alone most of the afternoon, and I needed the solitude, for I needed to think through two different things. The Ten Words belonged to everyone; the Ten Words were clear. But in another sense, the Words were not clear, for when I had observed Jethro holding his court and when cases had been brought to me, there were matters which were complicated, and the Ten Words were short, and too many things possibly remained open. In fact, the Ten Words, which only He could have had the intelligence to devise, were standards, they were not laws. I mean, laws tell what punishment a person is to receive if he breaks a law. Laws tell about courts, and about witnesses, and how to examine witnesses to know if they are telling the truth. Laws tell what the authority of a judge is and what authority he lacks. We needed laws, exact laws, definite laws. And since we had not inherited any laws from Abraham, Isaac, and Jacob, we had to start anew, beyond the Ten Words, and we could not wait for generations to pass and for laws to suggest themselves, or to come from the decisions of courts, and then to be gathered by some scribe into a collection for lawyers. We needed definite laws and needed them without delay.

And Aaron's dancing, in which the people had joined—clearly we needed that. But suppose that every time we had some occasion to assemble, some person, this one or that one, began to dance, and others fell in, and created all manner of chaos? We needed, so it seemed to me, some regulations, not to provide for animal sacrifice and dancing, but rather to arrange that these things did not become chaotic, or excessive. We have these regulations now, and they have become both elaborate and very specific. Caleb tells me how wise people consider me for having provided them with laws that instructed them in observing religious ceremonies and obligated people to do them. This is almost funny; the regulations were not to obligate people, but to deter them from too much, from the wrong time, from the wrong way!

Jethro had asked me if I were a venturous person. I do not know. Yet, who but me would have given birth that afternoon to the beginning of an idea: I would absent myself from the people, and ascend the mountain, and write out definite, specific laws for them? Who else would have had the temerity to think that by isolating himself on His mountain he could in privacy think through and then record all that needed to be thought of, to be weighed, to be assessed, and then to be recorded?

That afternoon, only the germ of the thought came to me. That night, more ideas came to me. By morning, a certainty arose in my mind. I would go up the mountain.

How long would I be gone? I did not know.

Who would go with me? Perhaps Joshua, perhaps Aaron. How far? All the way up the mountain? Or would that person only accompany me part of the way, and let me proceed the rest of the way myself? Perhaps some of the council of representatives, or some delegation, some seventy or so of the people, might go up with me, either all of the way, or only a part. All sorts of schemes occurred to me.

And whom would I leave in charge while I was away? Joshua? For military affairs, certainly he was the man, but for other affairs hardly, for he seemed to me cold and uncommunicative. Caleb? Possibly. But was he known and respected outside his tribe of Judah? My brother, Aaron? Surely not, for he was too much a dreamer to be charged with the responsibilities which could arise.

As I thought it over, Caleb was the man. It was known in the council that he was my close friend, and it might be thought that I was choosing him out of friendship, not out of recognition of his abilities. I went over in my mind the others on the council, and then I began to tell myself that some of the representatives, such as the men from Benjamin, were not men of great ability. Indeed, I had the uncomfortable feeling that some of the representatives tended to fawn on me, to want my approval, to agree with me, at least openly, despite what they might have thought in their minds.

I pondered too the name of Korah. Certainly he was able. Certainly he gave evidence of decisiveness, and he seemed to have followers. But I disliked him, whether simply because I disliked him or because I remembered a number of minor clashes with him. Also, I knew he disliked me. Would he not think me a weak person if I designated him to take my place while I was away?

The decision which I made was a foolish one. Let no one think it was an impulsive decision; rather, I spent many, many hours in thought. What I decided was to leave things in the hands of the council of representatives, not knowing that in failing to leave some single person in charge, I left no one in charge.

I can say in extenuation of my folly that I was moved to it by my recollection of the covenant of the blood. With what fervor our people have spoken the Ten Words! With what fervor they had danced! This was a people already instructed, already obligated to His Ten Words. Did they need some one over them?

I need not repeat for you the laws I brought down from Sinai. You should know them by now. Perhaps you may see in them that I tried to envisage both the remainder of our few days in the Wilderness, and thereafter our settling down in the land of Canaan, the fertile, empty land that had been promised to us. For the Wilderness portion, there had to be some way in which we could worship Him with an altar we could carry along, with equipment we could set up and dismantle. For Canaan, however, we would need laws of real estate, of property. I had not set myself an easy chore, and I did not myself recognize its difficulty.

I told the council that I was going to ascend the mountain. Fearful that I might not succeed in formulating the necessary laws, I did not tell them why I was going. I told no one why. I thought that in perhaps a week on the mountain, I could set down on parchment all that would be necessary for the Wilderness and for the beginning decades of our new life in the land of Canaan. Indeed, I implied to lovely Zipporah that I would be gone at most a week or two, not more. I kissed my children and left them.

The people learned from the council that I was going. Many accompanied me to the lower slopes of the mountain. Despite my decision to appoint no one, a voice called out to me, "Moses! Whom do we consult in your absence?" Near me were Aaron and my brother-in-law, Hur. I pointed to the two of them: "If necessary, consult them." But I added, "The council of the tribes remains here to guide you."

Aaron and Joshua went farther with me, Joshua carrying my food—cheese and dried meat—and Aaron, not knowing why I was going, nevertheless continually counseled me.

Since I spoke to no one of my purpose, not even to Caleb, it was assumed that He had summoned me. In the sense that He plants seeds of thoughts among men, He did. Our people now relate that He actually did summon me; what harm is there in this?

But Aaron was very fearful, and even Joshua a little so, that something evil would befall me on the top of the mountain. I was not afraid; I had no reason to feel afraid of Him. We ascended together part way, and then I told them to descend.

Joshua left me, but Aaron lingered for still another last word of encouragement, as if I were headed for some danger. "Take care of yourself, Moses," he said. He embraced me, and I him. Then, to compound my folly, I said to him, "You have been right, and I have been wrong about what people, even our people, need."

"I understand them," he said.

"Perhaps we do need priests, and a high priest."

"Will I be the high priest, Moses?"

I did not answer him. I did not say yes, I did not say no. I should have said something, for he went on to say, "Thank you, Moses! Thank you, Moses."

I had said too much and too little. How a leader needs to watch every word!

Alone atop the mountain, above the clouds, I experienced cold and hunger and loneliness, and anxiety about my purpose. I prayed to Him from time to time, and He answered my prayers. I wrote and scratched out what I wrote. Then, when still not finished, I became weary of writing; I found a huge flat rock, and on it I chiseled the Ten Words He had spoken; it was a double rock, as if two tablets of stone had been miraculously joined together.

The laws of property, of crime, of judicial procedures all came easy to me. More difficult was the need to fashion laws for worship, laws to limit sacrifices. Then Aaron's question about his being high priest recurred to me, and it troubled me. I remembered, too, how Korah asked to be the one to throw the blood. Was it better to have a designated priest, or better not? Was it better to have priesthood in a family, with the office to go from father to son, or to allow people to vie for the office, and possibly to resort to ugly maneuvering, or even misdeed, to gain the office? On the other hand, was it not dangerous to have such an office? I had to admit to myself that this was so. But so determined was I that I should not be thought of as ruler, or king, that I wanted there to be an important office which I would never hold. My laws must never be mine, must never come from the imposition by a tyrant of his will on a cowed and subdued people. Rather, my laws must be reasonable and just, and, hopefully, they could enable my people to be the unique people I needed them to be. In the interest of my role as the framer of their laws, I felt the need for a priest, a high priest, while I would always remain Moses without a title.

Who will believe me when I say that I thought of Aaron for that high office simply because I considered him the best man I could find? Did I anticipate that I would be accused of favoritism for naming my own brother? It adds to my bitter recollections that I gave no thought at all to such possible recrimination. Moreover, had I not inadvertently made what Aaron took to be a promise, but which I had not meant that way at all? And, above all, had I not neglected to say to him: Do not discuss this with anybody? So long as this remained between him and me, I could still abstain from deciding to have a high priest, or I could decide to have one and not name him. Yet, if I truly knew Aaron, it would have made little difference if I had enjoined him to silence! Was it not certain that he had already informed his four sons? And had he not already informed them of what he regarded as something very definite, something completely decided? Then why had I spoken to him so impulsively? Was it because I loved him as my brother, and remembered the misery he had gone through in the camps, and admired his mind which in many ways was superior to my own?

Or, maybe I was very unfair to my brilliant brother. Surely he was capable of his own kind of prudence, and when I should come down from the mountain, I would discover that that was so.

I wrote the laws on the sheets of parchment, trying to find different ways to express them. One way was to be very brief, for example: "Whoever kills a man is to be put to death." Another way was to be longer: "If one man lies in wait for another man, and kills him deliberately, he shall be put to death." I was fearful of being too wordy, fearful of being too terse. I wrote and rewrote, I thought and rethought, and again wrote and re-wrote. I imagined that I was a Hebrew, a hundred years later, in prosperous Canaan, and I wrote laws and regulations for worship, which seemed to me could be suitable for that future time.

In every single item which I wrote there was my conviction that we must be a special people, a kingdom of priests and a holy nation, a moral people, an elevated people. Surely without this conviction I would not have had the impulse to write, nor the persistence to rethink and rewrite and to press on and on. The laws, as you know, have been copied with some minor confusions. There comes in the midst of them now what I wrote as their very beginning: "Justice, truest justice must be our pursuit."

At last I finished what needed to be done. By my own tabulation, I had been on the mountain for almost forty days. I sensed that I had lost weight and that my strength had declined, that I had an acute sense of weariness. Yet my feeling was one of great accomplishment! Is there an artisan who is not proud of his work? I was proud of mine, and I know that I looked forward to the time when, after descending and showing my people what I had done for them, they would praise me. Aaron would praise me, and Caleb would praise me, and Joshua would praise me. And my lovely Zipporah would praise me. And I would tell my children that my days and my nights on sacred Sinai were much more significant than even what I had helped to accomplish in freeing us when we were slaves in Egypt.

I was proud of the clarity in the laws. I was proud of the regulations for the worship, for I had so expressed them that they were the right amount, neither too much, nor too little. How wondrously I had labored, how wondrously I had achieved! When ideas had eluded me, I had prayed to Him, and in His own way He had answered, and I knew from His answering that He too approved what I had done!

Now it was time to return. I finished in the middle of an afternoon, and I wondered if I could make the long descent and be back in the camp before it became dark. That did not seem possible, so I ate some of the last of the cheese and wrapped my clothes about me; and I slept through a happy night and woke refreshed in the morning.

I had the sheets of parchment before me. Should I bring down with me those sheets on which I had written the beginning of thoughts, the first efforts to express in words what needed to be recorded? I was undecided. I thought that I ought bring them with me, if only to have them to refer to, should someone some day ask this or that question. I separated the sheets into the preparatory and the acceptable. I arranged the sheets of the acceptable in their right order and smiled at myself for having forgotten to bring along needle and thread to sew the sheets together before rolling them up. I wrapped them in the cloth that I used to cover myself against the cold winds.

A strange thing happened. I was aware that the mountain was making its noises, and quite loudly, but I did not know if the noises had just begun, or if they had been with me all the time I was on the mountain! I tried to recall. For the most part, it seemed to me that the noises had been with me constantly, but I had simply not noticed them. Perhaps I had become so accustomed to them that I had failed to hear them. Perhaps, though, they had ceased, and only now were beginning again.

The noises did not frighten me. But some presentiment of evil came to me, and I wondered, if the noises were really beginning anew, how our people were responding to them—in fear and terror again? Or, if the noises had been continuous, had our people gotten over their fright? Had the period of forty days of noise increased their fearfulness? I wondered if all was well with my Zipporah and the boys, with the tribes, with all the people. Some intuition told me that all was not well.

I started down, but stopped. The two tablets of stone—should I leave them, or take them? A very loud noise came from the mountain, and a sudden cloud of thick smoke arose near me, seeming to come out of the ground. I dared not leave the two tablets. Heavy as they were, and weakened as I was, I picked them up, and burdened with them and the sheets of parchment, I began to go down the mountainside.

Within me, my sense of triumph over having finished my task fought with a nameless anxiety, as if I should find that some distress had struck us. Perhaps one of my children was sick, or Zipporah dangerously ill. Perhaps marauders had again attacked our people, and this time it had not been possible to drive them off. How easy it was to think of different kinds of calamities! How ironic that I did not think at all of the supreme disaster, the one which occurred!

I heard the noise of the camp before I was able to see it. I heard shouting and singing, and I was reminded of the dancing around Jethro's altar. Then I stepped onto a promontory, and looked down, and I could see the encampment not far below me. They were dancing, and my brother, Aaron, was dancing, and it was not around an altar they were dancing but a golden calf! As the men danced, they repeatedly pointed their fingers at the calf, singing, "Here is your god, O Israel!" Then, without ceasing to dance, they bowed to the calf and some even prostrated themselves, and then all arose and resumed the dance and from the way they danced, I could see that Aaron was leading them.

Someone saw me and shouted my name, and others stopped, looked up at me and shouted my name. The dancing slowly stopped, and the shouts turned into a horrible silence. I stepped to the edge of the promontory, and they crowded together below me. I spoke only these words, which all of them heard: "You shall have no gods besides me. You shall make no graven images, you shall not bow down to these." I heard some of them gasp, and I saw Aaron take a step backward. "Shame!" I cried. "Shame! Shame!" Then my fury welled up in me, and I threw down the two tablets, and I saw them fall onto a huge boulder and shatter. I unwrapped my garment and let the parchment sheets float down, pushed by the winds, and I did not care what happened to them.

That was my triumph! These were my people!

I cannot clearly remember the exact sequence of events. My people tell different things, and some things they do not tell.

I hear now that He spoke to me on the mountain, telling me what the people were doing below. My own recollection is only of a presentiment that all was not well. They tell, too, that He was even angrier than I, and wanted to destroy all our people except my family, and to raise from my children a new people to be His holy nation; perhaps. They tell that I called on the Levites to arm themselves, to kill as many of the Hebrews as their swords would reach; perhaps. This I do recall, that our people began to fight among themselves, and an ugly, bloody pitched battle took place before my eyes.

They do not tell about the sheets of parchment, which fluttered in the wind.

I did nothing to stop the fighting. When I stepped back from the promontory and made my way down the last hill, there were those who came to me as if to speak to me, but I answered no one, not Caleb, not Joshua. I made my way to my tent, and I embraced my Zipporah, and I lay down on my bed and I wept the most bitter tears I had ever wept. A kingdom of priests and a holy people! The Ten Words! "All that He commands we will do and obey."

Zipporah whispered to me, "Aaron has come to see you." I sat up; I could see through the opening of the tent that night had fallen. I did not answer Zipporah. She said again, "Aaron has come to see you."

"Send him away!" I shouted.

"Moses!" he called. "Let me explain to you—!"

"Go away! Go away and do not come back!" I lay back on my bed. I heard the sound of singing, sad, mournful singing. "Zipporah, who is singing?"

"The women whose men died in the fighting."

"Let them kill each other some more!" I said.

"Can I bring you some food, Moses?" I did not answer; I did not want to eat. "Are you angry at me too, Moses?" she said. "I gave no gold for the calf, I did no dancing. I did not worry as Aaron did that you were lost on the mountain and would not return!"

I sat up. "Tell me what happened."

She said, "I do not know everything. This much I know, that after you left, Aaron announced you had appointed him to be a priest for us, a high priest. Some did not believe him, but most did. Every few days he stopped by to tell me that he was worried because you were away so long, that the people were worried. Then someone came to me to say that Aaron was asking people to give him their golden jewels, and that person wanted my two bracelets and my earrings, but I would not give them. Someone told me that the gold was melted down over a very hot fire, and then someone made it into a calf for Aaron. And Aaron was building an altar and sacrificing lambs to the golden calf. The people sang and they danced. That is all I know, Moses."

My tears no longer flowed. Instead a cold fury, which is worse than a burning anger, overcame me. I lay there silent. A little later, Zipporah brought me a cup with some hot liquid in it and pleaded with me to drink it. Its taste was bitter, and I knew that she had put some medicine in it, for I began to feel as if I had been drugged. I fell asleep, to dream of golden calves even more gigantic than the one our people had bowed down to, many enormous golden calves, one after another, and there were dozens of Aarons leading our people in their dances.

I do not remember what happened the next morning. I have dim recollections of someone at the portal telling that the golden calf had been destroyed, of Aaron returning only to be sent away, of Miriam coming to tell me that I must see Aaron and listen to his account. I let no one into the tent; I did not leave it. Perhaps if my cold fury had turned to hot, finding some release for itself in either words of denunciation or in punishments which I might have succeeded in distributing, I would have recovered more quickly. Instead, I fell into a silence from which only my Zipporah and the children were exempted. The one outsider whom I saw was Joshua, reporting that all was quiet as far as desert marauders were concerned. He spoke to me, but I spoke not a single word to him, not even to say thank you.

The chasm between my people and me seemed beyond crossing. Not only their gross infidelity, but the way in which it came, so soon after their acceptance of the Ten Words and the covenant, while I was away on the mountain on their behalf, created in me a deep sense of the most acute grievance. Worst of all, it made me question that I could ever fashion this people into something special, something unique. I had lost my hope, and thereby I had lost that which sustains a leader.

Only once did my cold fury burst into heat. It was when Zipporah brought me a report, an infuriating report, that in reality no one, least of all Aaron, had made the golden calf. Rather, what had happened was that the golden jewelry had been thrown into the fire, and in it the golden calf had managed to fashion itself! Preposterous!

A few days later, seven days after my return from the mountain, Caleb came to see me, and I did not find it possible to refuse him the few words which he said he wanted to speak. He came in and we sat on the ground together. The smile that customarily hovered over his lips was missing. Each of us seemed to wait for the other to speak. After a bit he said, "Many bowed down to the golden calf; more did not, Moses."

I did not answer him. After another silence, he rose, and without another word, left the tent. Impulsively, I followed him, not that I meant to, but only because he was my friend, and he too was in deep distress, and I could not let him go away from me without some friendly word on my part. I called out to him, "Caleb! Come back!"

We sat again on the ground. I said, "Do you understand my agony? Can it be measured?"

"I understand. I could not measure it; who could?" He opened his mouth as if to speak, but no words came. He did this another time, and still another. Then he said, "When do we leave here and move on to Canaan?"

"Never!" I shouted at him.

He nodded. "But when will 'never' end? Tomorrow? Next

week? Next month? You can leave us, Moses, and we will perish. Or you can lead us, and we will move on further. Which will it be?"

It was then that my fury burst into words. I began to revile, to revile the calf, the people, Aaron, the tribes who had stolen the food—whom did I not revile!

At last my words ceased. He said, "When will your 'never' end?"

"Only when He tells me it should end."

"I wish He would speak to you soon, Moses!" He rose, and put his hand on my shoulder. I burst into new tears, leaning against his leg. I wept, and, almost as if he were a mother, not a man and my closest friend, he repeatedly patted my shoulder. From under his cloak he took out the parchment sheets I had written on on the mountain. "I picked these up that dismal day, Moses." He laid them beside me and he left.

Later, Aaron made his daily visit. This time I let him enter. I was appalled at his appearance, for his face was drawn, and his cheeks were sunken, and he was clearly in the deepest misery.

"What shall I say, Moses?"

"You can explain."

"Perhaps I can. I fear I cannot. We were in despair, for you were gone so very long. Our people feared you were lost. Our people needed reassurance. That is the explanation."

"You gave them reassurance by bowing to the golden calf? Whose idea was it—one of our Egyptians?"

"It was my own idea, Moses."

"Who gathered the golden jewelry?"

"It was I."

"And you were unaware of being faithless to Him?"

He hesitated. "Moses, I needed reassurance too. I needed it so much that I was unaware, unaware of the enormity of what I was doing. I felt compelled to do it, and I gave no thought to what it was and to what it meant. Only when I saw you standing above us did I understand; at that moment I understood." His voice broke. "Will you forgive me?"

I said, "No. It is not for me to forgive. You have betrayed me, you and the people who followed you. But He must forgive you. It is He against whom you have sinned."

"I am past forgiveness," he said. I did not answer him. "Past forgiveness! And I was so elated when you told me that I was to become our high priest—" He turned away from me, and I heard him sob.

I said, "Perhaps it is something in your favor that you have not lied to me."

He left. I felt all the lonelier when he was gone. Indeed, it occurred to me that I had not reviled him to his face. Should I not have done that? Should I not have scolded him, and cursed him, and belittled him, and humiliated him? Poor Aaron.

The dead had been buried—there were many too many—and many of the wounded had recovered. Now there was a restlessness among the people. Zipporah told me about it; I did not respond. Then Joshua came back to me. "The council wishes to know what they are to do? Do we stay? Do we move?"

I said with a sigh, "We make preparations. But we do not move. Not yet."

"As you say, Moses."

I sent for Caleb. "Did you read the parchment sheets?" He nodded his head. "Did you understand them? I mean, are they clear?"

"Some sheets would be clear except that other sheets say somewhat different things."

I knew that he meant the first sheets and the final ones. "Forgetting these differences, what did the parchments say to you?"

"They are laws to govern us."

"Do you approve of them?"

He looked directly at me. "Except for the disorder in them."

"Some sheets were only beginning attempts. I must look through, and throw those away."

He nodded. "There are things that need to be built. The Tabernacle, its vessels—"

"We shall stay here until these are completed."

"When do you begin to make these?"

"When He speaks to me."

"There is a fine artisan in our tribe, Bezalel, the grandson of your brother-in-law, Hur, by his first wife. I can commend him to you."

"Did you read the sheets which spoke of the high priest?"

"I did."

"What do you think?"

"In some you mention Aaron, in some you do not."

"What do you think?"

He shrugged his shoulders. "May I say this? From what you have written, you seem to give the high priest, whoever he may be, little room for thoughts of his own. Your instructions are very complete; I wonder about it."

I said, "My intention is to limit what the high priest will do. Perhaps I have had my brother, Aaron, unduly in mind. Aaron can follow instructions; I would be fearful for Aaron to have the right of discretion."

Caleb said, "You understand your brother."

"How can I designate him, after the golden calf?"

Caleb smiled. How good it was to see him smile! "Much better now than before. Now, he will surely never deviate from his instructions."

"But the golden calf—?"

"Moses, are there sins which are not forgivable? Our people are in great anxiety that He is holding some punishment in reserve for them, for they bear a heavy burden of guilt. Do you wish this? Or do you wish them to think that even this sin is forgiven? If Aaron is designated, they will know that sins can be forgiven."

"I must think this over," I said.

Perhaps when our people recall that period of anxiety, they confuse matters. Perhaps, too, some fathers tell their children one story, and other fathers a different story. Our people tell about me, that I have seen His face—even though He is invisible! They compliment me in this way! Some of them extend the compliment even to Aaron, Nadab, Abihu, and the seventy elders; they tell that these ascended the mountain with me, and that we all saw Him on a pavement of transparent sapphire—even though He is invisible! They tell still another story of me. As this story goes, we were on the verge of moving on from Sinai, and, since the route was unclear, I asked Him who would show us the way and even demanded that He reveal His face to me. Naturally, He replied that no man can see Him and live. Thereupon I said that unless He showed me His face and unless He went along with us, I simply would not go! To that He responded that He would set me in a cleft of a rock, cover it with the palm of His hand and then pass by, and after He would have passed by, He would remove His palm, letting me see His back. Thus, I would not see His face and die. But I would see His back!

These different stories, some contradicting others, amuse me. Perhaps other minds would notice only the little differences, and never notice the stories themselves; not so Caleb and I.

This story of the cleft in the rocks seems to have one part which is confused with a very important happening. It is told that when He passed by the cleft, He proclaimed His grace and His mercy. Fine! But those words do not belong there! They belong, though not in those exact phrases, in an important happening. That came about as I kept thinking to myself that the golden calf episode must in some way be ended, ended for all time. But how? That night when I prayed to Him, He gave me an answer. He told me to prepare another set of stone tablets like those which I had broken, and to ascend the mountain to Him again.

In the morning, I looked through the sheets of parchment, setting in one stack those which were to be thrown away, and in another those which were to be retained. I gave to Zipporah the ones to be discarded, telling her to throw them into the refuse area outside the camp. Then I took my sons with me to search for a suitable set of tablets of stone, and we found one very much like the one which I had broken. The rest of the day I spent preparing the two tablets. I told Zipporah that the next morning I must go up the mountain. "Again for forty days?" she said, somewhat sadly. I shook my head. "It will not be so long this time."

I convened the council after dark, for I did not want to see their faces or for them to see mine. We were together only long enough for me to say, "Tomorrow I go up the mountain to Him again." I waited for some question, or some comment; they were all subdued, even Korah.

On the mountain, I slowly and carefully chiseled in the Ten Words. As I was finishing, He spoke to me, above the rumble of the mountain: "I am a merciful God, and gracious, slow to anger, forgiving iniquity, trespass and sin." Those were His words. Those and no more. Not, as some tell it, that He also punishes sinners, even to the fourth generation. He did not say that to me. He may have said it to someone else, but not to me. And it was on the mountain, not in the cleft of the rock that I heard these words, in that important happening.

Now I knew the answer to Caleb's question: Sins are forgivable. Even the sin of our people with the golden calf.

My lingering despair disappeared; again I was the man with hope.

When I made my way down the mountain the next day, I looked carefully to find the same promontory on which I had stood, and from which I had thrown down the first set of tablets. I made my way to it, and I stood there, holding the heavy stone high above me, waiting for someone to see me and then to shout to the others that I was back. Soon I was seen, and our people gathered below me, as they had gathered before. I held the stones aloft, looking not at the people but at the sun which was bright enough to hurt my eyes, for I did not want the people to think that I was looking at them with reproach. I felt the need to say something. His words came back to me, and I spoke them to the people: "The Lord, the Lord is a God merciful and gracious, slow to anger, forgiving iniquity, transgression, and sin."

They remained standing, without anyone moving, all the while I made my way back from the promontory and then down the mountain; I passed among them, carrying the two tablets. No one spoke, no one moved.

I made my way to my tent.

∗ CHAPTER VIII

If you look in the encampment of the Levites, you can see the Tabernacle and the Ark in which the Two Tablets are borne, the Table for the showbread, the candelabrum—all the wondrous things which Bezalel either made himself, or else supervised in their making. I look at them from time to time with very mixed emotions, for I cannot completely overcome my remaining resistance. I remember so clearly, though, how our people rallied to the call to contribute their possessions, their time, and their talents to help in the making of all these things.

I had made the decision which had brought the people and me together again, and I had no regrets. But I felt a curious sensation, that though He had told me that He was gracious and forgiving, and presumably our people had received His gracious gift of forbearance, nevertheless, I persisted in regarding them as unforgiven. Perhaps, as moods of bitterness or cynicism recurrently arose to harass me, I even cherished enough resentment within me to wish, or to hope, that they were unforgiven. The truth is that though I had said most readily to Caleb that it was He whom the people had sinned against, I found myself believing that they had sinned against me. I told myself that this was wrong, that this was the way of a Pharaoh who believed that in some way he was a god, and that I must not think thoughts such as those; yet from time to time I thought them.

In the months that it took to make everything, I had countless enjoyable days with my sons, Gershom and Eliezer. Gershom was bright, quick to learn, and active. Eliezer lacked his brightness, but he was a sensible boy, with a disposition much sweeter than Gershom's. Perhaps because Eliezer was younger, he stayed near Zipporah and me, much more than Gershom did. Indeed, when the work began on the Tabernacle, Gershom seldom came back to our tent, for he worked with the men, making the staves with the carpenters as if he were one of them. Aaron, who frequently irritated good Bezalel with unsolicited advice, came to love Gershom as if he were one of his sons, and a deep friendship arose between Gershom and Aaron's eldest, Nadab, even though Nadab was much older, and, indeed, a grown man.

Over some opposition, I was able to persuade the tribes to create schools for the children. They were hardly real schools, not like the ones I had attended in Egypt. We had neither skilled teachers, nor, for that matter, educated teachers, except for a few Levites, and no scrolls for mathematics or astonomy. I asked Tat-Rin to help us. At first he refused, then grudgingly consented, and ended up enthusiastically with students recommended to him from all the tribes. He began with an insistence on teaching in Egyptian, though he knew Hebrew far better than any of the other Egyptians. As his enthusiasm grew at the brightness of the students, he progressively switched to Hebrew. What our Hebrew teachers taught was our release from slavery, the Ten Words, and the traditions of our fathers, Abraham, Isaac, and Jacob. The tribe of Ephraim faced the necessity to teach their children Hebrew— they were the most Egyptian of our tribes. I wanted our people, the grownups, to study the laws I had recorded on the sacred mountain, but I still felt so aggrieved at the golden calf that I did not at that time suggest this.

My father-in-law, Jethro, asked a favor of me, to teach him how to read and write. I could have gotten one of the Levites to teach him, but I was fearful that to do so might embarrass him. Jethro had become suddenly very old, and the bitter recollection of his children's disloyalty and cruelty to him weighed heavily on him. I taught him myself, having patience for a pathetic slowness which I tried to make light of. Often Zipporah sat with us, listening to the lesson. One day she too asked for a quill, and, in another day or so, she too became my student. She was as quick as Jethro had become slow, but never once did she let her father know that she mastered the parts of lessons which seemed to escape him. The evenings when we sat together, with quill and parchment, were tranquil and restful.

Often there were visitors: Aaron and Joshua and Tat-Rin, Anquru, and Qurmene and Nephros, and Elyaqim and Ben Onim. Often the tribal representatives came to me. The Benjaminite—I cannot remember his name—always fawned on me, overeager to please me and to agree with me, no matter what outrageous thing I might say. My cousin Korah was invariably resentful and even discourteous. He it was who, on a nasty evening, reproached me for having designated Aaron to become the high priest, and openly he charged me with having chosen Aaron only because he was my brother. I did not dispute with Korah; I let him speak, and I listened to his bitter words, and I said curtly that Aaron was my choice, and Aaron it would be.

I remember most vividly how completely and gracefully my Zipporah seemed to efface herself when visitors came, as if she were not there. She would sit in the corner, with her small lamp burning, and sew or practice her writing. I saw her look up in distress and anger at Korah, and for a moment I feared that she would say or do something. She said nothing and did nothing. I think that Korah never realized she was there.

My brother-in-law, Hur, came from time to time, my sister, Miriam, almost never. When Miriam did come, she ignored Zipporah, and complained to me about some kind of grievance or other, always tiny and always magnified far beyond its importance.

The best times of all were when Caleb came, bringing with him his wife, Leah, named for the wife of our forefather Jacob. Leah was short of stature, rather fat, and very jolly. When Caleb and Leah came, we knew we would have an evening of laughter. Sometimes Zipporah would become a little angry at Caleb, for she could become irked when he teased me. The teasing, even in those days, was not so much of me as about our people. When I had come down the second time with the Two Tablets, I had stood on the promontory, looking into the sun. Our people began to believe that, so brightly did my face reflect the sun, they could not look at me. Indeed, it was told that I wore a mask to shield them from the brightness of my face and would not take it off until the Tabernacle was completed, but that I would enter into the Holy of Holies without it. Sometimes Caleb's first words when he came were, "Is your mask on, Moses?"

It took a little time for Zipporah to learn that Caleb was not a clown. This she learned in time, and then spoke to me of the acuteness of his mind and the steadfastness which she thought she had discerned in him. One night after they had gone, I said to her, "If anything should happen to me, it is Caleb who should take my place."

I often ask myself if I ever, by syllable or word, let Caleb know this. Oh, he knew my affection for him. He knew my trust of him. He knew that it was he, and virtually he alone, whom I constantly consulted. Joshua, you must understand, was our military commander, and the best we could have had. But Caleb was my adviser, my counselor, the man to whom I could unburden myself about doubts and anxieties and to whom I could speak about my hopes. I said nothing to him; it was enough to have made the mistake with Aaron.

Yes, those were wonderful months. Especially because I was somehow able to persuade myself that I had reached the climax of what I could do: I had brought our people, with His help, out of slavery, led them to the mountain, skilled them in the Ten Words, and composed for them a book of laws which I would in due time give them. All that remained was for us to move steadily, in accordance with plans worked out in advance, to the land of Canaan. There was little more that I needed to do, little more that our people needed me for. I suppose that all men whose lives are somewhat different from ordinary lives come to regard certain events as the high point, and all that comes thereafter is a gradual, a peaceful settling down to rest and quiet. The journey to Canaan still lay ahead, but surely it would be no more difficult than the journey to the mountain, especially since by now we had the experience of having traveled. In Canaan I would rest.

The Tabernacle was completed, and all the vessels finished, and the garments which Aaron and his sons were to wear were all done. Naturally, Aaron wanted an elaborate ceremony for his investiture, and, of course, he recounted to me precisely what he wanted. He showed me how he looked in his priestly clothes—coat, girdle, robe, and over these the ephod, the most sacred of the garments; the silver breastplate, with Light and Truth on them; on his head the turban, and on it a crown of gold. Preposterous but wonderful!

I had said no to none of his proposals, and I even acquiesced in his request that I should myself participate in the ceremony to invest him. I did so. The anointing him with oil was pleasant, but the slaying of a bull and the two rams was not. When it was Aaron's turn to offer sacrifices, I envied him the zeal and pleasure with which he did so. And when, at the end, he lifted up his hands and blessed the people, I too was moved.

How good that I said no to none of his proposals! Even now, as I recall how he gathered his sons about him when it was all over, and how they kissed each other, I am deeply moved. Strangest of all is my recollection of the way in which Nadab called to my son Gershom to join them, as if he were part of Aaron's family. Nadab was Aaron's oldest son, and it was to him that the office of high priest would come next. With what joy Gershom ran to Nadab!

It was two days later that the tragedy took place. Nadab and Abihu were doing some work at the altar in the Tabernacle. Suddenly there were shouts, and smoke began to pour from it. There were some who were fearful of entering the Tabernacle. I was not close by, or I would have gone in immediately. When at last someone dared to enter, it was too late: Nadab and Abihu were dead, burnt to death. How did it happen? No one knows. Perhaps they thought the fire on the altar was out; perhaps they were trying to get it to burn higher, and somehow their clothes caught fire.

How majestically Aaron strode to the Tabernacle, unhurried and calm, to see what was happening; how broken and gray he was when he slowly came out. By then I was there. I spoke to Aaron; he did not answer. He went to his tent, and I went with him. He said not a word to me. He sat in his tent as if in some stupor, too shocked to speak, too stricken for tears. As I looked at him, I could not believe that this was the same person who two days earlier had so stirringly raised his hands to bless his people.

I stayed with him all that day and all that night. When at dawn I returned home, it was to hear the weeping of my son Gershom, and his bitter words: "Why did it happen? Why did He let it happen?"

What could I say to assuage my son's grief? This was his first encounter with what men cannot explain. Older men become accustomed to these things, and they do not ask the question with the same passion which I heard in Gershom's voice. He wept on, unconsoled, for I was not able to console him.

I have heard some explain that the death of Aaron's sons was the punishment of Aaron for the golden calf. Fine; but had He not led me to believe that He had forgiven? And why punish the sons, or punish Aaron through his sons? Again, there are those who say that the sons brought strange fire, that they should have let the sacred fire descend from heaven as it does on the morning of the equinox, and not have used their fire-bow for man-made fire. I know that people believe that sacred fire does descend, and quite possibly it does, but I for one have never seen it. Moreover, what possible difference could it make to Him whether it was one kind of fire or another? Or was it simply an accident? An accident, not something that He had caused to happen. But then why had He not prevented the accident from happening?

As to His punishing man, even though He had told me that He was gracious and merciful, could it be that because men, when wronged by other men, feel vengeful and wish to retaliate and to punish, they believe that He too punishes in retaliation? This I could not and cannot believe. It was wicked enough that man was vengeful; should He too be vengeful? It occurred to me that I must add to the laws I had written that men must not retain grudges or take vengeance. If vengeance was to be done, let it be Him who does it, never man.

But I did not think all those things as I sat with my son Gershom. I tried the best I could to comfort him, and so did Zipporah.

I did not succeed. But at least it was in the presence of the two of us that he did his searing weeping.

It was when night came that those thoughts came to me. After Gershom had managed to fall asleep, I left my tent and I walked beyond the encampment. Alone, I prayed to Him, asking Him to explain to me, so that I could explain to my son Gershom. I prayed long and ardently. Alas, He did not answer me. Perhaps He felt that in telling me that He was gracious and merciful, He had told me enough. Or perhaps He did not want me to understand these things. They are for Him alone to understand.

For a few days, I was more strongly concerned by the tragedy to Aaron, and Gershom's bitterness, than by the need to plan our further journey. I continued to teach Jethro and Zipporah how to read and write, and Gershom, being young, seemed to go about and to move about, and slowly he recovered something of his liveliness. Aaron's tragedy managed to slip away from all of us except Aaron himself. Because it slipped away, my recollection of that period, our months at the sacred mountain, now seem to me to be of an almost unbroken tranquility. Even in the days that are quiet for a people, there is a person here or a person there who experiences sorrow and tragedy.

But it was time to move on. I gave instructions for the Tabernacle to be dismantled, carefully, of course, so that it could be put together again. All was carefully organized for us to set out on our way, not so much toward the land of Canaan as away from the sacred mountain.

In the midst of the last preparations, Jethro came to me. "Moses, I must return to Midian."

I said, "How can you? They drove you out."

"Perhaps they have had time to consider what they have done, and they regret it. Perhaps they will welcome me back."

"And perhaps they will not."

"I have to know, Moses. I have to return to them."

"No!" I said to him. "You belong with us, with your daughter Zipporah."

"I must go back, Moses. As you went back to Egypt."

I said, "Forgive me, but you are an old man, and I was a young man. You have become very weak, Jethro. Without Zipporah to look after you, I am not sure you could manage the journey to Midian."

"My spirit is frailer than my body, Moses. It is my spirit which needs to be strengthened!"

We talked and talked; I could not persuade him. I sent for Ben Onim and Elyaqim, and told them of Jethro's desire, and asked if one or both would go with him. I warned them of what they might encounter when they came to Midian. Both were willing to go, out of their devotion to Jethro. Then Ben Onim said, "From what you say, Jethro needs a woman's care. Can his daughter, Zipporah, come with us to look after him on the way?"

I said I would ask her. Her first response was to say that Jethro must not go. Then she herself spoke to him, and she returned to me to say, "I will go."

Then Ben Onim came to me. "Moses, you may need one of us to help you through this Wilderness. Elyaqim will stay. I will take Jethro, if Zipporah comes along. It is only a half day's journey to Midian. We should be able to join you in a day or two."

I wept when I bade farewell to Jethro. I assured him that he was welcome to return to us. But I knew I would never see that great but broken man again. Then the three of them departed.

The next morning we began our journey. Our preparations had been excellent; all went smoothly.

That is, for three days.

Then, wearingly, the complaints began again. Complaints as before. Complaints over the food for the journey, for we could not eat as well when traveling as we did in the oasis near the mountain. How well I remember, at a meeting of the tribal council, the words of the representative from Ephraim: "We remember the fish which we ate, free, in Egypt: the cucumbers, the melons, the leeks, the onions, the garlic. There is nothing here but this tasteless manna." The free fish in Egypt! What silliness to remember what had never happened!

I found in myself an impatience and a resentment quite beyond anything I had experienced before at our people's complaints. I gave myself an explanation: when we had left Egypt, we were a rabble, not a people. We had fled from slavery, and had narrowly escaped being re-enslaved when the Egyptians had pursued us; we were then inexperienced. Now, no one pursued us. Now we had been at the sacred mountain, and, through the covenant in blood, we had become His sacred people; now we had the Ten Words, and we had judges; to be on the march was nothing new. Was I, in the light of all this, not justified in being irked, in being aggrieved, in being exceedingly provoked with our people?

Besides, I was worried that Zipporah and Ben Onim had not yet rejoined us. They were late, and I wondered why, thinking of awful things that had befallen them, and I even contemplated sending Elyaqim, if he were willing to go, to look for them.

In this way, I explain why I was angry, always remembering that Jethro had told me that there was anger within me, anger which I usually concealed and restrained. Now it so threatened to injure me that I went outside the encampment and I prayed to Him. Should I say I prayed? Should I not rather say that I poured out my bitterness? I said to Him that my task was no longer within my capacity, that I could not alone continue to lead the people; I needed men to help me. Do you ask, what about the council of the tribal representatives? Yes, I had that, and it was valuable. But they were strictly men each of his tribe, not men concerned for all the people of Israel. Numbering only twelve, with the Egyptian member a thirteenth, they were too few to be the voice of all the people. When He replied to me, it was to propose that I assemble seventy men whom I could consult. He told me also that just as He spoke to me from time to time, so He would speak to all seventy of us.

I have said before that I had no title, neither king nor ruler nor chief. This unique situation, however, that He spoke to me from time to time suggested not a title, but a name: prophet; someone to whom He speaks and who then speaks to the people. Unless I am mistaken, our father Abraham was called a prophet by some. I was a prophet; all the seventy were to be prophets.

Two of the seventy whom I selected, this after appropriate consultation, should have assembled with the others at the place to which I had convened them, outside the Tabernacle, but for some reason these two, Eldad and Medad, remained within the encampment. Joshua came running to me with the report that these two men, Eldad and Medad, were already prophesying in the midst of the camp, and he wanted me to confront them and to forbid them. I was too delighted to have the seventy share my burdens to be willing to silence the two men, and I told this to Joshua. What I did not say to him was that his zeal was misguided. Indeed, I think I was too subtle in chiding him, for I phrased what I said in this way, that Joshua did not need to be zealous for my honor. What I meant was that he did not need to be jealous of others who might rise to leadership. I think Joshua took no notice of my subtlety. He was at all times an exceedingly able and reliable man, from whom an occasional smile would have been welcome. I respected his capacities, and I urgently needed his help. I only wished that I could feel for him the deep affection which I felt for Caleb.

Since our people were tired of the manna and were remembering the glorious food they had been given in Egypt, He did a wondrous thing. He sent in flock after flock of quail. Here was a delicacy for our people, and how they seemed to crave it! There was an abundance, an overabundance of quail, and many ate more than they should. I walked among tents and encountered Elyaqim. I said, jocularly, "Are you enjoying the quail, Elyaqim?" He shook his head. "They are sometimes poisonous, Moses. A little quail meat is not dangerous, a lot is. I eat none of it." Immediately, I had heralds proclaim that people should not eat too much. But our people stuffed themselves in a most unseemly way. In the next days many of them became sick, and, to my horror, some died. Then had He done a thing truly wondrous in sending the quail? Or was He punishing our people for their yearning for Egypt? I said to myself, no, a better explanation is that it was an accident.

But I had to tell myself that this was not a much better explanation, for why did He allow accidents?

Miriam came to see me and was in my tent before I could keep her from entering. I could not recall when she had last come; it was enough for me that I saw her at the meeting of the council of the tribal representatives. I was as cordial to her as I could be. She asked for my health and told me she worried about my great burdens. Then she said, "Has your wife left you?"

"My wife is away. She has gone to Midian with her father."

"Has she left you for good?"

I did not answer her immediately. After a moment I said, "You will be sorry to learn that I expect her back at any moment."

She said, "I am indeed sorry to learn this."

"We have nothing to talk about, Miriam. Please leave."

"She is a Wilderness woman and not worthy of you."

"That will be enough."

"I have at times watched your tent. When you are away busy, and the children are out, she brings men in."

I rose and came to her, my hand uplifted to strike her. Then I saw in the light that came from the portal how old she had become, and how her skin had become pale, disfigured by red blotches. I lowered my hand. I raised it again, but only to point to the portal, and I stood there with my arm outstretched as if I were a statue. I whispered the words, "Get out." She must have found my words very menacing, for she arose and left.

Not for a moment did I believe that Zipporah was bringing men to our tent. Or, if she was, I had no suspicion that anything was amiss, for undoubtedly she had some worthy purpose—whatever it might be—in doing so. I did not send for Caleb, I ran to him. Together we walked outside the encampment. I said, "You are my friend, and you must tell me the truth. Have you heard tales of my wife bringing men to our tent when I am away?"

He looked directly at me. "Not tales, but a tale. Once someone said this to me—just a day or so ago."

"And is this a report that is known throughout our people?"

"I heard it from one person."

"And to whom have you told it besides your wife?"

"I have told it to no one, not even my wife."

"Who told it to you?"

He hesitated. "Aaron."

"Where and when?"

"We met as each was walking. He told it to me in great confidence."

I thought for a moment. "I ask you to do this for me. Question your wife, Leah, and let me know if she has heard this report. Come to me to my tent as soon as you have spoken to your wife."

I left him and slowly returned to my tent, acutely weary, and conscious that my heart was pounding. I could not contain myself in my impatience for Caleb to come to me, but strode up and down, clenching my fists and unclenching them. Caleb came to the tent. "Leah has heard the report."

"From whom?"

"From three or four women."

"And where did they hear it?"

"As best Leah could tell me, the source is your sister, Miriam."

Miriam and Aaron, my brother and sister!

"What more have you heard?"

"She has gone with her father to Midian, but only because she is enamored of Ben Onim. If she returns, it will be after dallying with him. But it is to be doubted that she will return."

"What men has she had in our tent?"

"That no one has told me."

I went to Aaron's tent. He greeted me, but I did not greet him. I said, curtly, "Come with me." Perhaps my countenance frightened him. He rose quickly and followed me, asking what I wished to speak to him about, but I did not answer him. I led him into the encampment of the Judahites, to the tent of Hur and Miriam. I said to her, "Come with me."

I led them outside the encampment. I turned to the two of them. "You will explain to me the slandering of my wife."

Miriam spoke. "It is not slander. It is the truth. Your wife is a whore. A whore like the Cushite whores in Egypt."

"You will tell me how you know."

"Men have been seen going to your tent."

"What men?"

"Several men."

"What are their names?"

"I do not know."

"Who saw them?"

"Various people."

"And various people have told you that my wife is a whore?"

"They have said that she has let men come to her tent."

I turned to Aaron. "What do you know?"

He stammered. "Only what Miriam has told me."

"And to whom besides Caleb have you gossiped about my wife?"

He took a step back. "I have mentioned it to only one or two people. Joshua and my son Eleazar."

I turned back to Miriam. "To whom have you spoken about my wife?"

"It is something people should know."

"You have spoken to many?"

"And why should I not?"

"Because I am your brother, that is why."

"She is a Wilderness woman."

Then words suddenly flew to my tongue, and I upbraided her and I cursed her. She tried to interrupt, but I did not let her. She fell to the ground, and Aaron said, "Moses, she is sick!" He bent over to her. "She has leprosy, Moses!"

I turned away. Then I said to Aaron, "Let someone attend her, outside the camp. And let her not come back until she is cured."

I returned to my tent. Joshua was waiting for me outside it. "We must discuss the route we will take to Canaan, Moses."

I said, "I must rest, for my head pains me terribly. I shall send for you." As he turned to go, I said, "My sister, Miriam, has leprosy. She has slandered my wife, and now she has leprosy." I told him where I had left her and Aaron. "Send some women there with medications. And tell them that she slandered my wife, and now has leprosy." I saw that men and women were nearby and must have heard what I was saying. To make sure that they did, I repeated it: "Miriam has slandered my wife, and now she has leprosy." Before I went into the tent, I asked Joshua to send Caleb to me at once.

I said to Caleb, "I ask you to tell your wife, Leah, but not in confidence, that Miriam has slandered my wife, and now she has leprosy."

"She does have leprosy, Moses?"

"Yes, she does."

"And people are to think that the leprosy has come because she slandered Zipporah?"

"Is that too dishonest, Caleb?"

"You are very harsh with Miriam."

"Zipporah is my wife."

"You are too harsh. I do not condone her gossiping. But you are blind to her virtues, Moses. And you have always been."

"She has slandered my wife. She has called my wife a whore. Am I to be grateful to Miriam?"

"You must remember her days in the slave— No; I am wrong, Moses. I can say only that Miriam does good as well as evil."

I said, "She is my sister, and she is my enemy."

He said, "When will Zipporah return?"

What could I answer, not knowing? I said to him, "I cannot go on, Caleb. I cannot bear the complaints of our people, the endless problems, like the sickness and the death from the quail— Now all the people have heard that my beloved wife is a whore, that she brings men into my tent! It is too much."

He said, quietly, "I have given it much thought, Moses. It is good to be a leader, as you are. But one must pay a price, a series of prices. One price is the disapproval by some, one price is the contempt by others, a third price is the disparagement by still others. Now your wife—this too is part of the price."

I said, "Would you pay the price, Caleb?"

"I am your loyal friend, for I know you. From time to time I hear minor slanders of you: that you are arbitrary, tyrannical, self-centered. I heard a great deal when you made Aaron the high priest. Ten thousand Hebrews can do better than you do, for you are incompetent! None of the gossip about you has accorded with the truth that I have known about you, but the gossip is there. Would I pay the price? How much do I want the power a leader has? How much am I devoted to my people, to withstand the problems, the abuse, the burdens?" He smiled. "I am a foolish man, Moses. I think I would pay the price. But I have not yet had reason to pay the price. So I do not know for sure."

I said, "I am worried that something has happened to Zipporah. At the hands of her brothers."

"If she were back here safe, you would not be so distraught at the gossip."

"I resent it!" I snapped, "My wife is chastity itself. I resent it." Then I said, "Who are the men who have come to the tent?" He shook his head. I said, "I do not believe there were any."

That was true. But I needed to be sure, beyond any doubt, that there had been no men. And my heart almost stopped beating as I said to myself, suppose there were such men?

Caleb left me. My head was a jumble of thoughts: that there had been no men, that there had been men. And Joshua wanted to discuss our route.

I did not sleep that night. The price of being the leader seemed to me too high.

Joshua came in the morning. "I have spoken with Elyaqim and with the Egyptian Tat-Rin who understands geography. Canaan lies more to the north than to the east. There are wildernesses to traverse. Then there will be a city called Hormah, and after that the city called Beer-sheba."

"Is not Beer-sheba the city where Abraham and Isaac dwelled?"

"So I have heard from my mother."

"What is the question about the route, Joshua?"

"There is no question. I wanted only to confirm with you that we will direct ourselves more north than east."

"Of course. Do you suppose—"

At that moment, Zipporah entered the tent, followed by Ben

Onim. As she and I embraced, Ben Onim said, "Moses! She is wonderful." I did not like his words of praise, not at that moment. "Wonderful!" Joshua said something about returning a little later and he left. I said, "You were gone so long."

"There was trouble, Moses."

"Her brothers," said Ben Onim. "She was wonderful. She made them obey her, made them take Jethro in, made them treat him with the respect due him."

"Is all well, Zipporah?"

"Now it is. At first it was not. They were mean, they were cruel. But I was not afraid of them!" She went on to tell what had happened, interrupted now and again by Ben Onim. Three times she said that all was well with Jethro, for that seemed more important to her than the account of how she had confronted her family, made her demands, and cajoled and scolded, and even threatened. Through all her words, to which I listened as carefully as I could, the question kept rising to my tongue, "Who were the men who came to our tent?" I restrained myself and did not ask it, not even when she had finished and had thanked Ben Onim for accompanying her. She was tired, for they had left Midian the day before, in the afternoon. I did ask, "Where did you spend the night?" She said, "We found a cave on a low hill. I slept inside, and Ben Onim outside." She blushed. "He went into the cave before I did, to see that all was well, and once I went into it, he would not come in, not even to eat our morsel of cheese." She yawned. The children came by for a moment, and I saw how lovingly they greeted her. Then who were those men who had come to the tent? I told myself that the way in which I, or the boys, could return to the tent at any moment made it silly to think that she brought men to the tent for unchaste reasons. Yet the need to ask her grew in me, for I had to know, I had to have some explanation.

I let her lie down to sleep while I sought out Joshua. The conversation earlier that day was mostly clear to me, but not all of it, and I could not give myself an explanation of exactly what Joshua had come to discuss with me. The names Hormah and Beer-sheba came to my mind. They were cities. There were traditions, too, about other cities, Abraham at Hebron, and Jacob at Shechem. Our father Jacob had seen angels ascending and descending a ladder into heaven at Luz which had changed its name to Bethel. Somehow the names of these cities which my mother, Jochebed, had mentioned did not seem real, for Canaan must be an empty land, or otherwise it could not have been promised to Abraham. Moreover, Abraham had enormous flocks as did his nephew Lot, and he had let Lot choose the part of Canaan he preferred, with Abraham to take what was left, so that clearly the land of Canaan was an empty land. Then how could there be those cities, if the land was empty? Or was it that the land was mostly empty, except for the few cities? From the Egyptians I had heard of only one city, Jericho the city of palm trees, where it was said that springs of warm water welled up, and men with stomach disorders could drink the water and find relief.

When I sat down with Joshua, I said to him, "We do not know enough about the land of Canaan. We should send some scouts to observe the land, to advise us how we should settle ourselves in the land."

He said, "That was my thought too."

I said, "Abraham had his flocks. Is any of the land farm land? Are there orchards? We should know before we all arrive there. And we should have some notion where each of the tribes will settle, for it would be bad if two tribes each wanted the same land."

He said, "I will be pleased to lead some scouts there."

I said, "I want you to go. But since this is not a military matter, I shall ask Caleb to be the leader of the scouts." I looked at him, to try to notice whether my mention of Caleb would be agreeable to him or not. Nothing in his countenance revealed his feelings.

I assembled the tribal representatives that evening, asked them to nominate each a scout from his tribe, and then announced that Caleb would be their leader. He came to me after the meeting, happy and expectant. "I thank you for your confidence in me, Moses. I shall lead them as best I can." I knew clearly from that moment that Caleb had his own private wish to be a leader. And he was a man whose qualities were such that I could entrust anything to him. That is, that evening I said to myself I could trust him for anything, anything at all. I am pained when I remember those thoughts.

The next day we had the meetings with the scouts. I told them they would go north through the Negeb to Beer-sheba and from there throughout the land. Especially they should study the cities, to learn their size and whether or not they were walled and armed, or seemingly peaceful. They were to bring back samples of the crops and the fruits. We would not move at all, I said, until they returned with their report.

Only after I arranged for the spies to leave the next day did the thought occur to me, suppose the land were not empty? Suppose the land had become peopled since the time of Abraham, through tribes which had moved in? Would there be room for us too? And would the tribes that were there receive us with the friendliness that our father Abraham found? And if not, what then? I dismissed the thought; it was too chilling. But I had to talk this over with Caleb, later that night.

The matter of the scouts had kept me very busy so that I had not had any real privacy with Zipporah. But that evening, as the scouts were preparing to leave, I was alone with her, and the children were away. I was about to speak to her of what was still very much on my mind; instead, she said to me, "I have heard that Miriam is outside the encampment, with leprosy."

I said, "Yes, that is so." I waited for her to say something more. She said only, "That is too bad."

Then I said, "Who told you?"

"Some of the women."

"What else did they tell you?"

"Nothing. What do you mean, Moses?"

Then I spoke the words. "Miriam has been slandering you, and she has become leprous."

"In what way has she slandered me, Moses?"

"She has said loathsome things about you."

Her lips began to quiver. "She has never liked me. What has she said?"

"That you have men visit you here in the tent when I and the children are away."

Her face became crimson and, to my surprise, she began to laugh hysterically. Then she ceased laughing and began to cry and even wail. "Has she called me a Wilderness woman? Or has she called me something worse? Tell me, Moses."

"She has never liked you, and I have never forgiven her for her discourtesies to you."

She came to me and lay at my feet, looking up at me. "You must tell me, Moses. Have you believed her?"

"I have not believed her, Zipporah. I have never waivered from my trust in you."

She said, "But suppose men did come to my tent, when you were away? Would it be to be a whore with them, Moses?"

"I have never thought that, Zipporah."

She rose to her knees. "Men have come here. I have asked them here. When you were to be away, away for more than a few minutes. Light another lamp, Moses!" My hand shook as I poured some oil into a second lamp, for I was profoundly disturbed that men had indeed come. She had risen and gone to the box in which she kept her few possessions. I saw her open the box and take out something wrapped in a black dress. Slowly she unwrapped the dress. "Bring the lamp here, Moses." I brought it to her. She threw the dress onto the ground, and she held up for me the parchment sheets on which I had written the laws. "Look, Moses, at the sheets you wrote. Look, too, at the copy I have made." She showed me the parchment with my own handwriting, and next to it, a parchment sheet, neat and orderly, with the letters drawn in beautiful form and clarity. "You taught me to read and write; I learned to write so as to make a copy of your writing for you. And I had some of the Levites who teach children come to me and read your writing and mine, to make sure that I have made no mistakes. They are the men who came here. I wanted to finish before I told you and showed you. I will tell you who the men were, men whom I swore to secrecy, so that you would not learn until the copying was done. They are—"

"I do not care who they are!"

"I insist on telling you, for you must know what kind of a whore your Midianite wife is!" She began to cry, all the while giving me the names of four of the Levites. "Ask them how it was to go to bed with the wife of Moses! Ask them, Moses!" Carefully she re-wrapped the parchment sheets, sobbing all the while. Then she lay on the ground and beat it with her fists. "A Midianite whore is your wife!"

I lay on the ground beside her, trying to quiet her, telling her what it meant to me that she was copying my parchment sheets. She suddenly seized me, held me tight. "Love me, Moses, as I love you."

Never have a man and wife loved each other as Zipporah and I loved each other.

I excuse my blindness because of the chagrin, the shock that my own brother and sister had maligned my wife. When one is a leader, he is well advised to look below the surface and to under-stand the real motives which prompt people to do things. In my indignation at the unjust calumnies against Zipporah, I took things as they seemed: that my sister, Miriam, hated Zipporah because she was an outsider, and she vented her hatred by maligning her. But was it Zipporah who was the target, or was it I? Was it far-fetched to suppose that Zipporah was only incidental to some half-conceived plan someone had made? If I, not Zipporah, was the tar-get, who was it that was aiming his arrow? Aaron? That seemed unlikely. Hur? What purpose could he have? Again, unlikely. Then who, and why?

The men Zipporah had had visit her were Levites, and Korah was a Levite, and Korah was hostile, and offended that I had named Aaron and not him the high priest. Was Korah behind it all, with Miriam an unconscious tool? Should I inquire into this, summoning the Levites and cross-examining them?

Or was I becoming suspicious, as in my youth I had been taught in the Egyptian schools that a king—in my case, a leader—needed to cultivate a judicious measure of suspicion? Was I creating a phantasy and turning it into a reality? Was there some undercurrent of rebellion flowing in our camp, accumulating strength so as to emerge into the open? And if it came into the open, what would I do?

When I summoned Caleb for the last talk with him about the scouts whom he was to lead, I had this matter very much in my mind. I left it for last. I told him what I wanted the scouts to find out. I reminded him that our fathers, Abraham, Isaac, and Jacob, had lived in Canaan, Abraham being an immigrant there and Jacob an emigrant, but they had lived there. Except for the unhappy incident of Dinah at Shechem, they had lived peacefully with their neighbors, and when Sarah had died, Ephron the Hittite had been honored to sell the double cave of Machpelah to Abraham. In that cave, Abraham and Sarah, Isaac and Rebekkah, and Jacob had been buried. But all that was generations ago, over four hundred years ago. For four centuries we had not been in the land. We needed to know how the land was now, and what peoples were there, and if the friendliness which our fathers had found would greet us too. My impression, which I conveyed to Caleb and about which he nodded, was that Canaan was an empty land, with only a small number of people, and few cities of significance. But most of all I needed to know the spirit of the people, whether they would welcome us as they had welcomed Abraham, or whether, with the passing of time, other peoples had come to settle, so that the land was no longer empty, and the friendliness gone. In short, what I wanted Caleb and his scouts to do was to confirm that Canaan was as it had been in the days of our fathers.

He and I understood each other. Fully. Then I turned to the matter that was much more on my mind. "Caleb, were the accusations about Zipporah directed at her or at me?"

He understood my question. He thought for a moment. "When a man has been a leader for a period of time, he makes his enemies. His actions prompt some to think that they are wiser and more able, and this one or that one thinks he would be a better leader." He smiled. "Your accomplishments have aroused envy, Moses.

You have made your position so lofty that a number of people wish it for themselves. Including me."

I smiled back at him. "And are you also plotting to seize my position?"

"I am a very poor plotter, Moses."

"Do you know who is plotting?"

He shook his head. "I know only rumors. It would be unfair to mention by name people about whom there is gossip."

"And what should I do?"

"Only one thing: be quiet in your mind, for envy of you is most natural. Do not be concerned about it. The moment when I learn that it should concern you, I will inform you."

We embraced, and he left.

I looked at the parchment sheets that Zipporah had copied. I remembered having asked her to throw away the early sheets. She had not done so. I had separated these from the final sheets, but somehow they had become mixed up. My laws were there, but no longer systematic or free from repetition.

I saw the copies the four Levites had made. They too were a mixture of the early beginnings and the last writings.

I wondered if I should not gather these copies together and substitute a carefully reworked version such as I had ended up with on the mountain.

I decided to do that, but to delay it, so as not to offend my beloved Zipporah.

I never got to that, for when later I tried to, there were already in existence copies of the copies, in some abundance!

∗ CHAPTER IX

Little of note occurred in the days the scouts were away. Miriam recovered from her leprosy, and, mindful of Caleb's words that I had been unjust to her, I personally joined with Hur in escorting her back into our camp. Or, perhaps it was not Caleb's words, but Zipporah's, for my wife, deeply hurt though she was, insisted that I must do my family duty to Miriam. When I came to Miriam with Hur, her appearance, though she was free of leprosy, gave Hur some anxiety, for she seemed not at all healthy, as if there were not many more months of life left for her.

Something in me had prompted me to want to send our scouts into the land of Canaan even before Joshua had mentioned it. Perhaps that something was only normal prudence, or else it was intuition that all would not be well. Twelve happy scouts set off for Canaan. None of them returned happy, and ten of them were very unhappy. I should have known better than to have them bring their report to an assembly of all the people, but I did this in the belief that our people would be encouraged by hearing how good it would be in Canaan. To their dismay, and my overwhelming distress, their report was gloomy. It told that in Canaan there were many cities, fortified ones, and fortified cities meant that warfare was usual. Moreover, though there was still empty land, the land was by no means empty. There were left so many traces of battles fought by the people of Canaan either against outsiders or among themselves as to give the impression of a land where soldiers and armies were the highest necessity. Moreover, our scouts had seen soldiers and military encampments, and they reported that the troops were magnificent human specimens, giants of men, and their equipment was of the best, especially to the north where the land was fertile farming territory. In the report of what the spies had seen, there was complete agreement, Caleb and Joshua too joining in.

It was the Benjaminite—I do not understand why I can never remember his name—who spoke the words which turned a peaceful assembly into a near-riot. As in the case of some other tribes, he was both their representative to the council and one of the twelve scouts. After Caleb and the others had given the report of what they had seen and showed the luxuriant grapes they had brought back, the Benjaminite spoke first. Before, at our meetings, he had seemed a mild person, and he had slightly annoyed me by agreeing with me too readily and too often. As I now remember the words he spoke, they seemed to say this, that all the scouts were in agreement in what they had seen, with their disagreement centered only in what it all meant. To him the meaning was clear: First, Canaan was a place of hostile, warlike people, devoid of any friendliness. Second, they possessed a formidable military might, beyond anything that we could muster. Therefore, if we were to go into Canaan, the only result could be the sheerest disaster, for we would be cut to pieces by the fierce soldiers of the land. Third, he could not say where we should go, but it was certain that we could not go to Canaan.

Since Caleb was the leader of the scouts, I let him reply. It was a very good answer he made, with his usual insight and his usual humor. The soldiers in Canaan were only men, not deities, and formidable as they might seem, other armies had been better in donning their armor than in fighting. They were normal men, but it would not surprise him, Caleb said, to hear reports that they were all giants, in comparison with whom we would seem as tiny as grasshoppers. There was no reason for panic, no reason for discouragement, he said. We had traversed the Wilderness, and surely a people who could do that had no need to fear entering Canaan.

Then the man from Manasseh, whose Hebrew was halting and whose Egyptian accent was marked, arose. About Canaan he said very little. "This opinion of Caleb ben Jephunneh of the tribe of Judah is absurd. It is silly to suppose that we, lacking trained troops and good implements of war, can dare to enter a land where military science is something carefully studied and pursued. The fact is, we are in a desperate situation. If we go into Canaan, we will surely die, and one can ask why we were brought out from Egypt—was it for us to be killed in Canaan? We cannot, we dare not go into that land."

With Caleb, the response had been silence. When the Benjaminite had spoken, there had been a murmur of anxiety. Now, with the Manassite, there was a loud response, for people not only agreed with him, but even shouted their agreement. At length they quieted down, and the man from Reuben—I remember his name, Dathan ben Eliab—raised his hand for silence. "We Hebrews must not deceive ourselves. It is bad enough that we have been deceived." He pointed a finger at me. "There is our deceiver, the man, Moses. There is only one thing that we can do: get rid of this man, Moses, and designate someone else who will lead us back where we belong, back to Egypt which we should never have left!" The response was tumultuous, and people one after another picked up the phrase, "Back to Egypt." And here and there someone shouted, "Down with Moses!"

With difficulty, some order was restored. Joshua seemed to wish to speak, and he came forward. When he began, there was so much noise that his first words could not be heard, and, moreover, his voice is not powerful. Gradually, the assembly became still, and Joshua was able to raise his voice a little bit. "We have heard how strong the Canaanites are in their armies and in their equipment, and that we have no real hope to be able to settle in that land, fertile and inviting as it is. Our scouts have been frightened, and our people are frightened. We have heard from Caleb of the tribe of Judah that we need not be afraid, but should simply move on. From Dathan of the tribe of Reuben we have heard that we should find a new leader and return to Egypt. In my opinion, neither of these views is a just one. My friend Caleb is right in saying that we should not fear, but it is one thing not to fear and quite another thing to succeed in a military endeavor. As to a new leader, this I shall not discuss, for I remember who it was who brought us out of slavery, and I want no leader other than Moses. As for returning to Egypt, have you forgotten the reality? Or, have you thought that perhaps our friend Dathan might go as your emissary and visit the Pharaoh and get from him a royal welcome, and special privileges, and even a rich subsidy? Between what Caleb has said and Dathan's irresponsible suggestion that we return to Egypt, there lies the one and only course of action: to move into Canaan but only after we prepare. Prepare! That means we become ready for anything that awaits us in Canaan. If some are to be farmers, they must train to be farmers. If we are to fight battles, then we must prepare to be invincible soldiers. Resisting marauders in the Wilderness is not the same as besieging a walled and armed city. Slowly and carefully we shall make the necessary preparations, and then we shall move on."

From the distance came the faint sound we had heard at Sinai. Suddenly the Wilderness sky was lighted up by flames which seemed to come from south of us, the south where Sinai lay. Joshua continued to talk, but no one listened to him, for cries of fear and terror arose among the people, and many of them seemed to flee to their tents, as if to hide.

I remained where I was, and I confess that I was frightened by the way in which the sky had lighted up, as if He had heard the words of complaint and was showing His displeasure. From the fringes of our assembly I heard sounds either of people fighting, or else some similar kind of disorder, for our people had become a mob, a discouraged, disconsolate mob. I strode away from the assembly, with some people hissing at me and others spitting on the ground as I walked by. Then I returned to the midst of the people and I raised my hands. "Tomorrow morning the assembly of the seventy and the council of tribal representatives will meet!" I said this over and over again to whoever would listen to me. I made my way to my tent.

It was not alone that I was disheartened by the report of the scouts and the disorder that had ensued, but I now found myself where no leader should be: caught in a crisis in which one could not know what to do, or how to do it. Zipporah lay beside me, partly understanding and partly not. Outside the tent there was still noise, of people shouting "Back to Egypt" and "Down with Moses."

I prayed to Him; He did not answer me.

Throughout the night I lay in fear that some group of them, five or six of them, might force their way into my tent, carry me out, and kill me. I, Moses, lay in fear of my own people! Before, I had had other occasions for fear, as when I saw the burning bush, or came before Pharaoh, or when the Amalekites had attacked us. I do not think that all fears are the same, for some are small and some are large, some are passing and some linger. That night I learned of a fear which was bitter, as if wormwood had come into my mouth.

My thoughts went back to the assembly. How gratified I had been with Caleb's courageous words! Yet, in all honesty, it was the words which Joshua spoke which seemed to me the most appropriate. Caleb with his warmth had not spoken as aptly as had cool, analytical Joshua.

In the morning, the two bodies, the council of representatives and the assembly of seventy, came together to meet with me. I said, "I have not brought you together to hear more speeches. I want to have answers. Caleb, will the tribe of Judah move on with us to Canaan?"

He said, "The tribe of Judah will move on."

One by one I called on the other tribes. Reuben said that it would not move on, Manasseh that it was returning to Egypt. Joshua spoke for Ephraim, that it would move on, Dan that it had not made up its mind. Only Joshua and Caleb spoke in favor; only Dan was undecided; all the rest were against it, though only Manasseh wanted to return to Egypt. Then I asked for silence. "The tribe of Manasseh wishes to return to Egypt. They have that privilege. I ask Anquru, the Egyptian representative: Will you lead Manasseh back to Egypt?"

Anquru came forward. "I will not."

"Is there anyone among your Egyptians who will?"

Anquru said, "I have discussed this with my associate Nephros.

He has promised personally to kill any Egyptian who tries to return to that foul and loathsome country!"

I turned to the representative from Manasseh. "Your tribe may go. You may leave us now and go! Arise, go, take Manasseh from us!" The man did not move. I said, "Any of you who want to go, feel free to leave! Even if you leave only Caleb and Joshua and me, we three shall journey on to the land where Abraham and Isaac and Jacob lived. I shall tell you why." A hush came over them, as they waited for me to continue. I said, "There is nowhere else to go."

For a long moment, no one spoke. Then a voice cried out, "Why do you say that?"

I said, "We cannot return to Egypt. We cannot live forever in the Wilderness. We must go somewhere. Where? To live in Midian, where a handful can survive, but a people as large as we cannot? To Edom, with its rocks and crags? They are our kinfolk, but will they have us? Who knows? Moab also are our kinfolk, but will they have us? Where have we a right to go? Is it not to the land where Abraham, Isaac, and Jacob lived? To a land which He promised them would be ours? Where else can we go? Nowhere!"

No one applauded my words, but also no one opposed them. I longed for Caleb to speak again, to say how inviting the land of Canaan was, so as to stir us to hope and to some warm expectation. He remained silent. We were a dispirited assembly, and when we parted from each other, there was no joy among us, and, so I feared, no courage.

No one spoke to me, except the man from Manasseh. "We will come with you, Moses. I will tell our people: There is nowhere else to go."

I sent for Joshua. "We shall move northward, passing near the city of Hormah, but our route must not take us too close to it. I want emissaries sent ahead, to the king of Hormah. They will explain that we are the descendants of Abraham, Isaac, and Jacob, on our way peacefully returning to the land where our fathers dwelled. They will explain that as Abraham bought the cave of Machpelah, so we will buy whatever land we settle in. They will say that we will dwell in peace and trust with their people. Now, select the emissaries, and let us move ahead."

We resumed our travels, slowly, but in an orderly way. There were no songs as we marched, and no laughter. We traveled because we could not stay still. We traveled without wanting to go where we were going.

The emissaries returned to us. "The king of Hormah replies to us: 'Keep distant from Hormah! Pass by to the west or to the east, but do not come to our city.'"

I said, "Will they trouble us if we stay far enough from them?"

"The king of Hormah did not say."

I asked, "Is Hormah a city of many people? Is there a large army we need to fear?"

"It is not a big city. Its army cannot be large."

I was relieved. We marched on.

The attack on us came at night, a fierce onslaught. Joshua had prepared our men, but the attack was still a surprise. Our soldiers fought bravely, even desperately. I cannot complain that our being dispirited kept us from fighting well. We did some damage to them; we took some prisoners. We did not drive them off; when they had fill of slaughter, they withdrew.

I did not need a detailed report from Joshua to know the extent of the catastrophe to us, for as one walked about the periphery of our encampment, one saw the corpses of our fine young men, and heard the cries of pain of the many wounded. I wondered how much of an army was left to us, for it seemed to me that there was none at all.

When Joshua came to me, he brought two prisoners. "Do you wish to speak to them, to ask questions, Moses?"

"Have you questioned them?"

"I have."

"What have you learned?"

"These prisoners are not soldiers of Hormah. These are from Arad, a city to the north of Hormah. It was not alone the army of Hormah which attacked us, but the armies of many cities, whom the king of Hormah persuaded to join with him."

"What language do these soldiers speak?"

"A form of our Hebrew."

I said to one of the soldiers, "Why have you fought us?"

"You are coming to take away our land."

"Have you not heard that we are coming peacefully, to live side by side with you?"

"You are coming to take away what is ours."

"The land is big enough for you and for us."

"You are coming to take away what is ours."

I made a sign, and Joshua summoned some guards who took the prisoners away. Joshua said, "I did not think we should send the emissaries to Hormah. In doing that, we prepared them for our coming. We should have sent no emissaries."

"You did not say that."

"I only thought it."

"Is there something you are thinking now, and not saying?"

"We can go into Canaan only by conquering it. We no longer have an army that is adequate for that conquest."

I said, "I do not want us to go into Canaan to conquer. I want us to settle there peacefully."

"The Canaanites will not let us."

"We shall still go peacefully."

"We must go prepared for battle."

"But we will go peacefully." He did not answer me. "We will go peacefully. We are not Egyptians, Joshua, to enslave other peoples. We will go peacefully."

"Provided that we are ready for battle."

"You will do the best you can to make our people ready for battle." I raised my hand, to indicate that we had ended. He did not move. "Is there something more?"

"Do you know, Moses, when we can be ready for battle?" I shook my head. "I will tell you. When the boys who are now lads grow into men. When the toddlers grow into lads, and then into men. We have a tiny army, with no young men to replace those who have fallen. We have undergone a total disaster, Moses. It will take years before we can move into Canaan."

"Years?"

"Years. Many years."

"That is impossible, Joshua. We cannot wait many years."

"We have no choice, Moses."

Many years! Now they have passed, and they have indeed been many.

It was bitter to turn about from our journey northward and to revert to the Wilderness, the Wilderness about which so often the taunting question had come, "Did you bring us out of Egypt to kill us in the Wilderness?" Before, the taunt had seemed to me the lament of the hungry, a lament devoid of real basis. Now it seemed all too real, for there was no certainty that we could ever survive the Wilderness. For the very first time, I was unsure of our ultimate achievement.

We were headed back into the Wilderness, and soon again we would find ourselves short of food and short of water. Maybe we were already low in supplies. I went to the supply wagons to learn what our needs were. I heard a biting answer: "Enough have died so that we do not yet lack for food."

If we were to raise a new army, of lads growing into manhood, then our training had to begin. I sent for Korah, my cousin, who hated me. "I ask you to fashion additional schools for our people, for our children."

"There are already schools."

"We need more of them and better ones. We need more teachers. We need men to train our boys to become soldiers."

He said, "So you can lead us into a new disaster?"

I said, "I will look elsewhere for teachers, Korah." I sent him away. I summoned the representative of the tribe of Dan. "Are there teachers in the tribe of Dan?"

"Teachers of what?"

"Teachers of learning, of laws, of mathematics, of astronomy—"

He laughed. "Not among us. No, we are the men with powerful bodies, strong shoulders, brawny arms."

"That training is needed, too."

"That we can do."

I sent for Joshua. "The tribe of Dan will train our young men and boys to be strong."

"Very good."

"How can we forfend against another assault by the Canaanites?"

"The farther we move into the Wilderness, the harder it will be for them to surprise us. I think that we can beat off an attack if we learn about it before it comes. I have created a system of roving sentries."

"Joshua, I have thought of a matter, but not thought it through. The short way into Canaan is to go north, past Hormah, and past Beer-sheba. There must be another way, even a longer way."

"We could go east, Moses, and then turn north, go past that strange lake which is of salt water, and then cross that river that descends so rapidly—they call it the Jordan."

"If we should go that way, perhaps the Canaanites will still expect us to enter from the south, and we would have an easier time."

"I will consider the matter, Moses. Perhaps that is what we should do."

We roamed about the Wilderness, as if aimlessly. It seemed to me that even our children caught the spirit of hopelessness which dominated most of us. It was my responsibility, I knew, to encourage the disheartened, but I was disheartened myself. The representative from Dan asked me to watch some of his teachers; I went to the classes. There were boys running and jumping, and shooting arrows, and casting spears. Then the teacher would call them together and ask, "What shall we do?" The boys answered, "We shall exterminate them!" "Say it again." "Exterminate them!" "Once more." "Exterminate them!"

I told the teachers how well they were training the boys, and hurried to my tent in agony. That was not the training I wanted! "Exterminate them!" That was exactly wrong, exactly against everything I believed in, everything that was precious to me. After a bit, I sought out Caleb, and told him of my agony. He said, "You want too much, Moses. You want to raise a generation of warriors, fine warriors, and you want them not to be warlike."

"If we are raising warriors and only warriors, in what way are we different from other peoples?"

"I think that you cannot have it both ways, Moses."

"I tried to get the Levites, through Korah, to teach our lads other things. He has refused."

"You are a Levite. Speak to other Levites. Speak to the men who have looked at what your wife, Zipporah, has copied. Perhaps there will be Levites who will teach, despite Korah."

I asked Zipporah to bring together the men who had guided her in her copying my law. I told them of my conversation with Korah and his refusal. "It is only among the Levites that there are competent teachers. Can you find me Levites who will teach, despite Korah?"

No one spoke for a bit. Then one man said, "We dare not go against Korah. He is a dangerous, violent man."

I said, "I will arrange to protect you."

"We dare not."

I wanted to press them. It seemed useless. I thanked them again for their work with Zipporah.

We needed the teachers. We needed our people to learn the laws, for I had prepared some of them particularly for our days in the Wilderness. Then an incident took place, a minor one, which I learned of only when it was too late. A man forgot it was the Sabbath and he began collecting pieces of wood for a fire. Immediately he was seized, the next day brought before a judge, condemned, and then taken outside the camp and executed—all in the name of me, Moses, and in His name! No one had asked why the man had desecrated the Sabbath; the judge had completely forgotten that there is such a thing as forgiveness and mercy. I was told about the incident as if I would applaud it. I said nothing; that was not the time to speak. My motive in the laws was for them to be the standards which would preserve people alive, laws through which men could live in freedom and safety; I had not devised laws so as to slay people.

I prayed in deepest agony. He did not answer me.

Then there came the most painful incident of all. I was seated in my tent, lamenting our lack of teachers. Joshua rushed in. "Moses! The tribe of Reuben has seized the supply wagons!" I followed him as quickly as I could, for he was running fast, and I could not. What I beheld was the Reubenites, armed with their spears and bows and arrows, surrounding the wagons, and with Dathan in front of them, telling them to pull them to the side. I shouted to him, "Dathan, what are you doing?" He did not answer me. I tried to walk to him, but men with swords blocked my way, and two men pushed me back. Then another man, who looked like Dathan, came toward me. "We are leaving."

"Then leave, but do not take our supplies."

Dathan called out, "Abiram, pay no attention to him."

Joshua said, "I will summon our soldiers to stop them—"

"Do not stop the men, but stop their taking our supplies. We must not hurt—"

There was noise behind me, where the wagons, which carried the parts of the Tabernacle, were located. I went there quickly, to see Korah and my brother, Aaron, standing face to face, shouting at each other. I came between them. "What is it, Aaron?"

Korah said, "We have had enough! Who are you two to raise yourselves over everybody else? We are taking the Tabernacle. It is as much ours as it is yours."

Joshua said, "There are some Reubenites seizing the Tabernacle."

Korah turned around and called to the men, "Move on! We join our friends of the tribe Reuben."

Aaron said, "Moses! Moses, you must stop them."

I said, "No. Let them go."

"But they are taking the Tabernacle and all the vessels—"

"Let them take them. We do not need them. Joshua, save the supplies."

Korah said, "The Tabernacle is ours. Dathan is our leader. We shall kill you, Moses and Aaron."

Someone behind him threw a spear. It missed me, but only barely. Then Joshua whistled, and at once his whistle was answered, and from here and there young men came running with swords and spears and bows and arrows.

In a few minutes fierce fighting broke out, as Joshua mustered his men. The Reubenites fought back, but our men fought harder, especially with Aaron urging them on.

I cannot bear to recall the havoc. It is easier to accept what Caleb tells me, that the ground opened up and swallowed Dathan and Abiram, and that fire suddenly consumed Korah and those with him. It is easier to accept that than to remember the needless killing that took place, of Hebrews killing Hebrews. It is bitter to remember the shouts from Korah's men, "Down with Moses."

Joshua lost men killed and wounded. Korah was killed, Dathan and Abiram were killed. Killing, killing, killing! Would it not have been better to have let them kill Aaron and me, than for our soldiers to have killed so many of them?

The rebellion was put down, smashed.

I had been dispirited. Now I became despondent.

Despondent, until indignation filled me. What right had Korah to try to seize the Tabernacle, Dathan and Abiram the supplies? How dared they speak against me in the ugly words that they used? Which of any of them was better able than I to have done what had been done, from the beginning, through the Exodus, through the journey to Sinai? Who could have done better? And why should I have had to endure the murmurings, the complaints, the taunts, and now the rebellion! Had I made myself rich at their expense? Had I taken their possessions to keep, or made concubines of their daughters, or slaves of their sons?

Let me confess it: I was glad, even happy, that we put down the rebellion by arms, happy that we had killed the leaders, killed the followers. I was their leader and entitled to be their leader, and they had no right to do as they had done. And I, I and no one else, would lead them finally to the land of Canaan.

Yes, those were the thoughts I had. I, and only I, could lead them! Does any leader ever think differently?

A sense of shame came over me, and silently I called myself a Hebrew Pharaoh. Was it not enough that I had had to do what was necessary? Did I need to gloat over what I had done, as if I and only I could lead them?

Now the Levites supplied us with teachers, and more and more copies of my parchment sheets were written. I would go to watch a class, and hear the Danite teacher say, "Exterminate them," and then the Levite would enter and say, "You shall not oppress a stranger, for you know the heart of the stranger, for you were strangers in Egypt." Sometimes a teacher would ask me to speak to the boys. I usually said the same thing: "We need soldiers. But Hebrews are more than soldiers. Hebrews are a holy people. Study law, learn law, obey law. Let justice be your pursuit. Let peace be your aim."

But sometimes I would say, "Be good soldiers. But let our greatness be that we honor teachers and prophets more than soldiers." Yet I wondered if they listened to me.

Joshua said, "We can think of moving east. But I should like to test our soldiers, and the result, if we are successful, can help us. I want to assault Hormah, with a special group of highly trained men. Assault it, take what supplies we can, and quickly leave. The Canaanites will hear and remember us and will continue to watch for us from the south, even when some day we enter from the east."

I gave him my assent.

To go eastward, I learned from Ben Onim and Elyaqim, would take us across the land of the Edomites, our kinsmen. If they would let us traverse their land, on our word to do no damage, we could save great distances. Moreover, there was a road which would make our travel easier, a road which was called the King's Highway. I therefore sent some emissaries ahead of us to the king of Edom, to speak of our coming in peace, pledging that we would do no damage to their land, not even depending on them for any supplies. I reminded the emissaries that we and the Edomites were kinsmen. I sent the emissaries off in some hope, but at the same time I feared that the Edomites would say no. The emissaries departed for Edom at the same time that Joshua led his troops in their wary, secret assault on Hormah.

Some days passed. Joshua and his men returned in high spirits. The assault on Hormah had gone most smoothly and effectively. Our few soldiers, highly trained, had carried out their assignments with skilled discipline. They took booty, they captured food, they brought back captives. From these we learned to some gratification the news that the Canaanites feared us greatly, but, to my greater consternation, that all of Canaan was pledged to oppose us by force should we enter the land. My hope that I would find rest and quiet in the land disappeared. We could go into Canaan only if we did so by force.

I visited the schools for our boys, hearing again the distasteful cry, "Exterminate them!" But I heard, too, the gratifying words which I had insisted that they learn: "Do not oppress the stranger, for you were strangers in Egypt." When I had Joshua accompany me on these visits, I saw his eyes light up when the children shouted, "Exterminate them!" They did not light up at the words about oppressing strangers.

It had not been, and still was not, my wish that we occupy Canaan by force of conquest. There was room in Canaan for the Canaanites and for us. And through our fathers we had as much right to that land as they had, for since the land was empty when Abraham came to it, those who now lived in it came after Abraham. We had to go into Canaan, for there was nowhere else to go, and He, who is the true owner of all the lands, had promised it to the descendants of Abraham.

Again and again Joshua spoke to me of his satisfaction at the raid on Hormah. "Our training is good; it must become better. Our forces are now small; in a few years, our lads will become men, and then we shall be strong enough." He worked at the training restlessly, tirelessly, for there was on his mind one single obsession, the conquest of Canaan. To him it was futile to speak of deeper things, of the distant future. There was no doubt in my mind that we could have no better military commander than Joshua. There was no doubt in my mind that a vision greater than mere conquest was even more important. When I spoke to Caleb, I could rejoice in his vision of the future, yet Caleb, bright and quick of mind and profound of understanding as he was, seemed unable to grasp that a military expedition is a matter of careful planning, of attention to strictest discipline, of concern for details, and reluctantly I had to tell myself that Caleb could not bring himself to understand military matters. In my conceit, I said to myself that I understood both the military and the limits of the military, but I was forced to conclude that there are among men some minds which can grasp a military need and nothing more than that, and some which can grasp the more ultimate purposes, but not the military necessities.

I had, and I have, no affection for the military mind. But I would have been derelict if I had not recognized that our military need was then more urgent than our ultimate purposes. I saw this clearly, even though it was a bit difficult to see it, for I loved Caleb, but Joshua I could only admire, never love.

We set out on the long, tedious journey around Edom. I think that in what I have told, and in what has been told about me, I have spoken of the death of people only when there was some disaster, some battle, or the rebellion. I think that I have not mentioned what must be self-understood, that people grew old, or sick, and they died. I must speak of this now, for our march had scarcely begun when my brother, Aaron, passed away. His loss I felt keenly, not only because I loved him, but because I remembered his suffering in the prison camp in Egypt, his unending suggestions, only some of which we accepted, his frailty in the matter of the Golden Calf. How splendid he was as the high priest; how tragic that at that high moment he lost his two sons! Aaron was not a perfect man—who is?—but he was a great and gifted man, and he had contributed much to our needs and purposes. After his death and burial, it was arranged for there to be an assembly of our people at which his son Eleazar appeared before us in the garments which Aaron had worn in his high office.

There were others who died, Hur and Miriam, my sister, and men whom I knew in the council of tribal representatives and in the assembly of the seventy. And noble Anquru. I was with him an hour before he passed away. He said, "Through you, Moses, I die a happy man. I have had my sorrows. But I die a happy man."

I had become inured to death, but an individual death was able to touch and move me.

I say this, though I cannot speak of my grief when my beloved Zipporah, too, passed away. I can say only that I would never have recovered from grief were it not for the obligation to our children who were growing up and who presumably would some day marry and have children of their own. So deeply did I love Zipporah in life, that it was impossible for her death to increase that love. I only wondered whether in future time there would arise another like her, a woman of alien people who would become one with us Hebrews, without reservation.

So Zipporah died, of some illness, not old age, and I mourned her beyond the others whom I mourned. Death seemed to become a daily experience, especially of our older people. I can understand why our people say that because ten of the twelve scouts we sent into Canaan returned with fear and infected our people with it, He decreed that we should not enter the Promised Land until all that generation had died out. It has seemed that way.

Some died of accidents, perhaps from a fall, or some collision occurring as we marched. A few died when they were bitten by poisonous snakes, and some who were bitten became sick but regained their health. I hear from Caleb that, at His command, I made a serpent of bronze, and anyone bitten by a snake could look at my bronze serpent and become well. What stories our people tell! Our lads were growing up; our older people were dying one by one.

We made our circuitous way around Edom, and then we turned to the north, until we came to the borders of Moab. We then turned eastward, to go around Moab just as we had gone around Edom. Our fathers, Abraham, Isaac, and Jacob, had not settled in Edom or Moab; we could probably have captured those lands and settled there, but we had no claim to those territories, so we went around them. Our route took us then to the land of the Amorites. Again I was willing for us to go around that land, though again this would add many weeks to our journey. I sent emissaries—how often and how futilely I did this!—to Sihon, king of the Amorites, humbly asking for permission to cross his territory.

Silly man! He did not know how well Joshua had trained our young men, nor that our army had grown in size. He came out to destroy us; we destroyed him! We entered his city of Heshbon without resistance. An ally of Sihon's, Og of Bashan, whose land was to the north, also came out against us, and him too we defeated.

Slowly we made our way westward in a route that kept us just north of the boundary of Moab. There were plains there, below the mountains, and we encamped there, east of the Jordan. That was the river we could cross when going into Canaan. Once we arrived in the fields near Moab, our Wilderness journey was over.

Not our trials. In the fields of Moab, unlike the Wilderness, there were people around, people not Hebrews, and they worshiped idols, and their temples were filled with sacred prostitutes. It did not take some of our people long to find these prostitutes and to eat food dedicated to images.

There was a horrible incident which took place. A man from the tribe of Simeon openly brought a prostitute—I think she was a Midianite, though what Midianites were doing so far north I do not understand—this man openly brought the prostitute into his tent. Phinehas, the son of my nephew Eleazar, our high priest, entered the Simeonite's tent and slew them both. As our people tell it, Phinehas slew them both with a single thrust of his spear. I did not see this.

But there were those who applauded Phinehas' deed, and some have even told me that had Phinehas not done so, He would have destroyed many of us in His wrath.

I do not hesitate to say that in my judgment, the Simeonite merited death. But death decreed by a court, consistent with laws and legal procedures, is different from the assumption by one man of the role of judge and executioner, this without a trial. Phinehas came to me proudly, to tell me of his achievement. He spoke as if sure I would praise him.

I said, "How did you dare?"

"How did I dare? I do not understand!"

"How did you dare on your own to kill these people?"

"But they were doing an abominable thing!"

"We have our laws. There are legal procedures—"

"This was urgent. This was a flagrant violation—"

"And so was yours, Phinehas! I do not praise you. I condemn you. In my judgment, your trespass is even worse than the Simeonites—" I said no more, for I suddenly became sick again. You ask, sick again?

Yes, sick again. For there is that part of the account which I have not yet told, and I save it until now.

At the time when my sister, Miriam, died, and we were at Kadesh, preparing to go around Edom, there took place still another incident of complaint, again the lack of water. By now I was used to these complaints and used to our being short of water. I no longer worried, for I knew that below the sands of the Wilderness there are hidden water supplies, which come to the surface and form oases. We could be without water, but we would find it. Our people needed no longer to lament as if something new had arisen.

Ben Onim and Elyaqim were digging around a huge rock, trying to find some way to fashion a lever to move it, so as to dig under it. Skilled men, they had begun to dig under the rock, intending for the rock of its own weight to roll away.

Our people were, as usual, impatient. What Ben Onim and Elyaqim were doing took some time, and the patience of our people became exhausted. I was a bit of a distance away, walking slowly and leaning for rest on my rod. Attracted by the noise, I made my way where the two of them were digging. One would have expected our people to remember about water; they did not. Again they shouted at me that I had brought them into the Wilderness to die.

Long before, Jethro had told me that there was anger in me. This time, I could not suppress my fury. I pushed my way among the people and scolded them, and I raised my rod to strike the rock, as if my feeble blow would move it.

An unbearable pain seared my chest. I dropped the rod, I fell to the ground, and I could not catch my breath. I gasped and perhaps I struggled to rise, but I could not.

I remember only dimly how I was carried away. A tent was pitched and I was put into it. I lay there for days, nursed by this person and that person, too feeble to eat, too feeble even to speak. I was sure that I would die.

How many days or weeks I lay there, between life and death, I do not know. How long it took before I could sit up, before I could rise, before I could walk, all this I neglected to count.

Before, I was, if not a powerful man, at least a strong man. Now I was a weak man, a sickly man. I had in part recovered, able to join in the march around Edom and Moab, but I was not the man I had been before. I was, and am, an old, sick, weak man, a burden to my children, a burden to my people. When Caleb tells me that they say I have not lost my virility, I know they mean the opposite; they mean that I am a very sick, a very feeble man. I have not long to live.

I know it. They know it. They tell now that because I hit that rock instead of speaking to it, as He commanded me, He has decreed that I shall not enter the Promised Land. Let them believe this and tell this. I know the part of it that is true, that I shall not enter that land. We need some more weeks of preparation, and then we shall cross the Jordan. But I shall not cross with them.

And Phinehas' deed made me sick again.

✳ CHAPTER X

I am old and feeble, but, unless I deceive myself, my mind is clear. Clear enough for decisions. For example, it has been I who have decided that Reuben, Gad, and part of Manasseh may settle here east of the Jordan, provided they cross with our people for the needs on the other side. It has been I who responded to some women who inquired of me about some rules respecting inherited property. It has been I who decreed that we should set aside cities of refuge to which someone guilty of manslaughter can flee, so that our people will not fall victims to blood feuds. Can I not say that the future of our people is still my greatest concern?

We have been here, at the foot of Mount Nebo, for several weeks. Throughout the journey around Edom and Moab, I faced the need finally to make a decision. Or, to speak the truth, I faced the need to act on the decision that I had already made; but I kept on deferring. When once we came to these fields, I knew that I could no longer postpone it.

I sent for Caleb, and he came to my tent. He is younger than I, an active, energetic man, while I am feeble. I said to him, "Every day we must set aside some time to talk. There are so few of my friends left, and you are and have been the closest."

He smiled, saying something funny, and I tried to laugh, but it was hard. Then I said, "If I were a king, Caleb, my throne would soon go to my son Gershom. I am not a king. My sons do not inherit my authority. It must pass to someone." At my words I saw an eagerness light up his face, so that I looked away from him. I felt a pain in my chest again, a sharp pain, but it went away. "If I were to choose my successor on the basis of love, I know whom I would choose. If I chose him on the basis of his wisdom, it would be the same man. We will soon cross the river, and bitter military campaigns lie ahead of us. I have made my choice in that light."

I looked at him. I saw his face become gray, even ashen. I saw him try to smile. I saw two tears, one from each eye, course down his cheek.

He did not speak. After a bit, he rose and he left. The pain in my chest returned.

The rest of that day and that night, I wondered what would happen in the morning, whether Caleb would come back to see me or not.

Yes, Caleb came, smiling as though nothing had happened the day before. But I know that he is hurt, and I think I know how deep that hurt is. I love him. But I chose Joshua.

I spoke that afternoon to Joshua. He is most competent. Perhaps it is wrong of me, but I had thought that he might speak some word of thanks for my having chosen him. He spoke no such word. He told me only that he would carry on, in hope that he would be a worthy successor.

During these weeks, there has been time to recall, to remember. To remember my triumphs, to recall my failures. To recall my hopes, to remember my mistakes. Granted that, through me, freedom came to our people, granted that I led them to the sacred mountain and into a covenant with Him, have I succeeded in making our people a unique people? How sad it would be to leave them, with the fear still in me that they were no different from any other people!

I have had this fear recurrently. Even now I have it. Yet perhaps I am too close to things. A month ago, that strange man came riding into our camp on an ass, that man, Balaam. What a spectacle he was, clumsy, his clothes torn, his beard unkempt, his breath horrible. How comic he looked! (Already, according to Caleb, our people are telling funny stories about him and his ass.)

He came to me, saying that he wanted to talk to me. That Balak, king of Moab, had spoken of us Hebrews, and he wanted to see for himself. "I am a student of people, Moses. Like a doctor who studies diseases, I study peoples. Not people, not persons. Peoples." I noticed that he kept moistening his lips. I asked him if he was thirsty or hungry. "Both," he said. "Thirsty and hungry."

I had water and food brought in. The water he guzzled, the food he devoured, and then he belched repeatedly. But I began to notice some turns of phrases, and it seemed to me that comic as he was, he had a mind, a good mind. I asked him what questions he wanted to ask. "I do not ask questions. I see for myself. I want to see."

I said, "What can we show you? How our troops train?"

He said, "No. Balak of Moab is afraid of you. If you show me the training, you will fear that I am a spy."

"How about the schools for our children?"

"You have schools?"

"Yes."

"Even though you have been traveling?"

"We have schools."

"Let me see them."

I wanted to go with him, but I was not well enough. I sent my son Gershom to escort him. I thought that they would return in a half hour or so; it was late in the day when Balaam returned to my tent. He spoke a single word: "Impressive!"

I said, "Sit down." I invited Gershom too to sit, but I suppose that he had had enough of this strange visitor, and he left.

Balaam leaned over to me; his breath was unpleasant. "Balak is no friend of you Hebrews." He straightened up.

"What was impressive?"

"Your young people."

"In what way? How they shout, 'Exterminate them'?"

He dismissed my question with a contemptuous guttural noise and a wave of his hand. "They are like all children, like all people."

"I am afraid our children mean it."

"I am impressed," he said, "with the other things I have seen. They read, they write. They understand law. And wherever I went, I heard them speak of justice and of peace. And—how does it go?—'Do not oppress the stranger, for you know the heart of the stranger, for you were strangers in Egypt.' I am impressed!"

My heart warmed to him. I wanted him to stay on; I felt weak. I said, "I am a sickly man. Can you come back to see me tomorrow?"

"Tormorrow I travel farther. I must go. But I will write you something. I am a poet, I am a prophet, I am a student."

He left. I was sure that I would never hear from him. Yet two days later there came to me a long parchment of poems. Some of it I have learned; I have given the poems to my son Gershom.

> From Aram has Balak brought me,
> Moab's king, from the mountains of the east:
> "Go, curse Jacob for me, go, revile Israel!"
> How can I curse him whom God has not cursed?
> How goodly are your tents, O Jacob,
> Your encampment, O Israel!

Yes, I have been too close to our people. I have seen only their blemishes. An outsider, one who knew other peoples, saw something different.

I keep remembering Balaam. Perhaps all has not been as sad as at times I have thought. Perhaps our people have often been just like other people, but still able to rise above what is common to peoples. Perhaps their shortcomings in the Wilderness which vexed me have not been so deplorable, but only the natural actions of people; but I have been prone to weigh them on a higher scale.

Do not tell me not to do this. Do not tell me not to expect too much of them. They are Hebrews; there is never too much to expect.

I sent for Tat-Rin. He seemed as young as the night I first saw him in the tavern in Egypt. I said, "When do you go to Chaldea, Tat-Rin?"

"Oh, very soon. Very soon."

I said, "I am deeply grateful to you."

He nodded. "We have worked together well, Moses."

I said, "I want to see Qurmene—"

"He is studying how we shall cross the Jordan."

"And Nephros?"

"Still powerful of arms and shoulders."

"Tell them to come to see me. Say that I asked for them. Good-by, friend Tat-Rin."

We embraced, and he left me. Then suddenly he returned. "I am sure I would earn more money in Chaldea, Moses. But I shall never find better students than my Hebrews. I shall stay with them."

"God bless you, Tat-Rin."

He smiled. "Thank you for His blessing. I still do not— If I believed, Moses, I would believe that your laws come from Him. Even not believing—Moses, your laws will endure. They are just laws, Moses."

I said, "And do our children learn them?"

"That is why I stay, Moses."

Nephros came, and Qurmene. And so did many of our Hebrews.

This morning Caleb came in to see me. He still smiles. If he is still hurt, or cherishes some rancor, he conceals it.

Joshua came in this afternoon. All business. He is most efficient. My choice is right. I wish I could feel warmly toward him.

I have here a piece of parchment which fell from his clothes. I should not have read it, but I did. Joshua is a man who always prepares. He has prepared for my death. The parchment is his eulogy of me:

There will never again arise in Israel a prophet like Moses, whom He has known face to face, whose career was marked with all the signs and wonders which He sent him to do in the land of Egypt, to Pharaoh and all his servants and to all his land, and with all the great and awesome deeds which Moses did in the sight of all Israel.

I do not care for this eulogy. I do not care for most of what it says. I am irked, though amused, by what it omits, for I want to be remembered as the man who dared to turn an enslaved rabble into a law-abiding people, and, perhaps, raised them to be a unique people.

But those words, or other words, are scarcely important. The future, into which I cannot peer, will tell me whether I worked well, or did not. I have confidence in Joshua. But if I am indeed a prophet, then the true legacy I leave will be my spirit. I shall speak to the people three times, hopefully having the strength to do so, telling them again and again what I expect of them beyond the inescapable military necessity. Then, some day soon, I shall ask my sons, Gershom and Eliezer, to help me up Mount Nebo. I know I am weak, but I am sure I am strong enough. They will take me to Pisgah, the peak, so that I can look to the west to the land into which I shall not go.

I will bless my children and ask them to leave me there. I have never been afraid of being alone on a mountain. I will not be there long. I am weary; in death I shall know my rest. I am not afraid. I have never feared Him, only loved Him.

My children will try to dissuade me, but I will prevail. I will say, when a Pharaoh dies, people build a pyramid. I want no pyramids, I want no physical memorials. I want no one to know where my grave is, lest people try to honor it. They will honor me best by forgetting me, the man, and by living by what I have tried to teach. When once my eyes will have seen the land, I shall be ready.

I will look at the land, for I want to see it. But more than the land, it is our unique people—our children, and their children, and their children—that I shall imagine I am seeing.